Premonition

Acknowledgments

Many thanks to Jim, Richard, and all the staff and customers of the Idle Draper for their help, knowingly or otherwise, in the creation of this novel. Without their input, interest and encouragement it would not have been completed.

Special thanks to Lorraine for providing the cover photograph, and for allowing me the time to spend in the Draper 'doing research'.

CHAPTER 1

4th October

His radio alarm was set for the same time each day, when it would play the news and weather forecast before reverting to snooze. He'd bought the alarm some months ago, set it, and forgot about it. Most days, John Braden wasn't even aware it had activated at all.

"Monarch Airlines has been put into administration. A total of 300,000 future bookings were cancelled as a result of the firm's collapse, the largest to hit a UK airline, and Monarch passengers were told not to go to airports because there would be no more flights. The Civil Aviation Authority (CAA) said it was working with the government to secure a fleet of more than 30 aircraft, flying to more than 30 airports, to bring 110,000 stranded tourists back to the UK.
A man has died after a violent attack outside a McDonald's in Huddersfield. The Homicide and Major Enquiry Team is appealing for witnesses to the assault which resulted in the death of Graham Bell, 37. Mr Bell suffered serious head injuries during the attack outside the restaurant in Kirkgate at about 12.40am on Sunday, October 1.
A Knottingley man denies murdering a man and his eight-year-old daughter by setting a fire to destroy evidence of a burglary at their home, a court heard."

"Persistent rain, sometimes heavy and remaining breezy throughout the day. Some clear spells expected during the evening before rain returns overnight."

He eventually woke and dragged himself out of bed to commence his daily schedule of banality. Toilet, shower, breakfast to start with, before the boring triviality of everyday tasks. Over breakfast, he checked the news and weather on his laptop, having missed it on the radio. Today's forecast was accurate, as the heavy rain pounding against the kitchen window confirmed. He checked his emails, deleted all the marketing pitches generated every time he'd accidentally checked, or failed to check, a box while ordering an item online. In truth, he still preferred to shop at a physical store, but often when he did, he immediately regretted it as the service he received was generally less human than when shopping online. The local shops where he was known were fine, but he hated having to shop in the city centre, some of whose stores seemed to have a policy of only employing staff with an IQ of less than 20.

Today being a Wednesday, he spent an hour doing his weekly cleaning, which consisted of a quick dust and vacuum of his small, one-bedroom flat, filling the washing machine, and occasionally, but only occasionally, ironing a shirt. The iron was a very under-utilised appliance in the Braden household. He had nobody to impress, and therefore felt it was sufficient that his normal uniform of casual wear should merely be clean. He had spent too many long years in uniform. Now nobody dictated what he wore.

Outside, the rain continued to fall. He put down his book just long enough to make a sandwich and a mug of tea for lunch, but continued to read as he ate, before eventually tiring of the book and putting it aside.

****

"Now those memories come back to haunt me
They haunt me like a curse
Is a dream a lie if it don't come true?
Or is it something worse"

John Braden was listening to a Springsteen CD, The River; he glanced at his watch. He pressed 'Stop' on the CD player, ejected the disc and placed it back in its case, leaving it on top of the player for later. He put on his coat and shoes and went down the stairs before stepping out of the door into the teeth of a gale.

As was often the case, he was the first customer through the door when the Idle Draper opened for business in the afternoon. It had become part of his routine. Since he retired, routine had become important to him. He recognised its value in bringing order, meaning and purpose to the long days. It was different now than it was when he was employed. Then his work involved the routine of establishing some measure of order into the horrifying chaos of fiercely burning buildings. Routine helped keep him sane. He'd recently watched a group of elderly people from a nearby Day Centre shuffling down the road to board a coach for a day trip. He'd thought at the time, very uncharitably, that they looked like extras from Zombie Apocalypse. He pushed the thought from his mind. There but for the grace of God.

The Draper had become his favoured watering-hole since it first opened almost a year ago, despite the fact it was a ten-minute walk from his flat and his journey there took him past a number of other pubs. He liked the Draper. It was his haven; his shelter from the storm. He felt welcome there and, depending on his mood, he could easily join in the general conversation or sit quietly on his own. Recently, he had more often opted for the latter. His mood was darkening. The frequent headaches didn't help; nor did alcohol, but he continually reminded himself he was in control. Besides, there were too many hours in the day, and too few activities to fill them.

It had been like this since he retired, or rather was forced to retire, from his career as a fire fighter. He'd failed his six-monthly fitness test. His VO2 Max test results were unacceptably low. The nature of the job had taken its toll on his lungs and on his mind and he was well aware that his physical and mental health would both decline further over time. The Fire Service had been his life for thirty years, but he accepted the generous pension and moved on. He kept in touch with his ex-colleagues, but contact had become less frequent over the months. He worked only occasionally now, helping out friends generally when they needed extra manpower on jobs, but never felt the need, nor had the desire nor the energy, to seek regular paid employment. Aged fifty-two, he could manage. He had a small rented flat and an ageing car, could afford to eat reasonably well and healthily, and kept a supply of good wine and whisky in the cupboard. He could even afford the occasional cigarette. But still he needed some contact with the outside world. And the Draper provided that. He drained his glass and took it to the bar.

"Same again, John?"
"Please, Nick. The Gold's on form today."
"Glad to hear it. What have you got planned for the rest of today, then?"
"Same as every other day. A couple of pints. Go home. Make some tea. Read a bit. Listen to some music. Maybe watch a bit of TV if I can find anything remotely interesting amongst all the dross. It's an exciting life."
"You still reading the book I lent you?"
"The James Joyce? Yeah. I can only handle a dozen or so pages at a time. It's too complex for me. Does my head in, to tell you the truth."
"I thought it might. I never finished it. Don't know why I bought it in the first place."
"So that people would think you were an intellectual?"
"Me? No. Somebody recommended it. Probably a joke."
"Probably. Would you be offended if I gave you it back?"
"Not at all. I'll just put it behind the bar so people will think I'm intelligent."
"Course they will."

John took his pint back to his seat, smiling at the fact that he no longer had to keep up the pretence of enjoying the book, Ulysses. He'd lost interest in it long ago. He'd lost interest in a lot of things even further back at around the time his divorce became absolute. More than three years ago. It had been on the cards for a while. It had always been an uneasy alliance.

"We married too young", he thought. "It's a wonder it lasted so long."

The only reason it lasted so long was the birth of his daughter, Jane, who finally arrived after years of IVF treatment. Jane blamed him for the divorce. John was an only child whose parents had died a few years previously, around the time of his acrimonious divorce, and he hadn't had any contact with his ex-wife since. There was only Jane, who left home as soon as she was eighteen and he hadn't seen her since, though he still received a Christmas card from her every year, and a brief text message every time she changed her phone number or email address. But no home address. He had absolutely no idea where she lived or what she did for a living or whether she was in a relationship. She'd just made it clear that her life was her own and since her father had screwed up his own life she'd rather he kept out of hers. He'd tried to phone her several times on her twenty-first birthday, but she wouldn't answer. In the end, he'd sent a simple text message wishing her a happy birthday and received a terse 'thanks' by text in reply.

The true reason his marriage ended was simply the fact that his wife couldn't cope with his mood swings. He had no doubt they were due to the enormous emotional stress his job imposed. He experienced sleepless nights and frequent vivid nightmares. During sleep he re-lived his experiences of firefighting. The adrenalin rush of entering a burning building, the fear, the screams of those trapped inside, the heat, the smell, the sounds. And most of all the utter despair he felt when dragging out the corpses. He knew he was not alone. It was common among his colleagues and all attended regular counselling sessions where they learnt coping strategies. But that's all they were. Those in his profession learnt to cope with the pain and the stress but there was a price to pay. And the price was often instability in close relationships.

There were a few customers in the bar now, most of whom he knew by name and who always acknowledged him when he was there. He remembered his first visit clearly. It was not long after the business opened, and the staff were still trying to sort the wheat from the chaff as they kept a close eye on the customers, occasionally coming across one who'd been barred from everywhere else in the area and was trying to ingratiate himself in the new bar. On that particular occasion, a scruffily-dressed woman, probably in her late sixties, but looking much older, was drinking pints of bitter while seated at the bar listening to the streamed music. Eventually, she felt obliged to comment in a loud, slurred voice.

"This is shite, this is. This modern stuff. Shite! I remember real music. The 60s, and all that. Good times. I was born in 1950, me. I remember 1967. Flower power. Hippies. The Summer of Love, they called it. The Summer of Love. Not for me, it wasn't. The only sex I got all that year was one lousy fucking blow job! And one swallow doesn't make a summer."

And she started cackling and subsequently coughing as she slid off the seat and on to the floor. She was helped out into the street and deposited on a doorstep across the road. She was never allowed back in and we discovered later she was a refugee from a pub up the hill. No-one else would offer her asylum. Thankfully, customers like that were few and far between and the majority of regulars, at least, were friendly and sociable.

He debated whether to have another pint having realised his glass was empty again, but his mind was made up for him when Foghorn Barry walked in. John had privately given him that nickname because he thought he would be best employed on a cliff edge, shouting at ships to warn them away from the rocks. Every time he came in he had another adventure to boast about. Loud and often littered with expletives, depending on his intake of alcohol, his stories became more exaggerated the more often he told them. Every situation was embellished with extravagant hand gestures as he held the limelight, regaling his captive audience with stories of arguments in takeaways and bars, boasting of his conquests of females of all ages, and how much alcohol he'd downed. The more he had to drink, the louder his voice became, to the point where John often thought the liquor bottles on the bar display shelves would vibrate and start to clink together, generating an impromptu melody. John frequently found it hard to believe some of his stories and mostly listened politely without comment, more often than not finding him highly amusing but just occasionally feeling the need to question his veracity. John had to admit, though, that every time Barry walked through the door, the quiet serenity of the bar was lost for the duration of his visit, but he was just the man to raise your spirits if you were down. It was simply impossible *not* to laugh. This particular time though, John just wasn't in the mood to listen. He took his glass back to the bar, zipped up his jacket and made to leave. In truth, he rarely stayed long, or had more than two or three pints. When his darkness came he preferred to drink at home, often to the point of unconsciousness, rather than face his demons in public. When his darkness came he could physically hear the crack of blazing timber, smell the acrid reek of smoke and feel the intense heat of the flames. Alcohol helped him cope by numbing his senses, taking the edge off his pain.

"Another one, John?"
"No, Nick. Thanks."
"We'll see you tomorrow, then."
"Probably not. I've a funeral to attend."
"Oh, well. Hope it goes OK."
"Me too. See you."
"Take care, John."

Light rain was falling as he left the Idle Draper so he pulled his coat collar up and walked at a brisk pace down the hill; nevertheless, he was soaked to the skin by the time he reached his flat. As he locked the outside door behind him and headed towards the stairs, he heard a familiar voice. Mrs Locusto, or Bella, short for Bellissima, as her late husband called her. Doris, her real name, was an eighty-six-year old widow who married an Italian Prisoner of War after he settled in the area following his release from Eden POW camp. She'd lived alone in the downstairs flat since his death and now had the onset of dementia to contend with.

"Is that you, Franco?"
"No, Bella. It's John. I live upstairs."
"Hello, John, dear. I haven't seen you for ages. How are you?"

We had this conversation this morning, thought John, but Bella couldn't be expected to remember.

"I'm fine, Bella. How are you?"
"I'm fine. Just waiting for Franco to come home from work."
"He'll be working late again. You know how busy he is. Best go to bed and see him in the morning."
"Oh, yes. He's always *so* busy."

John felt guilty of the fact that for some time he'd regarded Doris as a bit of a nuisance, but gradually he'd come to understand the nature of her illness. He no longer referred to her as Bella Lugosi and was as kind and understanding to her as he could be. Nobody knew what the future might hold. One day he might suffer the same terrible fate as Doris. He didn't have the heart to remind her that Franco, her beloved husband, died years ago.

Inside his flat, he stripped off totally and pulled on a bathrobe, hanging his trousers to dry over the bath, before pouring himself a large glass of Glenlivet and settling in his armchair. He tried to ignore the noise from the family next door having one of their frequent arguments, but in the end just turned up the volume on the radio to drown the noise. Pink Floyd's 'Comfortably Numb' was playing. Very appropriate, he thought, draining the glass and pouring another, smaller measure. His thoughts turned to the next day's funeral as he drifted off to sleep.

****

Amelia Walters was already seven miles into her run and feeling good, despite the rain and the wind in her face. She had been following her training program now for ten weeks, with twenty-odd days still to go. She checked her Garmin Fitness tracker; she was on schedule for an acceptable time considering the weather conditions. She knew she had to continue to step up her training distance so she could be sure of putting in a good performance on the day. She was determined. Just another two miles to go and she'd be back at the car park for the short drive home and a shower. She pushed herself just a little harder for the final stretch.

On the whole, things were going well for her. She was a twenty-seven-year old healthy woman, working part-time and married to Andrew, a self-employed web site designer with more work than he could handle. They were comfortably off, with a large detached house. Amelia managed his accounts and bookkeeping while bringing up their six-year old twin girls. The only blot on their landscape was the fact that Andrew's grandfather had recently been diagnosed with lung cancer. She was running for him, and others like him. The effort would be worth it. She'd started running after joining a local club over a year ago. She'd never quite managed to lose all the weight she'd put on in the course of her pregnancy. Running had helped her achieve her required weight loss while also keeping her fit. And she enjoyed it.

****

Two hours had passed before John woke suddenly, relieved to discover he'd finished his drink before sleep had overcome him. He hated it every time he'd woken up to find he'd spilt whisky – not because of the mess but because of the unnecessary waste of good alcohol. He rummaged through the freezer, selecting an acceptable ready meal, took it out of its wrapper, put it in the microwave, and set the dials before putting a knife and fork on the table. Hearing the 'ping', he coaxed the stodgy cottage pie concoction onto a plate. During his marriage, he and his wife had never eaten ready meals, and this particular one he ate neither with pleasure nor enthusiasm. It was simply poor grade fuel to get him through another day. Afterwards he made a mug of tea, drinking it as he washed up the items he'd used during the day. He only washed up once a day. What was the point of doing it any more often? He never had visitors, and he had enough cutlery, crockery, pans and utensils to see him through each day. Besides, it kept the water bill down. He poured another glass of whisky and watched an episode of some or other American crime drama before he went to bed.

****

5th October

"A Halifax man has died of stab wounds after an argument outside a night club late last night. Two men have been taken into custody for questioning by police.
Yesterday, a milk float crashed into railings outside a Birstall primary school as children were arriving. There were no reported casualties, but the local Fire Service team had to be called to clear the debris."

"Cloudy and cool with scattered showers to start. Remaining windy throughout the day with some sunshine expected later. Rain will return during the night, heavy at times."

And then the radio alarm reverted to a further twenty-three hours and fifty-eight minutes of silence.

John woke an hour later, showered, and ate a light breakfast of toast and cereals, swilled down with a mug of tea. He checked the local news and weather forecast on his laptop, groaning at the prospect of another damp autumnal day. He pulled the black-edged card from behind the clock to check the time of the service for the umpteenth time and lit his first cigarette of the day, coughing uncontrollably for several seconds until his seared lungs got used to the sensation. Someone had once told him a joke he'd never forgotten, about a heavy smoker who'd refused a lung transplant because he couldn't bear the thought of coughing up someone else's phlegm. He smiled at the thought as he dressed appropriately for the occasion in his only suit, with ironed white shirt and dark tie. He gave his shoes a quick rub with a cloth, pulled on his overcoat and left the flat, double-checking it was locked before walking down to the bus stop for the journey to pay his respects. He hated funerals but felt compelled to attend.

****

John Braden took a long pull on his cigarette, inhaled, held his breath for a few seconds, then let the smoke escape through his nostrils. However much he hated the habit, however much he wanted to quit, he still found it deeply satisfying. Especially at times like this. Standing in the drizzle under this old gnarled yew, his overcoat tightly buttoned and the collar up. He'd endured yet another funeral, with eulogies and tears, handshakes and hugs. To him each funeral signified one more friend gone and the list ever shortening until his own name eventually appeared at the top. On this occasion, it was a friend he'd known for many years, Phil Morrison. A good friend, only a couple of years older; in fact, it was only just over a month since he'd celebrated his fifty-fourth birthday. Fifty-four is far too young to die, he thought. Phil had been in a car crash on his way home from work. His car had slammed into a lorry on a bend. The Police said he'd been using his mobile at the time, which didn't surprise John, who reckoned he would probably have had a couple of pints as well. Old habits die hard. And hardened smokers die young.

John dropped the unfinished cigarette at his feet and ground it into the damp soil. He walked slowly away from the crematorium and up the long drive towards the car park and the exit. Passing row after row of headstones, some ornate, some plain, some plots well-tended, others overgrown. He knew how his plot would look when his time came. Neglected. Forgotten. Abandoned. Who was there to attend to it? Nobody.

He'd purposely left his car at home. Over the years he'd attended far too many funerals and always found the car to be a hindrance. Not that he ever went to the customary wake and drank heavily like some of the others. On the contrary, he preferred to walk to the nearest quiet pub and sit alone while reflecting on the life of whoever it was whose funeral service he'd just attended.

He could feel a headache coming on. He'd had quite a few lately. He stopped and closed his eyes for a few seconds. When he opened them, he felt confused and dizzy. He blinked a couple of times to regain focus. He must somehow have left the path. He was in a small glade. In front of him was a white marble wall, probably eight feet high and five wide. Carefully engraved in three columns were names, more than a hundred, in alphabetical order, with two dates alongside each entry, all picked out in gold paint. At first, he paid them little attention as he walked past. But then it dawned on him. There was something unusual about them. And it couldn't be pure coincidence. He looked at them again, carefully, checking each one.

His head was pounding now, impossible to ignore, as he took in the information engraved on the wall. It was no mistake. The names were all listed together because there was something linking them. There was a connection. Then it became clear. The dates! They all died on the same date! 29th October 2017. He counted the names. One hundred and three. His head was spinning. His brain could make no sense of it. How could all these people, all different, with different dates of birth, seemingly unrelated, all die on the same day? But the real conundrum was how could they all have died on 29th October, when today was only 5th October? And why was *his* name among them? He lost consciousness and fell on to the wet grass.

When he came to, he found himself being stretchered into an ambulance. His vision was blurred but he managed to recognise some of the faces of the onlookers. They were among the mourners. It crossed his mind that perhaps he'd just made their bad day a little worse, but some seemed genuinely relieved to see him conscious. After a quick check-over by the paramedics, he was soon on his way to the hospital where he was examined and pushed on a trolley for a CT scan. Two hours later, following a quick consultation with a doctor, he was discharged with a pack of painkillers and an appointment to return for a second CT scan of his brain, along with an MRI scan. In his damp and mud-smeared overcoat, he took a taxi home, paying extra for the use of a blanket to protect the seat. Once in his flat, he took two paracetamol tablets, had a shower and went to bed.

He slept soundly for a couple of hours before the nightmare started. The familiar scene of the burning house; the screams from upstairs as Red Watch made preparations to enter. He was laying the hose when the explosion occurred, blowing out the windows. Then the momentary silence, followed by the desperate scramble to get up the stairs regardless of the danger in the hope of finding a survivor. The two adults just about alive but badly burned and injured. The three-year-old child already dead. The adults were also dead by the time the fire fighters had got them out of the house. He had wept.

He got up and sat in the chair in the dark for a while, thinking, looking out of the window while he sipped a glass of whisky. Finally, he went back to bed. The fact that he'd had nothing to eat since breakfast didn't seem to bother him.

CHAPTER 2

6th October

"A body was pulled from the canal near to Globe Road, Holbeck, yesterday afternoon. Forensic tests are due to start today.
A cash machine has been ripped from the wall of a Co-op shop in a village on the outskirts of York in the early hours of the morning. The main street is still closed to traffic as the vehicle used in the raid has been abandoned in the street.
A severe accident involving two vehicles is causing traffic disruption on the M62 eastbound carriageway."

"A cold, sunny start, with some patchy cloud and more breeze along the coast. A sunny morning, before cloud increases from the west through the afternoon with the sunshine turning hazier."

Its task completed, the radio alarm silenced itself.

He woke suddenly, feeling tired and stiff. He'd had a weird dream. He was aware he'd had a dream but couldn't remember what it was about. But he knew it wasn't the usual nightmare. He could only remember seeing a list of names. He showered and dressed while trying to remember some detail, *anything* of his dream. But nothing would come to mind. He guessed it must be related to his loss of consciousness the previous day so he decided to go back to the cemetery to see if anything would jog his memory. He had a mug of tea and a slice of toast while checking the local news on his laptop. More doubts expressed about the ability of Theresa May to lead the party. This was the main political talking point of the day. John was uninterested, only half-concentrating on the text while finishing his tea before placing the crockery by the sink. The weather looked as if it would stay clear and dry for a few hours at least, so he put on a windcheater, grabbed his car keys, locked his flat and double-checked it was locked before descending the flight of stairs to the car-park, waving at Doris as she watched him from her kitchen window.

Within twenty minutes, he'd arrived at the cemetery. Leaving his car at the side of the road outside the main gates, he walked quickly towards the chapel where the service had taken place the previous day. The cemetery, unsurprisingly, was quiet. Deathly quiet, he thought. And then a date flashed into his head. October 29th. That was the date he'd seen inscribed on a marble wall. Yes, that was it! The same date of death for all those people whose names, including his, were inscribed on a white marble wall. How many? He racked his brain, but knew only there were a great many, a hundred or so. And it was in a glade, a shaded private area. Having reached the chapel, he walked in the direction he believed he'd taken after the service; the path towards the car park. But he'd reached the boundary wall without seeing anything which triggered his memory of any other events, anything unusual, prior to his blackout. He retraced his steps to the chapel, then walked off in a different direction. He covered every square yard of the cemetery without finding either the glade or the wall. Noticing two workmen carrying out some maintenance duties, lopping tree branches, he approached them not really certain what he was going to ask.

"Excuse me."
"Yes, mate."
"Is there a glade somewhere in this cemetery?"
"A glade?" No, mate. Nothing like that. This is council. Plain and simple."
"Well, is there a wall, a white marble wall? With loads of names engraved on it?"
"You could try the Garden of Remembrance."
"Where's that?"
"Behind the crematorium. Over by the far gates."
"So, there *is* a wall?"

"Well, people's names are engraved on plaques on a wall there."
"Thanks."

But the Garden of Remembrance wasn't the place he was looking for. There *were* names engraved on plaques attached to a brick wall. But it wasn't right. The dates were all different, all random. It wasn't what he'd seen, what he was looking for. Was he losing his mind? He returned to his car and went home with more questions and no answers.

During his drive home, a name dragged itself from the deep recesses of his mind and nudged its way into his memory. Emma? No. Anna? Annie? No. *Amy!* Yes, that was it. Amy who? Winter? No. Winterton? That might have been it! Amy Winterton. The final name on the list engraved on the wall. At four o'clock, he walked through the door of the Idle Draper. As expected, Nick was again on duty.

"Hello, John. Did everything go OK yesterday?"
"Far from it, Nick. I ended up in hospital?"
"Christ! Whatever happened?"
"I just passed out in the cemetery and someone must have seen me on the ground and called the paramedics."
"Any idea what caused it?"
"No. Might just be stress, I suppose. I've got an appointment for scans. Till then, I'm fine, so can I have a pint of Gold, please?"
"Coming up."

Taking his pint to a nearby table, he noticed a copy of the local evening paper on the end of the bar.

"Do you mind if I have a look at this, Nick."
"Be my guest. Let me have it back when you've done. I haven't read it yet."
"Of course."

He glanced at the front-page headlines. A report about council corruption in awarding contracts. Nothing new or of interest there. But when he turned the page, idly looking at the headlines, a name caught his attention. The reporter to whom one of the stories was attributed. Amy Winston. The name was familiar. That was it! The name had stuck. Amy *Winston*, not Winterton – the final name on the marble wall. He was certain. Or was he? No, maybe not. Maybe he was mistaken. He needed more information. Gulping down his pint, he returned the paper to Nick, waved hurriedly and was gone, leaving behind a puzzled barman.

Back in his flat after negotiating Doris at the door and assuring her that Franco would be home soon, he powered up his laptop and Googled 'Amy Winston'. Google returned over a million results. Mostly social media references. He tried to narrow the search, but was unable to remember the date of birth he'd read on the headstone. But at least he could narrow the search geographically to the local area. And soon he found what he thought he was looking for. Amy Winston, born in Bradford, freelance journalist providing interviews and features for local and national publications. That's where he'd seen the name. He checked her Facebook page and recognised her face too. They'd met. Once, some time ago. She was covering the opening of a brand new and long-delayed shopping centre in Bradford. He happened to be there and she'd asked him for his views. He was struck by how attractive and vivacious she was. It didn't matter that his interview was never published. So, had he really seen her name on a marble wall which no longer seemed to exist, or had she made such an impression on him that he saw her name the previous day in a dream? And now that he had a name, what was he supposed to do next? He ran options quickly through his head. If, as he thought, he'd had a premonition of a disaster, then he surely had a moral duty to forewarn the only victim, or *possible* victim, he could locate. But if he were wrong, the potential consequences could be equally catastrophic for Amy. And what if she simply didn't believe him? Thought he was a crackpot, stalking her? She'd probably try to have him arrested. And if he just kept quiet, then no-one would ever know what *he* knew, or thought he knew. He tried to put it out of his mind and poured himself a drink. Except he couldn't dismiss it. It gnawed away at him. He switched on the Hi-fi and inserted a CD without even checking what it was, but as the opening notes of Leonard Cohen's Suzanne played he began to relax and concentrate on someone else's issues.

He played music from his CD collection for most of the evening after he'd eaten, trying to free his mind of the problems he knew he had to face; the decisions he knew he'd have to make. But how could he make a decision when he didn't know what the problem was? The only decision he made that evening was that he had to share the problem with someone. His dilemma was choosing who to share it with. He didn't know anyone who wouldn't think he was insane.

****

Amelia was in the shower. Andrew had already put the twins to bed and prepared a light meal for his wife. His working day was over now – apart from the washing up – so he poured a glass of wine for himself and would sit at the table while Amelia ate. He'd taken a phone call while she was out. It was an enquiry concerning a sales pitch he'd made recently to a large company. They'd discussed what he had to offer and would like him to come back in for further talks relating to a possible contract to set up and maintain their corporate website. He couldn't wait to tell Amelia.

****

7th October

"The head of Swedish journalist Kim Wall has been found, two months after she disappeared on a trip with a Danish submariner, Danish police say.
In Bradford, two men have been jailed for the manslaughter of a man knifed to death following a row over a television.
As stargazers looked up to the Harvest Moon on Thursday, people in Leeds were treated to a spectacle of light and sound around the city centre. Tens of thousands of people were in town for Light Night, a collection of more than 60 illuminated artworks, activities and performances.
A cow which fell down a sinkhole in its field had to be rescued by firefighters. The "distressed" animal was found on Birks Close Farm in Norwood Green, Halifax, at about 09:20 BST on Thursday. West Yorkshire Fire and Rescue Service (WYFRS) said the cow's back leg was stuck, with crew members and the farmer digging around the limb to free it.
Police were called following a vicious assault in Idle village last night where a man suffered facial injuries after being attacked by a group of youths. Investigations are ongoing into the incident."

"A lot of dry and bright conditions, especially in the east, but remaining windy with some showery rain at times. This rain mainly affecting the Pennines during the morning. Feeling slightly warmer than Friday."

Unusually, John was wide awake and, listening to the news about the cow, he reflected that he'd attended several such incidents during his time in the FRS. They were traumatic for the animal, but much less so for the rescuers for a change. He pushed the thought from his mind and prepared to face the day.

The Catholic Church of Our Lady's Immaculate Conception stood opposite The George, close to a junction of the main road towards Leeds, and set back a little, with a car park at the side. John coaxed his battered Fiesta into a vacant space and switched off the engine. He sat there for ten minutes, thinking how best to phrase his predicament. He knew Father Brennan would sympathise, but whether he could offer any practical advice was another matter. At least he could unburden himself.

In for a penny..., he thought, and got out of the car, locked it and strode purposefully towards the church where a stout, grey-haired priest approached him.

"Nice of you to call on us, John. It's been a while."
"Sorry, Father. It has. I've been.... busy."
"So, have you come for Confession?"
"No, Father."
"So, what is it, then?"
"I need your advice. I think that something terrible might possibly happen."
"Ah. Your nightmares again?"
"No, Father. This is different. This wasn't a flashback of something that happened. This was a premonition of something that's going to happen."
"John, are you sure it's not just your mind playing tricks with you again? You know you were ill for quite some time."
"That's finished, Father. I'm over all that. I'm OK these days. Yes, I have the nightmares of things past, but this is the first time I've seen into the future. And it's frightened me."
"Then come through, John. We'll sit in private with a glass of malt and you can tell me all about it."

They sat for about thirty minutes as John struggled to put into words what he understood from what he believed he'd seen. Father Brennan said nothing, but occasionally raised his eyebrows, and listened without commenting until John had finished.

"So, Father. What do you make of it all?"

There was a long pause before Father Brennan replied, obviously giving careful thought to what his response should be.

"John, I have absolutely no doubt that you believe what you saw. And, by the same token, the Bible records many such events, or 'signs from God'. Indeed, the Bible teaches that, in ancient times, God relayed His messages through the power of the Holy Spirit, to His chosen servants by visions and dreams. But it's a very dangerous assumption to believe that every dream is a message from God."
"I understand that, Father, but what should I do?"
"Trust in God, John. You are a good man. When the time comes, you will know what to do. God will guide you. But as for the lady you mentioned, I think you should tell her what you believe. And let her make her own mind up about it. That way, at least, you will have warned her."
"Thank you, Father."
"Now then, let's just have another small glass and you can tell me why you've been avoiding Confession these last few months."
"Ha, that's easy, Father. I've done nothing I need to confess to."
"I don't believe that for a minute. So, how's your daughter? And your wife, sorry, *ex*-wife?"
"Exactly the same, Father. And I don't expect things will ever change."
"Sometimes these things are meant to be. But don't close the door. Everybody's entitled to a mistake. And a change of heart."
"I'm sure my ex-wife is better off without me. But I miss my daughter. I wish I could see her again. Or at least speak to her."
"I'll pray for you, John."
"Thank you, Father. And thank you for taking the time to listen."
"I wouldn't be doing my job if I didn't listen when someone needed to talk to me."

They shook hands before John took his leave. He felt strangely comforted that Father Brennan had not dismissed him as a deranged psychopath. After all, he'd taken a sly peek at his counsellor's notes once during a psychotherapy session, and it was clear from what was written that even back then he was considered borderline.

John ate a light lunch in his flat before firing up his laptop and searching for contact telephone numbers, or email addresses of journalists employed by the local newspapers. He noted the information he needed, and made a call to the Press Desk. After the first ring he terminated the call, realising he had no idea what to say even if he did manage to get put through to Amy. He made some hasty notes, re-read them, re-organised them, read them again and finally tore the page off the pad, screwed it up and threw it in the bin.

Do it, John. Bite the bullet, he told himself. He called the Press Desk again. His call was answered on the third ring.

"Good afternoon. Press Desk. You're through to Angie. How can I help you?"
"Hello. Could I please speak to Amy Winston?"
"Can I ask who's calling, please, sir?"
"My name is John Braden."
"And may I ask the nature of the call?"
"I have some information which Amy really needs to know."
"About what, sir?"
"Information concerning an event in the near future which will have a profound effect on her life."
"Thank you, sir. Amy normally only comes into the office on Tuesdays, just to discuss assignments with the editor, but if you wish you can leave a message on her answerphone. Sometimes she checks that. Please hold while I put you through."

The recorded music seemed endless as John waited for a connection, but finally a voice came on the line.

"Hello, this is Amy Winston. I'm out of the office at the moment, but please leave your number and the reason for your call after the 'beep' and I'll get back to you as soon as I can."

When prompted, John was ready with his prepared spiel.

"My name is John Braden, phone number 07549832508. I need to talk to you urgently. I believe your life may be in danger. Something is going to happen on the 29th of this month. Please call me and I'll explain fully. Thanks. 'Bye."

He terminated the call and sat for the rest of the afternoon waiting for a response. It didn't come. It being a Saturday, he didn't really expect a reply anyway. He took a ready meal out of the freezer and microwaved it, eating with the phone on the table, in front of him. After spending all evening in his flat, waiting for a call, he poured a glass of whisky, downed it in one, got washed and went to bed, leaving the phone on the bedside table. He lay awake for a while, reading, frightened to sleep for fear that the nightmare would return. It was past one o'clock before he put down his book and turned out the light.

****

8th October

"Hurricane Nate has brought strong winds, torrential rain and a threat of storm surges to the US Gulf Coast. The storm, with maximum sustained winds of 85mph (137km/h), made landfall near the mouth of the Mississippi River in Louisiana, late on Saturday.
Police are appealing for witnesses after 11 people were injured in a crash at London's Natural History Museum. A black Toyota Prius hit people outside the museum, in South Kensington, at about 14:20 BST on Saturday, sparking initial fears it was a terror attack. But police later said the

incident was not "terrorist-related" and is being treated as a road traffic collision.
A man who raped three young women has had his "unduly lenient" prison sentence extended at the Court of Appeal. Lee Duffy carried out "violent attacks" on women aged between 16 and 19 while he was between 19 and 22 years old, the Attorney General's office said. The 26-year-old from Bradford was convicted of four counts of rape at the city's crown court in June."

"Largely dry with variable amounts of cloud and bright or sunny spells. Cloud may thicken over the Pennines later with a few spots of drizzle. Feeling pleasant in the afternoon sunshine with winds remaining light."

It was unusual for Amy to be in the office on a Sunday, but she desperately wanted to file a report on a story she'd been following for weeks. She wanted it to be in the Editor's in-tray when he arrived for work in the morning. The first thing Amy did was switch on her laptop, and check her phone messages while the computer powered up. Her phone indicated there were two new messages. She pressed the 'play' button. The first message was from a member of the public thanking her for the sensitive way she'd reported the story of the caller's eighty-year old father who had been beaten up and mugged on his way home after collecting his pension from the post office. As a result of the story, members of the public had sent donations totalling over five hundred pounds, for which the caller wished to express her gratitude. Amy made a note to call back during the week and get further details for a follow-up story.

Amy was logging into her laptop when the playback of the second call began. It stopped her in her tracks. She listened intently, then played it through again, this time making notes. When it had finished, she sat for a while, tapping her biro on her teeth. Then she typed 'John Braden' in the Google search bar. Roughly half a million results were returned. She narrowed the search, including the words 'Bradford' and 'UK', but the results yielded nothing of interest. She tore her notes out of the pad, put them in her bag, and turned her attention to the tasks she had scheduled for the day. Then she had a second thought. She picked up her phone and punched in a three-digit number.

"Research. Jackie speaking."
"Jackie, it's Amy."
"Hi Amy. What can I do for you?"
"I didn't really expect anybody to be working on a Sunday, but since you are, you must be busy."
"I am. I'm just trying to get on top of things before I go on holiday next week."
"Well, if you get a minute, can you see what you can find about a John Braden. Probably local. His phone number is 07549832508. Discreet, please."
"As always, I'll see what I can do. I'll call you back before I finish for the day."

The call came shortly after four o'clock. Recognising the extension number displayed, Amy picked up immediately.

"Hi Amy. It's Jackie."
"Hi Jackie. Any luck?"
"Possibly. I found an old report about a fireman called John Braden. Bradford born and bred. In the fire service until he retired due to health problems. In his early fifties. The report concerns a house fire in Eccleshill, where a family of three died. Arson, apparently. Anyway, Braden was seemingly so traumatised, he seemed to go off the rails for a while. He appeared in court charged with assault and got a suspended sentence. Nothing since then."
"Thanks Jackie. I really appreciate this."
"All in a day's work. Bye."

Amy sat at her desk for a while, thinking about John Braden's message before dismissing it and continuing to work on the story which had caused her to come in to work in the first place. That was her priority for now. She would give the other business some serious thought later.

****

9th October

"The White House has tied any new deal on young undocumented immigrants to a clampdown on illegal immigration, including a border wall with Mexico. US President Donald Trump is asking for funding for the wall, speedier deportations and the hiring of thousands of new immigration officials.
New research claims that hands-free mobile phone use is as bad as drinking and driving. It suggested dual-tasking drivers take on average 1.6 seconds longer to react to hazards than motorists who are not distracted.
Police officers in Sheffield seized two weapons and drugs under stop and search powers over the weekend. Hundreds of people went through metal-detecting knife arches at popular night spots across the city.
Morrisons High Court data leak trial begins today. Thousands of Morrisons staff are going to sue the West Yorkshire-based supermarket for damages after a data leak. It follows a breach of security in 2014 when a former internal auditor at the Bradford headquarters posted the payroll information of nearly 100,000 employees online."

"A dry, but often cloudy day, although one or two places could see the odd spot of rain or drizzle, mainly across the Dales. However grey skies could break later, with sunny spells developing, especially in the east."

The buzzing of the phone aroused him. He looked at the bedside clock as he reached for his phone. 9.15am.

"Hello?"

"Hi, it's Amy Winston returning your call."
"Oh, hi, Amy. Thanks for calling me back. I..."
"Before you start, if this is some kind of sick joke, I'm telling you now I'll report it to the police. I've got your number."
"Hang on, Amy. Please listen. I know this is going to sound very odd to you, but I've received information that both of us will die on the 29th of this month...."
"OK, that's enough. I've heard enough. Do you realise how many crank calls I get every month? I'm reporting you...."
"Wait! Please don't put the phone down. Something terrible is going to happen. More than a hundred people are going to die. I just know it. You have to help me."
"You need to see a psychiatrist."

The tone told him she'd disconnected. He sat on the edge of the bed for a while, pondering his next move, then he walked into the bathroom where he was violently sick.

Later, having eaten a slice of toast and drunk a mug of tea, he got out his laptop, found Amy's email address and sent the following:

"Hi Amy,
I'm sorry you didn't take me seriously earlier. But I *am* deadly serious. I have seen something which tells me we will both die on 29th October. As yet I don't know how or where, but I would be grateful if you would meet me to discuss what we can do. It would also be useful if you could let me know what plans you have for that day, so I could corroborate the fact that we will both be in the same place at the same time at some point during that day.
I know this must be difficult for you to accept, but my life is at stake too. Please meet me. You choose the time and place. Bring a minder if you wish, but I swear I mean you no harm. Perhaps together we can stop whatever it is which is set to kill us both.
John Braden."

He read it through several times before finally hitting the 'send' button.
Then he waited.

He was still waiting at ten to four. He picked up his laptop and went to The Draper.

****

Amelia was back at her car, panting heavily. She'd just finished ten miles, over a hilly course, and she'd found it difficult. Difficult, but not impossible. She knew that in less than three weeks she'd be ready and in good shape. It had been a good week's training and she was on course. She felt strong, and confident. She drove home to help prepare the meal her husband would no doubt already have started. And after they'd eaten and washed up, the family would have some time together before the twins went to bed.

CHAPTER 3

10th October

“Theresa May is to challenge public services over how they treat people of different races. The prime minister says institutions must "explain or change" any variations when data is released later on Tuesday.
BAE Systems is planning to cut almost 2,000 jobs in military, maritime and intelligence services, the firm says. A total of 750 posts will go at the Warton and Samlesbury plants in Lancashire where parts for the Eurofighter Typhoon are manufactured.
A driver stopped by police was found to be almost eight times over the legal drink-drive limit. The man was stopped as he was "driving erratically" in the early hours on West Lane, Baildon, near Bradford, said West Yorkshire police. The man, 34, from Shipley, was arrested on suspicion of drink-driving.”

“Starting cloudy with a few showers, but these will die away this morning to leave the rest of today dry with bright or sunny spells. It will become rather warm despite the breezy conditions.”

John Braden never heard the news and weather forecast. He was already up and in the shower. At eight o’clock, he was waiting across the road from the entrance to the newspaper’s office. He’d been up since five-thirty worrying about how to tackle this next move. Now, standing with his hands thrust deep into his overcoat pockets, and stamping his feet to keep warm in the light drizzle of this chilly morning, he kept close watch on the people making their way to work. He toyed with the idea of popping into the Costa Coffee shop just along the road but decided against it. If he missed her, he might not get another chance.

He watched a succession of buses pull up and disgorge their passengers at the end of the road. Amy was not among them. It was quite possible, of course, that she didn't use a bus but he had no way of knowing for sure. Nor did he know if she was even going to be at the office on that particular day. He was simply making assumptions and would have to consider other options if this failed. And by the time the City Hall clock struck nine, he was ready to give up his vigil. And then he saw her. Walking briskly along the road towards the entrance to the office. Glancing quickly both ways to check traffic, he crossed the road to intercept her.

"Amy".

Hearing her name called, she stopped and turned as the man approached her. She didn't recognise him, but that was not unusual. People were always approaching her, simply because *they recognised her*, but she met so many different people in the course of her work and couldn't remember all of them. Still, she met every single one with a smile.

"Yes. Can I help you?"
"Amy, my name is John Braden. I need to talk to you."
"Look, Mr Braden. I really don't know what your problem is. You're harassing me. I'm calling the police..."
"No. Please, wait. Please just give me a minute to explain. This could be the biggest story you've ever handled."

Amy paused for a moment. John sensed that he'd chosen the right approach. Appeal to her journalist's instinct. The possibility of a scoop. How could she walk away without at least listening to the whole story? He decided to press home his advantage.

"Please just give me ten minutes of your time. If, after that, you're not interested, well, at least I tried."
"Ten minutes. OK. Let's grab a coffee."

They walked down the road in silence towards the coffee shop. John knew he had one chance to make his pitch. He had to make it count. He opened the coffee shop door for her, allowed her to enter first, and insisted on paying for the drinks. Once they were settled at a corner table, John took a deep breath and started.

"I know this is going to sound very odd and very unlikely to you but please let me tell you the story and if you think I'm mad, then feel free to tell me so. But listen first. OK?"
"OK. But this had better be good."
"A few days ago, I had attended a funeral, and afterwards, I broke away from the rest of the mourners to have a smoke. I wasn't going to the wake. I didn't know his family that well, though we'd been good friends for years. Anyway, as I was walking through the cemetery, I suddenly came across a sort of memorial wall. White marble. Names were engraved on it in gold paint. More than a hundred. A hundred and three to be exact. In alphabetical order. Each name had two dates alongside it. The first was obviously the date of birth. The second was the date of death. And here's the weird thing. They all died on the same day. And even weirder, that day was 29th October, nineteen days from now."
"I'd like to see this wall."
"You can't. That is, I can't find it. I went back and it's not there now."
"This is beginning to sound a bit far-fetched, John."
"I know. But the weirdest thing of all is the fact that both our names were listed on the wall."

He paused for a moment to let his last comment sink in. Amy, though, was less than convinced.

"I'm sorry. But I find all this just too hard to believe. And without any evidence it ever existed…"
"I *saw* it. I know I did."
"Where's the proof? Why didn't you take a photograph, or something?"
"I… I fainted."

"You fainted?"
"Yes. When I came to, I was in hospital."
"And what did they say was wrong with you?"
"I have to go back for some tests…."
"Well, I'm sorry, John, but I just don't think I can go anywhere with this. I just have difficulty in believing it all."
"But I saw it!"
"You believe you saw it. I'm not so sure."
"But what if I *am right*? Don't you want to know when and how you're going to die? So maybe you can prevent it happening?"
"So, tell me. You say I'm going to die on the 29th. Where? Where am I going to die? How? How am I going to die? You know what I think? I think you're a stalker. And maybe you're the one who's dreaming about killing me. Well, I'm not playing your silly game. Please don't try to contact me again. Or else I'll have you arrested."
"Suit yourself. But I'd still like to know where you're going to be on the 29th. Just so I can make sure I'm somewhere else."
"Nothing would please me more."

And with that she was gone, slamming the door behind her so hard that several customers looked up from their coffee. John continued to sit for a while, pondering his next move, watching the rain continue to fall ever more heavily.

****

Back in her office, Amy was also contemplating her next move while checking through her assignments for the week. She wondered whether it would be possible to handle them all, or perhaps re-schedule some, from the safety of her office. She had this nagging fear that if she stepped out into the street she'd be immediately confronted by that madman Braden. She'd experienced violence before, having had a number of unsuitable, short-term relationships. She'd had a tough childhood as the only child of a loveless union. Her mother was verbally abused and frequently physically assaulted by her drunken husband. She bore the scars and bruises stoically. Until eventually, she knifed him one night during a struggle after both had been drinking heavily. Amy was 11 at the time and was put into care, and had to endure jibes and bullying at school until she left aged sixteen. She found a job working in a department store and went to night school before winning a place at university to study journalism. That was now her life. She was 43 and single, never having married or even seriously considered it. Relationships somehow never quite worked out. She worked long hours and refused to be dominated by any man. Nobody would ever take control of *her* life.

Eventually, she rose from her chair, walked down the office corridor, and knocked on the Editor's door.

****

John continued to think about what kind of event could conceivably cause so many fatalities. He took a sheet of A4 from his pocket, thought for a moment and then printed in neat biro in a numbered list.

Fire – department store, office, concert venue, sport stadium
Building collapse
Plane crash
Train crash
Explosion – gas
Explosion – TERRORIST!!!!!

He read back through what he'd just written. All were feasible. Some were more likely than others. For instance, he would not be on a plane under any circumstances, so a plane would have to fall on *him and Amy*. Or else, she'd have to be in a plane which fell on him. In all the circumstances he had considered, all depended on the two of them being in the same place at the same time. But none were preventable unless he knew where they were going to occur. He guessed it would have to be in Bradford, otherwise why would the names appear in a Bradford cemetery? He folded the sheet of paper, put it in his inside pocket and made his way across town to where he'd parked his car. He drove home, his head pounding.

****

On the second floor of the West Yorkshire Police HQ in Wakefield was a windowless office. Electronically locked, and recognisable from outside only by the inscription North East CTU on the door, this is where Don McArthur and his seven colleagues were usually to be found, poring through local tip-offs, the latest alerts from GCHQ in Cheltenham, and their partner agencies abroad. Detective Inspector McArthur, now nearing retirement, had lost none of his enthusiasm for the job he'd been earmarked for as he rose through the ranks. He was an imposing figure, six feet two tall and weighing thirteen and a half stones. He commanded respect. His service record was flawless including the time he spent serving in the army in Northern Ireland during The Troubles. His two full-time active colleagues DS David Lee and DS Brian Peters were both recruited for their specific analytical skills, and were nominally 'analysts', but were nevertheless hard-bitten, front-line policemen, who did everything legally, and occasionally illegally, to get results. McArthur referred to them as 'Peters and Lee', and whistled 'Welcome Home' whenever they entered the office together, a joke which was lost on them as they were both too young to be familiar with 1973 UK chart records. David was 31, good-looking and single, a fact that caused his colleagues to ponder his sexual alignment. The truth was, he preferred living with his parents, and didn't want anyone to distract his full attention from the career he'd chosen. On the quiet, though, he had a regular lady-friend with whom he liked to spend what time off work he could get. Maybe in a few years he would feel differently, but, for now, that was how it had to be. Once a promising young Rugby League player, he'd given up a potentially lucrative career in the sport to join the force, and was comfortable with the decision he'd made. Brian joined the force straight from school; it was always what he'd wanted to do. Now 33, he had been happily married for seven years to Sarah. They had one child, Daniel, aged 3, and were trying for a second. Whenever Brian arrived a few minutes late for work, usually due to heavy traffic, he knew that whatever excuse he offered, as far as the others were concerned, he'd been 'trying'. The rest of the team in the office were analytical and clerical staff, and liaison officers, back-office staff who dealt mainly with information from members of the public, and ensuring all intelligence received was entered into the system and made available to all authorised interested parties. They were highly trained and dedicated, and McArthur, Lee and Peters, being the only members of the team who regularly worked outside the safety of the office, were all authorised to carry firearms.

When the phone rang, it was David Lee who answered it.

"Lee."
"Morning, sir. It's Constable Hopkins at Trafalgar House."
"Morning. What can I do for you?"
"Well, sir. A call was put through to me a short while ago. From a member of the public. She was quite worried, sir, that she was being stalked and threatened. But when I spoke to her, I got the impression there was a little more to it, sir."
"And why should this affect my department, PC Hopkins?"
"Well, sir. Her 'stalker' kept going on about an impending disaster where hundreds of people will die. I think it's possible this man may be dangerous, sir. I consulted my superior and he said I should pass it on to you, sir."
"Thanks, PC Hopkins. You did the right thing. Now give me some details…."

David Lee made a careful note of all the information Hopkins had gleaned from his caller, thanked him and took it straight to his boss. As he expected, McArthur authorised him to follow it up, but not to spend too much time on it. Lee made the call immediately and Amy answered in a matter of seconds.

"Amy Winston speaking."
"Amy, my name is David Lee. I'm a Detective Sergeant with the Police Force in Wakefield. Your call has been passed to me and I wonder if you could please give me some more information."
"Yes, of course. What do you need?"
"I understand you have a nuisance caller? Or a stalker?"
"Well, yes. I think so. I discussed it with one of my editors – I'm a freelance journalist – and he thought I should contact the police."
"Do you have the stalker's name and address?"
"I don't know his address, but I have his email address and he said his name is John Braden."
"John Braden. And what exactly has he been saying to you?"
"His first call said that my life was in danger. He said some disaster was going to happen and I would die along with about a hundred others. He said something about seeing all these names on a wall at the cemetery and all the dates of their deaths were the same. 29th October 2017. Oh, yes. He also said he'd die as well."
"Anything else?"
"I asked him to show me the evidence and he said it wasn't there any longer. He'd fainted and gone to hospital. He sounds a real sicko. Anyway, he was waiting for me as I got to work this morning. He said he had to speak to me urgently. I agreed to go for a coffee with him. But he was just creeping me out. So, I left him, went to work and told my boss. He advised me to contact the police."
"You did the right thing. Anything else?"
"He sent me an email. I've kept it."
"Forward it to me, please. And don't delete it. We'll want a hard copy of the original. Now, could you please give us a description of this Mr Braden?"

“Early fifties. Short dark hair. White. Average height and build. Oh, and he did say he’d been taken to hospital last week if that’s any help.”
“That’s fine, Amy. I’ll have a word with this Mr Braden. He shouldn’t bother you again.”

He ended the call and phoned the A and E department in Bradford. The administrator was able to confirm that a Mr John Braden, a white male in his fifties, had attended A and E at the Bradford Royal Infirmary the previous week, and had been released for out-patient treatment. David Lee noted the address of the patient, and entered the information gleaned so far into his computer database. Finally, he searched all records he had access to for any other information relating to John Braden and appended the notes from his Fire Service counselling reports to the database file.

After lunch, McArthur, Lee and Peters held a meeting, where Lee outlined his progress on his current task.

“David, in your opinion, is this man currently a threat to national security?”
“At the moment, no. But I do think he may be a threat to this Journalist, Amy Winston.”
“So, he’s just a stalker?”
“I’m not sure. It may be that he’s planning some offensive. I certainly think we ought to speak to him, rather than just passing him back to the local force to deal with.”
“I agree. The two of you go tonight, mid-evening. Go armed. And it goes without saying, but do what you have to do.”

****

At four o’clock, John walked through the door of the Idle Draper and nodded to Nick behind the bar.

“Evening, John. How are you today?”
“Fine, Nick. A pint, please.”
“Usual?”
“Please.”
“Have you been back to the hospital yet?”
“No. My appointment is this Thursday.”
“You’re looking a bit pale round the gills.”
“I’m still getting these headaches. The beer will probably help.”

He’d tried to sleep during the afternoon but couldn’t relax. The headaches had been getting progressively worse. He guessed it was the stress. He hoped his scans on Thursday would bring some clarification. And, hopefully, a cure. But for now, alcohol would have to suffice. He took his empty glass back to the bar and ordered another pint. Soon the bar started to fill and he got into conversation with a couple of the regulars, one of whom, Scouse Billy, was always good for a laugh. He enjoyed the company as the hours slipped by.

****

There was no answer when Lee and Peters knocked on John’s door so they decided to try to catch him in first thing in the morning. As they were leaving they noticed a Silver Fiesta with some minor front wing damage. Lee checked his notes. John Braden had a Fiesta, and the number plate indicated the car was his.

“Are you thinking what I’m thinking?”
“It would be nice if we could talk to him tonight.”

Lee took out a long flat-blade screwdriver, inserted it behind the seal of the passenger-side window and pulled outwards sharply. The glass shattered into tiny square fragments. Reaching in, he opened the glove box, pulling out the contents and scattering them on the passenger seat. They walked quickly away back to their car and drove off, parking up a mile or so from John's flat. Lee called it in to the local police.

"DS Peters and I have just called to have a word with a Mr John Braden. He wasn't in, but we noticed that someone has broken a window of his car. If he reports it tonight, can you please pass it on to us, as we'll be in the area for a few hours yet."

He relayed the details and sat in the car exchanging small talk with his partner. They waited until ten o'clock when the return call finally came. Peters started the engine and drove the short distance to Braden's flat. He answered the door immediately.

"Good evening, sir. Mr Braden, is it?"
"Yes."
"You called the police regarding damage to your car, sir. Can we come in?"
You were quick. I've just phoned."
"We were in the area, sir."
"Can I see some ID?"
"Of course. My name's DS Lee and my colleague is DS Peters. Check the warrant cards, please."
"That's fine. Please come in."

They sat in the living room, where Peters took a statement, while Lee had a quick look round the flat, having excused himself to use the toilet. After completing the formalities, they inspected the damage to the car, issued a crime number, and left after assuring Braden that they'd do everything in their power to apprehend the culprit, but that it was highly unlikely they'd find him. Once back in the car, they discussed their findings.

"I found nothing out of the ordinary. He seems just a regular bloke who's been out for a few pints and come home to find damage to his car. He was calm, almost resigned to it. No sign of paranoia. You find anything?"

“Nothing at all. Nothing unusual in the bathroom cupboards, nothing in the bedroom. And nothing unexpected in the kitchen cupboards. And he was quite happy to let us in.”
“Perhaps he’s got a lock-up somewhere.”
“Then why leave his car outside?”
“Perhaps his lock-up, wherever it is, is full of explosives.”
“OK. Tomorrow, we find out who owns the lock-ups round here. And we’ll see if CID can put a tail on him for the day. Let’s call it a night.”
“What about the devices?”
“In place.”

CHAPTER 4

11th October

“The US has conducted a joint military exercise with South Korea, flying two strategic bombers over the Korean peninsula. The B-1B combat bombers were joined by two South Korean F-15K fighter jets, and carried out air-to-ground missile drills off South Korean waters. It comes amid heightened tensions with North Korea over its nuclear programme.
Taxpayers' money should not be spent on preparing for a "no-deal" Brexit yet, Chancellor Philip Hammond has said. Writing in The Times ahead of next month's Budget, Mr Hammond said he would spend only when it was "responsible" to do so.
Two 14-year-olds have been charged with murdering a teenager who was stabbed to death, police have said. Saif Abdul Magid, 18, suffered multiple knife wounds in an attack in Tanfield Avenue, Neasden, north-west London, on Friday afternoon.”

“A cloudy, windy start with outbreaks of rain, heavy and persistent over western hills, drier in the east with some brightness. Rain gradually clearing to the south later in the afternoon with sunshine and showers following, and winds easing.”

The alarm woke him up momentarily, and he listened to some of the weather forecast before it fell silent. His head pounding, he struggled to get back to sleep with the help of paracetamol.

Just before 11am, John was outside his flat, watching as the man from Autoglass completed fitting the replacement glass in his car’s window. He’d contacted his insurance company first thing and they’d been quick to organise the repair. He signed the necessary paperwork, thanked the fitter and was about to go inside when a police car pulled up next to his car. Two uniformed officers got out.

"Morning, sir. Are you Mr Braden?"
"Yes, I am."
"Could we talk inside, sir?"
"Two of your fellow officers were round last night. They took a statement about the car…."
"We're not here about the car, sir. Can we go inside?"
"OK. Come in."

They sat in the living room. The officers declined John's offer of a cup of tea and came straight to the point.

"Mr Braden, we're here to investigate a claim of harassment which has been made against you."
"Don't tell me. Amy Winston."
"That's right, sir. She says you've been stalking her. Waiting for her outside her office. Sending emails, making phone calls. And death threats."
"I think she's blown this up out of all proportion. Yes, I did phone her, only twice, and left messages, and she called me back once. I also sent her *one* email. And on one occasion I waited across the road from where she works and asked her if she could spare me ten minutes of her time. She agreed and we went for coffee. I told her what I had to say. She didn't believe it and walked out. I haven't bothered her since, nor will I again."
"And what exactly did you say to her, sir?"

John knew how ridiculous his answer was going to sound. But how else could he explain his behaviour? Better to tell the truth.

"A few days ago, I had been to a funeral. Afterwards, walking through the cemetery, I collapsed and while unconscious I had what I thought was a premonition of a disaster. It's bothered me ever since and I've really no idea

what I ought to do. If I report it, will anybody take it seriously? Or will they lock me up in a nut house?"
"So how does Miss Winston fit in with this dream, sir?"
"In my 'dream', as you call it, I saw a list of names. Over a hundred. They were inscribed on a memorial wall, all with the same date of death. Miss Winston's name was on it. So was mine. So, I only thought I was doing the right thing in informing her. What I thought was, if I knew where *she* was going to be on that day, then I could make sure I was somewhere else. That way, this 'disaster' couldn't kill us both. So possibly, it may not even happen."
"And what exactly is this 'disaster, sir? And when is it going to happen?"
"I've no idea what is going to happen. But the date I saw was 29th October 2017."
"Right, sir. We'll make sure this information is passed on up the chain. But in the meantime, sir, we would advise you not to make further contact with Miss Winston, or she may wish to press charges."
"I see. Thank you. Could I just ask one question before you go?"
"Fire away."
"Why do two uniformed officers investigate a potential disaster, and two plain clothed officers call about a broken car window? Petty vandalism isn't in the remit of CID, is it?"
"I can't really comment on that, sir. We were very busy last night. It's quite possible CID officers were in the area and took the call to help us out. It happens frequently, sir. Efficient use of resources and all that."
"OK. Let me see you out."

****

Back at the station, having written up his report, PC Stanford phoned Amy Winston to inform her they'd advised Mr Braden not to contact her again or charges may be brought. She thanked him and put the phone down. She was relieved. She could now get on with her life without anyone watching her every step.

****

Lee and Peters each sat in a chair facing Don McArthur's desk while he read their written report, occasionally asking for clarification on one or two points.

"So, you responded to an incident of petty vandalism to a car. Rather lucky you were in the area, then?"
"Yes, sir. He wasn't in when we went earlier, but we noticed his car had been damaged. So, we called it in and then stopped off locally for a bite to eat, and as it happened we were still in the area when Mr Braden reported the crime, so we told the locals we'd take the call."
"OK, your report is fine. You can file that. Now, I want to know the bits which are missing from the report."
"Yes, sir. As per standard practice, while Peters took the statement from Mr Braden, I went to use his toilet. I had a good look round the flat and installed the bugs, laptop included. With your permission, sir, we'll gain entry after a few days and remove them. Make it look like a burglary. No-one needs to know otherwise."
"Agreed. This stays between us. If this became public, it could void any prosecution. But if it all turns bad, I can get retrospective authorisation. In the meantime, we need to find out what he does on a daily basis. Where he goes, who he meets. I want to know everything about him. Get one of the girls to follow him about discreetly. Usual stuff. Bump into him accidentally. By coincidence, just happen to be in a pub when he walks in. Might be worth seeing if there's an empty flat she can move into close by where he lives. In the meantime, I want one of you at all times keeping track of his movements."

****

John Braden paced the floor in his kitchen. Something wasn't right. His car window being broken. A complaint from Amy Winston. Was there a connection? His brain felt too muddled to reason clearly. He had another fierce headache. Rather than take any more painkillers, he put on his coat and went for a walk. He was only vaguely aware of the rain that was falling steadily. His mind was elsewhere. He was worried about tomorrow. He hardly noticed the black Audi whose driver got out and followed him at a distance. But he *had* noticed him. He was fairly sure it was one of the officers who'd called to take details regarding his car. John's coat gave him sufficient protection against the rain and his boots were appropriate for the weather. He wasn't too worried that his legs would get wet.

Let's see how far he's prepared to walk in this filthy weather. John smiled.

David Lee gave up the surveillance when it became clear John was heading through Thackley and downhill towards the canal towpath. There was no way he was going to follow him all the way to either Shipley or Apperley Bridge. The rain was falling more heavily now, to the extent that his trousers were soaked from the knees down and his feet were wet through.

"Fuck this for a game of soldiers", he cursed, before walking briskly back to the warmth of his car.

****

John had reached the canal towpath, outside the water treatment works. He stood for a while close to the wall, seeking what shelter there was available. From there he had a clear view of the path he had walked down. Whoever was following him had evidently given up the chase. He waited ten more minutes before retracing his steps into Thackley and from there up to the Draper. The rain had stopped and his pint tasted good as he dried out in the warmth of the pub. He decided to spend an hour or so in the pub before walking home and his mood lifted immediately when the Foghorn came in with a new story.

"You'll never guess what's just happened to me."
"Someone's stolen your megaphone?"
"No. Silly bugger!"
"What, then?"
"Well, you know that second-hand Lamborghini I bought?"
"Yes."
"Well, it was a reasonable price and all that, but I was passing the dealership where I bought it this morning, so I just dropped in. And I asked this guy, real smarmy, with his smart suit and all that, if he had a minute. You know, a typical, high-value car salesman. All they see is money. And as soon as he realised I wasn't interested in buying a car, because I'd already bought one, he didn't want to know. He wanted to get rid of me as soon as he could. So, I said 'Fuck you, pal'. And I went over to the service desk. And there's people behind the counter there who actually work for a living. So, I asked this fella how much it would cost for a service for my car. And he asked me for some details, make and model, and age, and that. The car, I mean. And he got his calculator, and then he said, no word of a lie, £945, including VAT. I don't know how he kept a straight face. I thought fuck me! I said to him, £945, including VAT? It's a Lambo, not a Boeing seven-0-fucking-seven."

****

12th October

"The death of British IS recruiter Sally-Anne Jones, reportedly killed in a US drone strike in Syria in June, has been confirmed. Jones, from Chatham in Kent, joined so-called Islamic State after converting to Islam and travelling to Syria in 2013. The BBC's security correspondent Frank Gardner said Jones had been a useful propaganda agent for IS on social media and her death would be "significant".
Brexit Secretary David Davis and the EU's chief Brexit negotiator Michel Barnier are expected to sum up the state of negotiations on the UK's departure from the union later.

The fifth round of talks - the final discussions before a crucial EU summit on 19 and 20 October - are due to end. The UK has been hoping EU leaders at the summit will decide enough progress has been made to open trade talks.
A body has been discovered on moorland by detectives investigating the disappearance of a man who went missing six weeks ago. Tyron Charles, 29, from Denholme, Bradford, was last seen on 6 September. West Yorkshire Police said the body was found near Nab Water Lane, in Oxenhope, earlier and that officers were now working to identify the deceased. A woman and two men have been arrested in connection with Mr Charles' disappearance.
Two men were injured in a shooting in Leeds last night. Armed officers were called in after a shotgun was fired twice at a car in a targeted attack. It happened at about 23:15 on Maud Avenue, Beeston, when three men were sitting in a Toyota Yaris. A black BMW, which had a number of men wearing balaclavas in it, pulled up and shot at the other car, leaving a 21-year-old man with a shotgun pellet wound in his hand. A 19-year-old man was left with minor injuries from flying glass - both men were taken to hospital and later released."

"Mostly dry, bright and breezy with sunny spells, although cloud tending to increase later in the west. This may bring outbreaks of rain to the Pennines later in the evening."

John Braden sat nervously in the waiting area at the hospital Radiology and Imaging Department, dressed in a hospital gown. He'd filled out the medical questionnaire and signed the consent form, and the procedure had been explained to him. He'd been injected with a dye and was waiting for his name to be called. At that moment he wished he could speak to his daughter. But even if she was prepared to speak to him, he wasn't able to make a call as his phone was stored in a locker along with items of clothing and his watch. He heard his name called and soon he was lying stock-still on the CT scanner table as it moved back and forth through the scanner. He held his breath when the instructions to do so were given.

Twenty-five minutes later he was on his way to the waiting area for his MRI scan where a similar procedure was carried out, lasting a similar amount of time. After retrieving his clothes and personal items from the locker, there followed an interminable wait until he was called in to see the specialist. He rehearsed different scenarios in his head so that he could be prepared and could act pragmatically whatever the outcome.

"I've been in life or death situations before. This is just another one," he told himself.

He neglected to remind himself what a terrible toll the previous ones had taken on his well-being. His name was called. He took a deep breath and walked in to the Radiologist's office. The news was every bit as bad as he expected. He sat ashen-faced as the Radiologist explained.

"Mr Braden, the scans we've taken today show conclusive evidence of a tumour in the temporal lobe of your brain. At the moment we have no idea how long it's been there or how quickly it may be growing. Therefore, at this time, I cannot, with any certainty, tell you the probable outcome. It could be a very slow-growing tumour, in which case we can treat the side effects and simply monitor the growth. On the other hand, it may grow rapidly, and you would require surgery and radiation and chemotherapy. I'm afraid that's all I can tell you today. I'll complete my analysis and forward my report to a specialist. You can expect an appointment at the beginning of next week. In the meantime, if you would please take this prescription to our pharmacy, they'll provide you with corticosteroid medication to reduce any inflammation round the tumour and an anticonvulsant to prevent any further seizures. It is very important that you take this medication exactly as and when prescribed. The pharmacist will advise you regarding the dosage and frequency."

They shook hands. John Braden followed the directions to the pharmacy, collected his prescriptions and walked slowly back to his car, in time to see a parking enforcement officer checking the time on his ticket. He shouted,

"Hey. Wait a minute!"

John was fortunate that the officer was a reasonable man who fully understood the stress involved in clinical visits and since John was only five minutes overdue, the matter was overlooked and common sense prevailed.

Not like his officious colleagues in the city centre, John thought.

He drove home carefully, not feeling fully focused on the job, but, thankfully, traffic was light. He parked the car, took his medication into the flat, and checked his watch. It was after 4pm. He'd left the house at 12 to attend his hospital appointment.

At least it killed some time until opening time, he thought, a smile on his face for the first time that day.

He walked to the Draper. Nick, as usual, was on duty and there was already a dozen or so customers in the bar.

"Hello, John. You OK? You're looking a bit pasty."
"Yeah. Fine, thanks. I've just got a lot to deal with at the moment."
"Not all bad, I hope."
"Most of it. Someone broke a window in my car. Didn't take anything. Just mindless vandalism, I guess. And on top of that, someone's accused me of stalking and harassment."
"Surely, that's not true."
"'Course not. In future, though, I'll be careful who I talk to."

"Well, you know you're always among friends here."
"I do. And on top of that, I had a hospital appointment this morning for a brain scan."
"Did they manage to find it?"
"Very funny."
"Sorry. I mean, did they find anything nasty?"
"Potentially. They found a tumour. I have to go back next week for a repeat performance."
"Well, let's hope it's good news next time."
"Let's hope so. I've got some tablets to take, but I haven't read the info on them yet. Just in case it says 'Do not take alcohol'. So, I'll have a pint, please. Oh, and on top of everything else, I think someone's been following me."
"Paranoia, John."
"Perhaps you're right."

And he had several pints, was in good company, listened to and laughed at Foghorn Barry's latest escapades and thoroughly enjoyed himself before leaving and calling for a takeaway on his way home.

Eat, drink and be merry, he quoted to himself, for tomorrow, we die.

Back at the flat, he did his best to eat his takeaway. He managed to eat enough to satisfy his hunger, but he ate without enjoyment. It was simply a matter of ensuring he had something in his stomach prior to his customary assault on the malt whisky. There were other things he could have done. The surfaces of the furniture had a thin film of dust which he chose to ignore. He hadn't made the bed. There was a pile of washing up. No matter. It could all wait. He took out his packs of medication, read the instructions and took his prescribed quota. That task accomplished, he opened the whisky and poured a large glass, then sat in his customary chair, reflecting on his day.

Across the street, in the shade of a tree, DS Lee reported back to base the news that John Braden had returned home and appeared to be settled for the night. He was given permission to end his surveillance for the day.

****

13th October

“The EU is to begin preparing for its post-Brexit trade negotiations with the UK, while refusing to discuss the matter with the British government. An internal draft document suggests the 27 EU countries should discuss trade among themselves while officials in Brussels prepare the details.
Uber has filed an appeal against the decision by London authorities to deny it a licence to operate in London. Last month, Transport for London (TfL) refused Uber a new private hire licence, saying the ride-hailing firm was not fit and proper. TfL said it took the decision on the grounds of "public safety and security implications". The appeal process could take months, during which time Uber can continue to operate in London.
More than £500,000 has been spent on new power boats to help West Yorkshire Fire and Rescue respond to flooding. The service says that if there's a repeat of the Boxing Day floods of 2015 it will be better prepared. The new equipment will be stationed in Yorkshire, but could be deployed anywhere in the country.”

“A cloudy and windy day with outbreaks of rain. The heaviest of any rain will be over western hills. Drier with bright or sunny spells in the east. Feeling warm.”

Friday 13th, John mused. I wonder what catastrophe is going to befall me today. Worst thing would probably be the Draper running out of ale.

But at least he did not die, which thought had crossed his mind the previous evening, although he felt deathly ill with diarrhoea, nausea and a full-blown hangover. He hauled himself out of bed and spent a half-hour in the toilet before feeling well enough to make a cup of coffee. Thereafter, his day proceeded slowly as he gave his brain time to clear and his body time to mend. He didn't know whether the severe headache was down to his hangover or his tumour, or a mixture of the two, but at that moment he didn't really care. He re-read the instructions, particularly the part relating to side effects, on the packets of tablets and took them as prescribed. While filling a glass of water at the sink, he noticed through the window a removal van opposite. An attractive blonde, probably in her late thirties, early forties, casually dressed, and with her long hair tied back, was supervising the movement of furniture and boxes into a flat just down the street on the opposite side. Had he been feeling better, he would probably have shown more interest. As it was, he went back to slump in his armchair. Eventually, he fell asleep, waking occasionally and, if it was close to the appointed time, taking the stated dose of each of the various medications he'd been given. He'd expected he would experience at least some of the side effects. It seems that extreme lethargy was one of them. Unless, of course, his severe headache was due to a hangover. He'd sleep it off, and if he felt better later, then perhaps he'd consider going out for a pint.

****

One of Don McArthur's 'girls' was Ellen Stevenson. A high-class 'escort', she had often provided her services as an undercover agent for the Counter Terrorism Unit, and could be trusted to do a good job. Within hours of being briefed for the job, she was moving into a flat opposite where John Braden lived. Everything except her personal belongings and clothes came out of CTU's stores where they'd been since the last covert surveillance. While supervising the removal men, she'd briefly seen John's face at his kitchen window. She hoped he'd noticed her. After dismissing the removal men, she unpacked only what was necessary for what would most likely be just a short stay. From a suitcase she pulled out an A4 envelope, opened it and laid the various sheets of paper on the table. She memorized the floor plan of John's flat, and read carefully through all the accompanying notes. She put them away carefully in the suitcase, locked it and placed it in the back of a cupboard. She put on her coat, picked up her bag and walked out, carefully locking the door behind her.

Laden with carrier bags, she returned an hour later, methodically putting away her groceries before making a light meal which she ate at the kitchen table. For a second time she took out her notes and re-read them thoroughly, taking in all the detail. She liked to be fully prepared for her assignments, regarding herself as a professional. She washed up and made sure the flat was tidy before having a shower. She dried her hair and applied a little make-up, selected some smart casual clothes, dressed, checked her look, applied a touch of her favourite perfume, quite light and floral, put on flat shoes and her coat, and took a walk round the neighbourhood, familiarising herself with her new environment, before arriving at the Idle Draper shortly after opening time. She stopped outside for a moment to ensure she was fully prepared, then took a deep breath and pushed the door open. She immediately felt a little deflated. John wasn't in; in fact, there were no customers, only the man behind the bar.

****

Nick looked up from his newspaper when she walked in. It was unusual for his first customer to be a woman, let alone a beautiful one. He put on his best smile.

"Good afternoon. What can I get for you?"
"I'd like a large Shiraz, please."
"Coming up. If you'd like to take a seat, I'll bring it over for you."
"If it's OK with you, I'd rather just sit at the bar. That is, if I'm not taking anyone's regular seat."

"The seats don't belong to any specific customer, although there are some who think they own the place. You can sit wherever you like, love."
"Thank you."
"There you go. Six pounds, please."
"Thank you. Is it always so quiet at this time of day?"
"I can't really answer that, love. We've only just started opening earlier on Fridays. We used to open at 4pm, so customers are not used to the new hours yet. I'm sure we'll have a few in soon. John's usually in early on, but he had a skinful last night."
"A celebration?"
"No, not exactly. He was just a bit down. Health problems."
"Well, if he comes in, tell him I hope he's feeling better."
"I will. I'll introduce you to him if you like. That would make him feel a lot better, I'm sure. I'm Nick, by the way."
"Ellen."
"Pleased to meet you, Ellen. This is your first time in here, isn't it?"
"Yes. I just moved in down the road today. Marchmont Gardens."
"Really? John's your neighbour, then."
"What a coincidence. When I meet him, he'll be able to tell me who to trust and who to avoid in the area."
"Who to avoid? That'll be a long list."

But she didn't meet him. Not that night. She left the bar at seven after a group of men, including Foghorn Barry, came in and made leering remarks about her. She'd seen it all before and heard it all before so it didn't faze her; she just went straight home. As she put the key in her front door, she turned and looked in the direction of John's flat. It was in darkness, apart from the dim light of what she assumed must be a table lamp in the lounge. She opened a bottle of wine, pouring a large glass to spend some time planning her activities for the next day. Before leaving the Draper, she'd noted the opening times.

She dialled the number she'd been given for CTU, and left a short report of her fruitless first day.

****

John was fast asleep in his armchair until 10pm when he woke, bathed in sweat, from his regular nightmare. He poured himself a large whisky, then changed his mind and poured it back into the bottle, spilling a small quantity and cursing under his breath. His medication was overdue. He took his final dose for the day and went to bed, thankful, at least, for the fact that he'd survived another day. He was still awake when he checked his clock to find it was after one o'clock. He got up, walked naked in the dark into the kitchen and sat in his chair, whisky in hand for a further hour.

I'm dying, he thought. Why forgo one of the few pleasures I still have in my life?

He finished his drink, put the empty glass in the sink, and went back to bed.

CHAPTER 5

14th October

“Global powers, including key US allies, have said they will stand by the Iran nuclear deal which US President Donald Trump has threatened to tear apart. Mr Trump said on Friday that he would stop signing off on the agreement.
People caught twice carrying acid in public should receive a mandatory six-month prison sentence, the Home Office has proposed. It is aimed at curbing the number of acid attacks committed, which has more than doubled in five years. Home Secretary Amber Rudd said she intended to ban the sales of corrosive substances to under-18s.
A family left terrified by an armed police raid on their home say officers told them they had got the wrong house. Zaffar Iqbal's wife Nasreen was at home with their two teenage children on Thursday night when police arrived, shouting at her to open the door. Mr Iqbal said after four hours of being in their Dewsbury home, they told him "sorry, we've got the wrong house". West Yorkshire Police said it was acting on intelligence and apologised for any distress caused.”

“Cloudy through the morning with outbreaks of rain and drizzle, more especially across the Pennines. The rain should weaken into the afternoon, allowing some drier, brighter spells to develop in the east and feeling warm here. Breezy at times.”

A ringing noise woke John. It wasn’t his alarm; that had gone a while ago, though as usual without his knowledge. His phone! Where the hell was it? He turned over and swung his legs over the side of the bed. He tried to stand, but fell back on to the bed. His head was pounding. His sight was blurred. He would have to ignore it and hope the sender’s number was recorded. It was already light outside but he’d no idea what time it was. He thought about taking the first of the day’s dose of his new regime of medication but the sheer effort of getting up to get them was just too much for him. He lay back, trying to sleep.

But he couldn't sleep. He got up, took his medication, vomited, had a quick wash, got dressed and went down to his car. He drove straight to Lister park, arriving just in time for the start. He recognised a few faces – people he'd run with previously, in the days when running was a regular part of his exercise regime.

"Hi John. Good to see you. You've just got time for the start if you're quick."
"If it's all the same to you guys, I won't be running. I just want to walk the course. To see if I'm still capable."
"Are you OK? You don't look too good."
"I'm just a bit under the weather, that's all. The walk will clear my head."

He walked slowly round the course he'd run so regularly in the past, as runners sped past him. Many were on their third and final circuit before he'd finished his first, and, exhausted, he gave up at the end of the first circuit. He spoke briefly to a few of his old friends before taking his leave and returning to his car for the drive home. As soon as he'd locked himself in his flat, he collapsed on to his bed, fully clothed. His 'tail' followed at a distance, and once John was safely home, made the call to McArthur.

"Hi, boss. He's back home and I've passed the baton to Ellen. He's been to Lister park, for the parkrun."
"What the hell's the parkrun?"
"It's an exercise initiative. Very popular these days. Happens in parks all over the country on Saturday mornings. It's a 5k run."
"You're telling me Braden's been for a 5k run?"
"No, boss. He just walked once round the course. Talked to a few people."
"Tell me, Brian. Do they run past any statues?"
"Statues?"

"Yes, Brian. Statues."
"Just let me check, boss. I took some photos.... Yes, here. Yes, they run right past a statue near the main gate."
"Thanks, Brian. Send me the photos."
"Will do."

While he waited for the photos to come through, McArthur did a quick search for 'parkrun'. He'd remembered reading a report some years back regarding a plot to blow up a statue in Lister park, and the information he was now reading about parkrun heightened his suspicions. Around four hundred runners, running past a statue. Plus, onlookers, marshals. Was the plot about to take place? Could Braden have been mistaken about the date? Could it have been 28th, which would be a Saturday?

****

When John woke the light was fading. His head was clear, as was his sight. He got out of bed and made his way slowly into the bathroom where he threw up while counting out his tablets. It was already five thirty. He could take a dose now and another at bedtime. Only missed one dose.

Can't make that much difference now, he told himself, then re-considered. Carry on like this and you might not make it to the 29th. Get a grip on yourself, man.

He made a mug of coffee, drank it and took a shower. Drying himself, he went in search of his phone and found it in his jacket pocket. He checked for missed calls. None recorded. As he turned to go back into the kitchen, he noticed the envelope on the doormat. He picked it up and examined it. The envelope bore the name and logo of the local health authority. He tore it open. Inside was a letter detailing his appointment for Monday morning to discuss the result of his scans and determine actions to produce the best clinical outcome. The 16th. That was quick. He made himself a promise that this weekend, or at least what was left of it, would be different. He dressed and went down to the local convenience store for a ready meal for the microwave, walking straight past the racks of alcohol without paying them any attention.

Back home he heated the chicken dinner and ate it without much enthusiasm. To drink he poured a glass of tap water, thinking he would rather wash his meal down with a glass of Malbec, and finished off with a banana, rather than his usual malt whisky. He washed up and sat in his chair listening to a Lou Reed album.

****

Ellen left the Idle Draper at eight-thirty after another wasted evening. She'd been chatted up by several customers, had a few drinks bought for her, but her target had failed to show once again. Approaching her front door, she looked across the road and saw the light in John's living room.

"At least he hasn't done a runner. At least I can report *something* positive."

Once inside, she took off her coat and shoes, poured herself a small glass of red - the last for the night, she promised herself, and phoned the CTU number. Peters took the call.

"What have you got for us, Ellen?"
"Nothing, again, Brian. I watched his door all day and never saw him at all. And thinking he might possibly have left the flat before dawn, I went up to his local, stayed a few hours, got pawed by some grubby customers who couldn't possibly afford me, and just came home. But at least I can report that there's a light on in his living room."
"OK, Ellen. Better luck tomorrow. Talk later."
"'Bye."

She drained the glass of red, then poured another.

"So much for good intentions."

She thumbed through her phone contacts list and called another number.

"Hello."
"Hi. I'm in Bradford. Can we meet for a quick catch-up?"

****

15th October

"Forty people have died and hundreds are still missing in California after six days of wildfires that have devastated swathes of countryside and destroyed thousands of homes. California's governor said it was "one of the greatest tragedies" the state had ever faced.
A man has died after being injured at Kempton Park racecourse in Surrey. Saturday's fixture was abandoned with two races remaining when the man in his 50s was injured in the stable yard. A Surrey Police spokeswoman said the death was being treated as unexplained and inquiries were ongoing.
Manchester City Council has been honoured by its historic rivals for its response to the bomb attack on the city's arena which killed 22 people. The authority was presented with a special award at the annual Yorkshire Awards, held in Leeds on Friday. Six people from Yorkshire were killed in the attack on the Manchester Arena."

"Dry with variable amounts of low cloud around, but this should break up during the day to allow spells of warm sunshine. The low cloud will mainly affect western hills with hill fog. Winds will become lighter through the day."

John woke early, feeling refreshed. He'd slept well and had only a mild headache. He made a mug of coffee and a couple of slices of toast, and took his medication. An hour later, showered, shaved and dressed, he was on his way to the convenience store for the Sunday paper and a pack of bacon and a dozen eggs. He knew he should have made a shopping list. He was vaguely aware he needed something else but couldn't recall what it might be so he walked along every aisle hoping that something would jog his memory. Rounding a corner, he collided with a blonde woman distractedly checking her shopping list.

"Oops, sorry, love."
"Don't apologise. I should watch where I'm going. I've never been in here before. I don't suppose you could tell me where the washing up liquid is?"
"Far end of this aisle. Bottom shelf, right hand side."
"Thanks."
"My pleasure."
"One other thing. Is there a local taxi firm you could recommend? I'm not going far, but I've quite a lot to carry."
"There are some numbers on the notice board by the exit. But if you live close by, maybe I can give you a hand carrying your shopping."
"I don't want you to have to go out of your way. I live on Marchmont Gardens."
"I thought I'd seen you before. You've just moved in across the road from me."
"What a coincidence."
"So, I'll help you carry your shopping home."
"I'm Ellen."
"John. Pleased to meet you."

They made small talk as they walked back to Marchmont Gardens until they arrived outside Ellen's door.

"Thanks, John. I really appreciate your help. I'd invite you in for coffee but the place is still a tip. Perhaps another time?"
"No problem. I'm sure I'll see you around."
"Bye, then. And thanks again."
"Bye."

She went inside, closed the door, and began to plan the rest of her day.

****

John was simultaneously cooking bacon and eggs while making toast and a mug of coffee. He had forgotten to switch on the extractor fan and the familiar high-pitched tone of the smoke detector alerted him to the fact that his toast was burning. He switched off the grill and pulled the tray out from under the element. The toast was charred and smoking. He opened the window and waved a towel under the smoke detector to disperse the smoke. But it continued to beep. He pulled out a chair, stood on it and tried the reset button on the alarm. That failed to have the desired effect so he decided to unscrew the cap and remove the batteries. It was then he noticed the black wire protruding slightly from the rim of the alarm. He removed the cap and found a tiny microchip attached by a clip to the battery terminal. He'd seen enough smoke alarms in the course of his career to know this device was not a part of the alarm mechanism. It had been put there for a specific purpose. He removed it and put it in his jacket pocket. He ate his breakfast in silence. Twice he took the microchip from his pocket and turned it over in his hand before replacing it in his pocket. He'd decided what he would do.

He stacked the dirty crockery at the side of the sink then conducted a methodical and laborious search of his flat, starting in the kitchen. He searched all the cupboards, unscrewed the door bell and inspected inside the cover. He checked all the appliances, pulling out the microwave and peering behind and under it. He unscrewed each electrical switch panel carefully, inspected each one and replaced the covers. He took down the wall clock and removed the cover enclosing the batteries and, once satisfied it was 'clean', replaced it on the wall. He moved on to the extractor fan, taking the opportunity to give it a much-needed clean while the cover was off. Satisfied, he turned his attention to the bathroom down the corridor, searching methodically as before. Clean. Next, the walk-in cupboards. Stacked with boxes and things which had no rightful place anywhere else but which he'd never got around to throwing away, he nevertheless took out every item, inspected it and replaced it. He'd find time some other day to take them to the tip. Then the bedroom. He took everything out of every drawer, inspected it and replaced it. He removed the drawers themselves and checked behind and underneath. He moved every piece of furniture, looked behind the photos hung on the walls. He checked the curtain rail, and finally, attached to the back of a picture light, he found another bug. He removed it and put it in his pocket, and continued his painstaking search.

Back in the living room, the one room where he'd remained all the time the officers were in his flat, he sat, mentally ticking off everywhere he'd checked, but with the gnawing feeling he might have missed something. It came to him. Whenever he left the flat, he had a habit of putting his laptop in the bottom of the wardrobe, underneath the drawer. He'd only just returned home that night he called the police about the damage to his car and they arrived quickly. The laptop would still have been hidden in the wardrobe! He set it on the table, and carefully unscrewed the back. He wasn't totally familiar with the innards of a laptop, but it was patently obvious the tiny black chip attached to the motherboard was not factory installed. He removed it and powered the laptop up, running a virus scan immediately. His AVG software did its job and reported that a keystroke recording program had been installed. He followed the recommended actions to remove it.

He made a mug of tea and sat for a while, thinking about recent events, trying to recall anything out of the ordinary that had occurred over the past few days. The fact that two plain-clothed officers had attended an incident of petty vandalism was clearly the most important factor. He recalled that one of the officers had left the living room for a few minutes. It seemed obvious he had used the time to plant the bugs. Thinking back, he felt sure he had not said anything in the flat which could incriminate him. He hadn't recently performed any internet searches which might be deemed illegal or immoral. He was sure it must all be a mistake. Or some kind of giant conspiracy.

****

David Lee was in the office even though it was Sunday. He often popped in primarily to catch up on outstanding work but he had nothing better to do and realised that the more he put into the job now, the better would be his chances of career progression later. His first task was to check the monitoring equipment. His jaw dropped. The three monitors marked JB1, JB2 and JB3 all reported 'No signal'.

Shit! he said out loud, though he was alone in the office. Either there's been a transmission fault or he's found them and disconnected them.

He played back the audio recorded up to the point of the error. Nothing usable. No phone calls. No conversation. No recognisable noises except those associated with someone going to the toilet, and hours of music. And the occasional expletive. And the loud beeping of a smoke alarm at the very end.

He phoned his boss with the news and within half an hour the three senior members of the unit were in the office to discuss the next step. Peters was able to lighten the gloom by announcing that Ellen had managed to make 'accidental' contact with Braden earlier that morning, and he felt sure her 'methods' would yield some valuable information.

"Is it worth breaking in to the flat and just checking so we know for certain whether the equipment is faulty or whether he's found it?"

"I think the fact that the smoke alarm had been activated and shut down tells us all we need to know. Besides, the bugs have yielded nothing useful up to now, so let's just write them off and give Ellen a chance to use her skills."
"Do you want us to continue monitoring his movements?"
"Yes. Between you two and Ellen. I want to know where he goes, who he talks to, what he does. Sort it out between you."
"Does that mean we'll be paid overtime?"
"Just do it."

****

John wasn't hungry although it was past six o'clock. He'd spent most of the afternoon thinking about the bugs. And on top of that he was worried about his hospital appointment in the morning. He'd eat later; maybe a takeaway, but now he fancied a pint. It was quite warm outside, certainly unseasonably warm, and calm and dry so he just slipped a jacket on and made his way to the Draper. Walking through the door, he couldn't help but notice the tall blonde sitting alone at a table facing the door. She smiled at him.

"Hello again, John. Fancy meeting you in here."
"It's my local."
"Well, it's nice to see you again. Now perhaps I can thank you for helping me this morning. Can I buy you a drink?"
"If you insist."
"I insist."
"A pint of Gold, then, please, Ellen."
"Gold? Is that beer?"
"Just ask for a pint of Gold. They'll know what you mean."

When she stood up and walked to the bar he got a good look at her legs for the first time. Impossibly long and shapely, below the shortest miniskirt he'd seen in a long time. It was a sight to stir his soul. So much attention was he paying to her body he never noticed Jim Tate sat at a corner table. Clockwork Jimmy, so called because everyone wound him up, got off his seat and walked straight over to John. He moved close, speaking in a conspiratorial low voice, so low that John had to really concentrate to hear what he was saying.

"I hope she is worth it, John, though I don't know how much you paid."
"What are you on about?"
"Sorry, John, I'll talk to you later. Just be careful."

Clockwork Jimmy moved quickly away back to his table as Ellen returned with the drinks.

"What was that about?"
"Jimmy? Oh, don't worry about Jimmy. He's always nattering me for something or other. He's harmless."
"So, John. Why don't you tell me all about yourself?"
"There's not much to tell. I lead a very boring life."

Mindful of what Jimmy had said, he was determined to give away as little as possible, until he discovered her *real* motives. He decided to turn it back on her.

"Let's talk about you, Ellen. I'm sure your life is much more exciting than mine. So, what brings you to this area where nothing exciting ever seems to happen?"
"I've just walked away from a bad relationship. I needed a clean break."
"But why here? What's the attraction of this place?"
"I got a job offer. Found accommodation and arranged the move and everything. And then the job fell through. And since I'd already put down a bond and paid three months' rent upfront, I thought I might as well move and see how a new area works for me."
"So, where did you move from?"
"Nottingham."
"I know Nottingham quite well. Did you ever drink in the centre?"

"Not really, I never really got out much at all. I told you. It was a bad relationship."
"Shame. There are some nice pubs in the centre of Nottingham. So, what kind of work are you looking for?"
"Anything clerical, really."
"Well, you shouldn't have much trouble. Have you tried signing on with any agencies?"
"Not yet. I haven't got around to it yet."

All non-committal stuff, he thought. She's not giving anything away. Well, neither am I.

He bought a round of drinks, and then it was her turn to quiz him.

"So, John. Your turn now."
"Nothing to tell. A very boring existence. I live alone. Took early retirement, because I could afford it. And now I spend my life going for long walks, reading, listening to music. And going to the pub. That's life."
"No special person in your life?"
"Nope."
"Never married?"
"Yes. And divorced."
"Any kids?"
"One."
"Boy or girl?"
"Girl."
"Does she live with her mother?"
"I don't know. Lost contact with her."

The fact-finding conversation had gone as far as either party was prepared to allow, and the silence was palpable as they sipped their drinks. John decided enough was enough.

"Well, Ellen, I'm sorry but it's time I went home. I've got a very busy day tomorrow and I need an early night. So, I'm sorry, but I'll have to leave you to it."

"I'll walk home with you if that's OK. I've had enough to drink."
"Fine."

They walked in silence until they reached Ellen's door.

"Fancy a nightcap, John?"
"Er. No, thanks. Not this time."
"Sure?"
"Sure."
"OK. Goodnight, John."
"Goodnight, Ellen."

****

Back in the flat, he considered Clockwork Jimmy's warning, and wondered if there was anything in it, or if someone had been winding him up with a false story. He had known Jim Tate for many years, socially. They had grown up together in the same area, although they could never be considered close friends. John's opinion was that Jim was basically a good guy, honest and straightforward, who just had a tendency to trust too easily in what people told him. He was just a little naïve, that's all. And people took advantage of him because of it. John could feel he had a headache coming on. He took his medication and sat in his chair in the dark, glass of whisky in hand.

****

Across the road, Ellen saw his light go out, picked up her phone and called in her report.

"David?"
"Yes, Ellen. What have you got?"
"Not much, but at least we had a few drinks in a bar together. He's not opening up much yet, though."
"You couldn't get him into bed, then?"
"No. He said he had a busy day coming up tomorrow."

"You're losing your touch. OK. We'll get someone to keep an eye on him. Thanks, Ellen. I'll see you soon. Goodnight."
"Goodnight, David."

Ellen sat at her kitchen table, a glass of red wine in front of her. She swished it around the glass distractedly as she wondered how she could conjure up a situation which would bring about a breakthrough with John. She thought of, perhaps, inventing a household emergency she could get him to fix. Maybe a fuse to change, or a light bulb, so she could look like she needed a man. Surely, he couldn't resist her if she played the role of damsel in distress. And if she could get him into bed, she could get into his mind. That, when it comes down to it, was what she got paid to do.

****

John continued to sit in his chair until close to eleven o'clock. He'd spent his time wondering why Ellen had taken such an interest in him and what would have happened if he'd accepted her offer of a nightcap. Would he also have been offered sex? He wasn't sure, in his present state, whether he would be able to perform anyway. Apart from the effect his medication might have on his libido, it had been a long time since he'd had sex with anyone but himself. He drained his glass, had a wash, took his medication, stripped off and went to bed. He was asleep in minutes.

CHAPTER 6

16th October.

"Clashes have been reported between Iraqi and Kurdish forces after Baghdad sent troops towards disputed areas held by the Kurds in Kirkuk province. State TV said government forces had taken control of some areas, including oil fields, "without fighting". But Kurdish officials denied this. An exchange of artillery fire is said to have occurred south of Kirkuk city.
Theresa May is to travel to Brussels later for a dinner with EU leaders in a bid to end a stalemate over Brexit. The meeting, with chief negotiator Michel Barnier and Commission chief Jean-Claude Juncker, comes days after the pair said talks were in "deadlock". Brexit Secretary David Davis will join Mrs May for the meeting, ahead of this week's summit of EU leaders.
The Met Office has warned of "potential danger to life" as the remnants of Hurricane Ophelia head for the British Isles with 80mph (130km/h) winds. An amber warning for Northern Ireland, parts of Wales and south west Scotland is in force from midday."

"Largely dry but increasingly windy, although the odd spot of rain is possible at first, mainly in the north. Some warm sunshine is likely to develop, especially towards the coast. However, cloud will thicken later in the west, with gales likely."

The alarm clock woke John at 7.00 with the news and weather forecast. His headache was intense as he lay still with his eyes closed. Eventually he hauled himself wearily out of bed and made his way to the bathroom. After a shower and a light breakfast of cereals and coffee, he took his medication. Finally, his headache had reduced to a tolerable level. Even at eight-thirty the sky was still quite dark, with rain seemingly imminent. He pulled on his coat, grabbed his keys and laptop and drove down to the car park close to a row of small shops. Unusually, he found a space without a problem and walked the hundred yards to the Computer Shack, his laptop under his arm. The atmosphere was humid. A storm brewing.

Ahmed, the owner of the Computer shack, knew John as he'd repaired his laptop previously. John trusted him, and his prices were reasonable.

"Morning, Ahmed."
"Morning, John. How are you, mate?"
"OK, Ahmed. You?"
"Yeah, good, mate, yeah. What can I do for you today?"
"Can you give the laptop a deep clean?"
"Been downloading naughty stuff?"
"No, mate. Someone installed a bug. Here, check this."
"Let's have a look."

He examined the device, then connected it to a PC. He initiated a program which swept it for viruses, then read its contents.

"It's a keystroke recorder, mate. It just transmits to a base station so someone can follow what you've done online. I don't think there's a virus installer on it, but I'll clean the laptop anyway."
"There are another two bugs, Ahmed."
"Christ! What are you? Some sort of secret agent?"
"Nothing of the sort. But for some reason unknown to me, someone is watching me. Very closely."
"OK. Let's have a look at the others."

Ahmed hooked them up to his diagnostic equipment one after the other, and gave his verdict.

"Audio transmitters, mate. Listen."

He played a section. John could clearly make out the sound of his music on the Hi-fi, the scraping of the chair as he rose from the table, the clink of the whisky bottle on the edge of the glass, and a host of other sounds he could recognise as those he made as he shuffled round the flat. Even the unmistakable sound of a loud fart was recognisably his own.

"Nothing incriminating there, mate. You can't be locked up for farting in your own house."
"Any idea where this might be transmitting to?"
"No idea, mate. I haven't got any equipment that would find that for me. Sorry."
"No worries. Can I pick the laptop up today?"
"Yes, mate. Be ready in an hour."
"Thanks, Ahmed."
"Take care, mate."

John went straight back to his car and drove across town to the hospital. Distracted by his imminent appointment, he didn't notice the black Audi which followed him, two cars behind, all the way. He parked and made his way directly to Radiology, where once again he endured CT and MRI scans, before sitting patiently in a corridor until he was called into the Consultant's office. He was understandably nervous. In the room were the Radiologist he'd seen the previous week, and a well-dressed, silver-haired gentleman who introduced himself as Alexander Coleman-James. His general air of authority, and the silk handkerchief neatly tucked into the breast pocket of his well-tailored suit, gave the very strong impression that he was in charge.

"Good morning, Mr Braden. I have looked through your notes from your visit last week, and examined the evidence of this morning's scans. I am sorry to have to tell you that your tumour has shown significant growth since your last scan. As I believe you were informed last week, the tumour is in the part of the brain which can produce hallucinations. I understand you have already experienced one such episode linked to a seizure which led to your admittance to A & E."

He paused to let the news sink in, watching as the colour drained from John's face, then continued.

"My colleagues and I have reached the same conclusion, Mr Braden. And you must be aware that we cannot offer guarantees of a completely successful outcome. Our proposal is this. We book you in for surgery as a matter of urgency. Assuming surgery is successful, we then commence with chemo- and radiotherapy. There will be quite a cocktail of drugs to be taken throughout your treatment, for instance to control the pressure in your brain, to prevent the seizures, ease the pain. And on top of those, of course, there will be yet more drugs to alleviate the side-effects caused by the rest...."
"How long before the surgery?"
"I'm not certain at this moment, but possibly within two weeks."
"Please schedule it for after the 30th. I need two weeks."
"We'd rather sooner than later, Mr Braden. This is a race against time..."
"Two weeks, and then you can do whatever you want."
"If that is what you wish, Mr Braden, in the full knowledge that the sooner we start the treatment, the higher the likelihood of a positive outcome."
"It's what I wish."
"Then, if you'd just sign these forms of consent, please, Mr Braden."

He walked slowly, wearily, back to his car, checking the time on his ticket before he slid into the front seat. He had unexpired time left on his ticket, which he made use of to sit and think. He questioned whether he'd made the right decision. After all, he'd evidently experienced a hallucination. No more, no less. It had *seemed* very real, but that was because his brain had attempted to make some sense of it. Obviously, he was the only one who thought it was real. And, of course, he was the one with the brain tumour. He could surrender himself to an early operation which might just take away the nightmare scenario of impending disaster which was now firmly lodged in his head. On top of that was the fact that he was being spied upon and was not sure who he could trust any more. But could he live with himself, or, more realistically, die with the knowledge that, if only he could convince the right people, then a potential disaster could be averted? He took the ticket from the dashboard, put it in his pocket and started the engine.

Driving home, he checked his mirror before signalling to turn right. He noticed a black Audi behind him. He had a fleeting thought that he might have seen it behind him earlier that morning.

Paranoia, John, he whispered to himself. You're losing your mind.

But he continued to check his rear-view mirror at regular intervals during his drive home. On the way, though, he stopped at the Computer Shack, pulling into a parking space right outside. He sat in the car, watching the Audi drive past, then entered the shop.

"Hi, mate. It's all ready for you."
"Thanks, Ahmed. Find anything?"
"No, mate. Just ran a 'clean'. No threats reported. It's all fine."
"Thanks. How much do I owe you?"
"Thirty OK?"
"Fine. Thanks for your help."
"Any time, mate."

Taking the laptop back to the car, he could see no sign of the black Audi. He shrugged his shoulders. Probably just another hallucination, he told himself.

****

The driver of the black Audi, David Lee, called in his report to CTU, was given permission to stand down, and went for his lunch. Five minutes later, Ellen called CTU to report that John Braden had now arrived home.

****

John gathered up the post from behind the door and threw it on the table after a quick glance. There was nothing which required his immediate attention. In fact, there was nothing which required his attention at all. He'd deal with it later. He had more urgent matters on his mind.

He placed his laptop on the kitchen table, took off his coat, filled a glass with water, counted out his tablets carefully, checking against his prescription, and swallowed them one by one, washing them down with the water. He put the kettle on, spooned coffee and sugar into a clean mug and made a sandwich for his lunch. He ate his sandwich and drank his coffee at the kitchen table, staring at the closed laptop. His mind was still replaying the events of the morning, particularly the conversation he'd had with the Consultant. His time was running out, yet he had refused the offer of early intervention because he needed to be somewhere on the 29th. The Consultant's words leapt into his brain. He'd called it 'a race against time'. That was it! He reached over and opened the laptop, powering it up and waiting impatiently until it was ready for input. In the Google search bar, he typed 'races in yorkshire' and pressed 'enter'. The displayed results were mainly for horse racing, though there were others concerning road races. John thought for a few seconds then, deciding a local race would be a more likely subject, he changed the search parameters to 'races in bradford'. As an afterthought, he narrowed the search by adding 'october'. The results appeared in an instant. There it was at the top of the list after the sponsored results. 'Bradford City Runs - Racebest'. Although the description gave the date as 28th October, he clicked on the site anyway, reasoning that there may be two consecutive days of races. When the site opened, the date in the top right-hand corner stated 29th October 2017. He paged down, clicking the links and then opened a different site for Bradford City runs. This yielded the information he was looking for. Four races over different distances, including the Bradford Half Marathon, all on the morning of 29th October 2017. That had to be it. The Race Against Time. He remembered seeing posters advertising the event around the city centre, but it just hadn't registered as being of any significance at the time.

He checked a number of entries for events taking place on the same day, but always came back to the Half Marathon. Nothing else really measured up, in terms of the impact, or the likely crowd. All he really needed to know was whether Amy would be there. He considered calling her, but thought better of it as she might consider pressing charges against him for stalking her. But as far as he was concerned, the Half Marathon, or one of the associated races, was the target. Now he could start to make specific plans. He switched on his printer and printed out the route. But there was not enough detail. He would need to enlarge it many times over to get the required detail. He took the printout, folded it and put it in his inside pocket and went out to his car. He pulled out on to the main road and checked his mirror. No-one was following him.

Fifteen minutes later, he had parked in Forster square Retail Park and was making his way on foot into the city centre, his destination being The Broadway Centre. He knew there was a WH Smith store there, and though it was a number of years since he'd bought such an item, he felt sure they'd stock it there. If not, he'd order one online. But really, he wanted it now.

He entered the Centre from Market Street and consulted a store plan, from where he was able to navigate his way directly to the stationer's. He approached the first assistant he saw to ask where he could find what he needed. She took him straight to the display at the end of an aisle. He quickly found it. A Leeds and Bradford A to Z street guide. Forget the digital world. For now, this was exactly what he needed. He paid for it and walked back to his car, on the way passing a number of posters advertising the Half Marathon on the 29th. He wondered how many other people had seen the same or similar posters and decided to get out on the streets on the day to support the event. Several thousands, he imagined. He drove home in silence, planning how best to tackle the problems of identifying the specific location where the disaster would occur. On a circuit covering a distance in excess of thirteen miles.

The closer he got to home, the worse his headache became. He was able to park up, lock the car and enter his flat before he passed out in the kitchen. When he regained consciousness an hour or so later, all he could remember seeing in a dream was a hooded figure in the midst of a large crowd. He made a mug of tea, sat silently at the kitchen table and ate a chocolate biscuit as he regained his energy. He checked his watch. Three-thirty. He took out his phone and spent almost ten minutes composing a text to his daughter, before finally pressing 'send'.

Only now did he pick up the envelopes which arrived in the post. Typically, due to the time of year, they were all random mailshots, none of which were of even remote interest to him. He was dying. Why on earth would he require a hearing aid, a two-for-one offer on spectacles, gardening implements, a universal remote control, or any of a host of cut-price electrical appliances? Fortunately, a couple of the mailshots had kindly supplied pre-paid return envelopes, so he gathered up all the offers and stuffed as many as he could into the envelopes before sealing them and putting them in a pile for posting.

Let's see how they enjoy finding a pile of useless crap in their post, he thought, smiling.

At 4pm, as Nick unlocked the door, John was waiting on the steps of the Draper having posted his junk mail back to the mailing companies on his way there.

"Hello, Nick."
"Hi, John. Come in and tell me how you did it."
"How I did what?"
"How you managed to make small talk with the tall blonde woman."
"Pure charm."
"Well, she was in on Friday and Saturday and cold-shouldered every customer who approached her. Yet she took to you immediately. Almost as if you were the one she'd been waiting for."
"We met in the shop yesterday morning. Turns out she lives just across the road from me."
"She's probably after your pension."
"I'm not sure what she's after, but I doubt it's my pension."
"Well, let me know all the sordid details."
"You wish."
"Let's see if she makes a beeline for you tonight."
"What time does she normally get in?"
"Any time. I've not worked out a pattern yet. I guess she'll be here if she thinks you'll be in."
"I'll risk an hour, then."
"If I see her coming, I'll give you a nod and you can run out of the back door."
"Thanks."

John tried to relax at a table with his pint, but jumped every time the door opened. He drained his glass and took it back to the bar.

"Another, please, Nick."
"OK. I forgot to ask, John. How did the appointment go?"
"Not well. I need an operation."
"Is it that bad?"
"Without the operation, it will kill me. With it, I've got only a slight chance of surviving any length of time."

"Did they give you any idea how long?"
"Well, put it this way. I won't be renewing my TV licence."
"Between you and me, I don't bother with one anyway. When does yours expire?"
"End of January."
"Well, at least you'll be able to watch all the Christmas spectaculars legally."
"Won't that be a treat."

They'd taken their eyes off the door, and failed to see Ellen enter before she'd seen John. He had no option but to look pleased.

"Hello, Ellen. Would you like a drink?"
"Oh, yes, please, John. Could I have a large Shiraz?"
"Large Shiraz for the lady, Nick, please."
"So, what have you been up to today, John? Anything exciting?"
"Not really. Just a routine hospital appointment. Nothing to worry about. How about you?"
"Looking for work. I've done as you suggested and registered with a couple of local agencies. And I've applied for a clerical job in Shipley."
"Well, that would be handy. Direct bus from just up the road."
"Well, I'm sure I'll know in a few days. In the meantime, I shall enjoy the freedom."
"I'm sure you will. I'm sorry, but I'll have to leave you here. I have some things to sort out."
"Oh, that's a shame, John."
"Sorry. It can't be helped. Another time, maybe."

He said his goodbyes and walked home briskly. He locked the door behind him and put the security chain on – something he never did before bedtime – then made a mug of tea, sat at the kitchen table and checked his phone. No messages. No missed calls. He considered sending another text to his daughter, but it seemed pointless. She would either reply to the one he sent earlier, or ignore it, in which case he was unlikely to hear from her ever again. He took his prescribed tablets with a glass of water, poured the rest of his tea down the sink and refilled his glass with whisky. He flipped idly through the channels on his DAB radio, switching stations every time a record he hated came on, which was a frequent occurrence. In the end, in frustration, he switched it off, enjoying the silence.

Every bloody station's the same. The first time you tune to one, it's like a breath of fresh air. Songs you haven't heard for ages. Then the next day, the same songs are on again. And the next day, it's the same thing. Same songs, just in a different sequence. It doesn't matter whether you tune in to Radio Awful, or Radio Rubbish, or Radio Abysmal, every single one has a limited playlist which they run through daily, day in, day out, every day the same old crap, he moaned.

It was one of John's pet hates, his Room 101 subject, which he complained about, loudly, almost daily, to anyone who'd listen. He drank his whisky and poured himself a refill.

John had just started his second glass when his phone vibrated on the table. He picked it up and answered without bothering to check who the caller was.

"Hello?"
"Dad?"
"Jane! How are you?"
"I'm fine, dad, but, how are you? The message you sent me has got me worried."
"I'm sorry, Jane. There was really no other way of saying it…."
"That you're dying?"
"Yes."
"Is there nothing anybody can do?"
"No. It's going to happen. And I wanted to hear your voice again before it did."

"Dad, I'm so sorry…."
"You don't need to apologise. I drove you away. I'm the one who should apologise."
"Can I see you?"
"Yes, of course. I would love that. But it's better if I come to see you. If you'll tell me where you are, that is."
"I'm in Derby. Come whenever you can."
"Tomorrow OK?"
"Absolutely. How will you get here?"
"I'll drive, if you'll give me an address."
"I'll text it to you after this call."
"Promise?"
"Promise. And, dad, be prepared for a surprise or two."
"OK."
"Dad, I'm really looking forward to seeing you. I've so much to explain…."
"Let's put the past behind us, Jane. I'm really looking forward to seeing you tomorrow."
"OK, dad. Let me know when you get close so I can look out for you."
"OK. 'Bye, Jane."
"'Bye, dad."

He ended the call and placed the phone on the table. His eyes were wet with tears as he powered up the laptop so he could plan his journey as soon as the address came through. Five minutes later, armed with the address and postcode, he had clear directions to an estate on the northern outskirts of Derby. He printed off all the information he required and made a short 'do list' for the morning, including filling up with petrol and checking the tyre pressures, and making sure he took his medication with him. He didn't want to be stranded seventy miles away from his life-prolonging tablets. Before he went to bed, he reset the alarm for a much earlier time than normal. And set it to ring loudly.

****

Ellen left the Draper five minutes after John. She went straight back to her flat, noting that John's kitchen light was still on. She sat at the kitchen table and phoned CTU with her report. Another disappointing day. She would have to work harder at it. Usually, by now, she would have made much more progress. Was she losing her touch? Or was John Braden simply too good an adversary. She took the briefing notes from her suitcase and re-read them for potential clues as to his character, and possible ways to find out the information she was paid to discover. But no matter how many times she read the notes, she was unable to find any obvious chink in his armour. Perhaps the direct approach would be best. Perhaps she should just go up to him and offer him a 'no-strings-attached' shag.

CHAPTER 7

17th October

“The US has called for "calm" after Iraqi government forces seized the northern city of Kirkuk and key installations from Kurdish control. State department spokeswoman Heather Nauert urged all parties to "avoid further clashes". Iraqi soldiers moved into Kirkuk three weeks after the Kurdistan Region held a controversial independence referendum.
A man has died and two others have been injured in a stabbing outside Parsons Green Tube station in London. The attack happened just after 19:30 BST on Monday at the station where 30 people were injured in a terror attack last month. A 20-year-old man died in the stabbing, which is not being treated as terror-related. The two who were injured were taken to hospital and one was subsequently arrested.
Brexit negotiations should "accelerate over the months to come," says a joint statement from the UK prime minister and the president of the EU Commission. Theresa May and Jean-Claude Juncker met in Brussels on Monday for a dinner they called "constructive and friendly"
A police investigation into the death of a boy found hanged did not find any evidence of bullying, despite claims to the contrary from his parents. Asad Khan, 11, from Bradford, was a pupil at the city's Beckfoot Upper Heaton School. He was found hanged by his mother at his home on Tile Street, on 28 September 2016, an inquest heard.”

“Very strong, gusty winds initially but these gradually ease. It will also be largely cloudy across the region, with outbreaks of rain, although these will be mainly across the Pennines as bright or sunny spells will gradually develop for many eastern areas.”

After an early night and a fairly restful night’s sleep, at least by his recent standards, John switched off his alarm clock as soon as it rang, got out of bed and went through to the bathroom. It was just after 5.30am. Considering the time and the present state of his health, he felt remarkably alert. By 6.15am he was enjoying breakfast of coffee and toast, and had taken his first batch of daily tablets. He dressed, packed a flight bag, checked his wallet, switched on the bedside light, put on his coat and went out to face a cold damp and still dark morning. He locked up and went around to the car, pleased to note that no lights were yet visible in Ellen's flat. He set off across town to pick up the motorway south.

****

When Ellen awoke at seven, her first reaction was to check the status of John's flat. Peeping through her front window, she could discern the faint glow of a light emanating from what the floor plans told her would be John's bedroom. Satisfied that he was still in the flat, she went for a shower. From her viewpoint she was unable to tell that John's car was not still parked up.

She emerged from the shower, refreshed and ready to face another day, and was drying her long hair when she heard the familiar buzz of her mobile. The tone told her the call was from the CTU. She switched off the hairdryer and reached for her phone.

"Hello."
"Ellie, it's Brian. Is the target still in sight?"
"I checked not too long ago, Brian. His bedside light was on."
"Have you *seen* him this morning?"
"No. I just assumed…."
"Is his car there?"
"I don't know. I can't see from here."
"Well, let me tell you. It's not. At the moment, it's on the Eastbound carriageway of the M62, a few miles from the M1 junction."
"Shit!"

"Just as well we bugged it, don't you think? I think it's time you came in for a word with our boss. Can you manage that, do you think?"
"Yes, Brian."
"Well, do it today, then."
"Will do."
"Oh, and Ellie."
"Yes."
"Don't bother unpacking any more stuff."

The line went dead as Brian ended the call.

****

John pulled the car into the M1 service station car park and parked between two white Transit vans in one of the few empty spaces close to the entrance. He placed his flight bag securely in the boot and jogged through the drizzle towards the services, looking first for the toilets. That need satisfied, he became aware that he had a more urgent requirement. He was feeling dizzy and his head ached. He bought a bottle of water and dug into his jacket pocket for his tablets, his hand shaking as he coaxed two capsules from their foil pack and swallowed them. He bought a coffee and sat for thirty minutes until he felt stable, and then bought a bacon sandwich which he chewed slowly, until finally he felt well enough to continue.

He pulled out of the slip road, re-joined the main carriageway, and was cruising along at seventy when he became aware of a slight rattling noise. He ignored it. That had always been his way. Drive a car, whatever the condition, and when it stopped working, get it fixed. Slight noises didn't unduly worry him. But as he neared his exit, Junction 25, he was aware it was becoming louder. He turned up the radio to drown the noise while he followed his printed route round the outskirts of Derby, finally turning left off the A38 to enter a suburban estate. He soon spotted the pub he was looking for and turned immediately left after he'd passed it. A couple of hundred yards on the right was number 61, his destination. He drove past, to the end of the street and stopped. He took out his phone and called Jane.

"Hello."
"Hello, Jane. I'm nearly at your house now."
"How long do you think you'll be?"
"About thirty seconds."
"Thanks for giving me advance notice. See you in about thirty seconds."

He smiled. Nothing he did could upset her these days, it seemed. All that had passed. He pulled up outside her house, a neat semi with a paved driveway and a narrow strip of garden at the side. She was standing at the front door, arms folded. He switched off the ignition and eased his tired body out, stretching his back to relax the knotted muscles. Jane nodded towards his car.

"Bit noisy, isn't it?"
"Yes. It started a few miles back."
"I'll ask Mark to have a look at it."
"Mark?"
"My boyfriend. He can fix anything."
"So, how are you, Jane?"
"I'm fine, dad. Come in and we'll have a cuppa."
"Thank you."

As soon as the front door was closed, she threw her arms round his neck and buried her face in his chest.

"Dad, I've missed you so much."
"I've missed you too, Jane. And I'm so sorry about everything that happened...."
"Dad, no more, please. We've both suffered as a result of your breakdown. I admit, I blamed you for a long time, but since I met Mark, I see a lot of things differently. Now I realise it wasn't all your fault. We were all to blame. But

let's put it behind us. I want to start again, even if we don't have long..."

With that, Jane started to cry. Great heaving sobs. All he could do was hold her until they stopped. She pulled away, and wiped her eyes.

"Let's have that cup of tea, Jane, and you can tell me everything that's happened in the last few years."

And over a cup of tea in the well-equipped kitchen, they had a heart-to-heart chat.

"You know, dad, that until I met Mark and did a course at college, I didn't understand where all your anger came from. Mark taught me a lot."
"Tell me about him."
"Well, he's six feet tall, slim and absolutely *gorgeous*. He's twenty-four and works for Rolls-Royce, except at the moment he's back at Uni doing a Post-Grad Engineering course."
"What about the house? Rented?"
"Good god, no. We've got a mortgage."
"Serious, then?"
"Absolutely. I can't wait for you to meet him. You'll love him. He'll be home by lunchtime. Only morning lectures today."
"And what about you, Jane? Do you work?"
"Three days a week at the moment. Then next September I was hoping to start training as a psychiatric nurse."
"Good for you."
"Well, I'm not sure that's going to happen now."
"Why's that?"
"I'll explain when Mark gets here. I'll need to get something ready for when he gets in. We usually just have sandwiches at lunchtime. Is that OK with you?"
"Fine."
"Well, just sit back and relax. He won't be long."

Five minutes later, John saw a white Ford pull on to the drive.

"I think he's here, love."

John stood up, Jane at his side as Mark came through the door. He came straight to John.

"Hi, I'm Mark. You must be Mr Braden."
"John, please, Mark."

He extended his hand and Mark shook it warmly.

"I've been really looking forward to meeting you. I'm so sorry to hear of your illness."
"Thanks. At least it's brought us all together again."
"Has Jane told you our news?"
"I was waiting for you to arrive, Mark. We can tell him together."
"Tell me what together?"
"We're getting married."
"Congratulations. When?"
"March 24th."
"Not sure I'll be able to make it."
"I know, dad. I'm sorry."
"Not your fault, love. You'll have a wonderful day whether I'm there or not."
"There's one more thing, dad."
"What's that?"
"I'm pregnant. Thirteen weeks."
"Congratulations again. Do you know the sex?"
"A boy, dad."
"Well, when he grows up, don't let him become a fireman."
"He'll be a really clever engineer, like his dad. Oh, before I forget, Mark. Will you have a quick look at dad's car before lunch? It's making a noise."
"Yeah. I'll do it now. Do you want to come with me, Mr Braden?"
"It's John, Mark."

"Sorry, John. Can you show me the problem?"

Mark had the car jacked up in no time and was peering underneath.

"Thought so," he said. "Your exhaust tail pipe is rusted. You really need it replacing, like now."
"OK. After lunch I'll take it to a Kwik-Fit."
"I'll go with you. There's one not far from here. There's another problem, though."
"What's that."
"Well, how do you explain this?"

He was holding a small, square box, a couple of inches square.

"What is it?"
"I think it's a tracking device. It was magnetically attached to the underside of your car. Looks fairly recent. Are you in some sort of trouble, John?"
"Come inside. I think I owe you both an explanation."
"Are you sure you want Jane to know?"
"It's about time I showed her some respect, don't you think?"
"I'll just get rid of this first."

Mark walked quickly to the end of the street where a taxi was parked at the roadside outside a takeaway. He bent over to put his head in the open passenger window frame. He engaged the driver in conversation, asking the price of a ride down to the university, and so distracting him while he reached down with his left hand and attached the bug just inside the front wheel arch. He thanked the driver for the information and walked back to an admiring John.

"That was good work, Mark. Where did you learn that trick?"
"I've watched a lot of American TV crime dramas. You can learn all sorts of stuff from them."

"Well, I'm impressed."
"Whoever it is doing the tracking is going to be kept busy. The taxi driver's just about to start a twelve-hour shift. Anyway, let's go in. We'd like to know what's going on here."

Over lunch, John told them the whole story while they listened in silence.

"So," he said in conclusion, "instead of being someone whose sole aim was to alert someone to the fact that I *really believed* she was going to die, along with many others, I've become the suspected perpetrator of this disaster. My house, my laptop and my car have been bugged. I'm being followed. I've had a visit from the suits, rather than uniformed officers, to investigate a broken car window. None of it adds up. I'm not the villain here. I'm a dying man who was just trying to do the right thing one last time, that's all."
"It's a weird story, John."
"I know. And I understand why nobody would believe me. I don't really know if I believe it myself. All I know is that I had a premonition, or, as the doctors tell me, a hallucination which my brain has tried to make sense of by giving it the context of an impending disaster. But what if I *am* right?"
"I don't know what to say, John. But if the authorities don't take you seriously and something catastrophic does happen, they're going to blame you for making it happen."
"That's what I'm afraid of."
"So, what do you plan to do next?"
"Travel the route. See if I can work out the most likely site. Gather as much information as I can. Then hand it over to the authorities and hope to walk away from it unharmed. Whether I'm successful or not, we'll know on the 29th."
"Dad, please be careful."
"Whatever happens, Jane, I'm glad I've been able to see you and talk to you, and to know you'll be OK. The two of you will be great parents, I know that for sure."

While Jane cleared up after lunch, John and Mark took the car to have a new tail-pipe fitted on the exhaust. The three of them then spent a few hours together, sifting through a box of old photographs of Jane as a child. And after a light early evening meal he reluctantly took his leave, stopping the car once it was out of sight of the house to take another dose of medication. He knew he shouldn't be driving. He'd refused their kind offer of a bed for the night because it was too comfortable for him to stay. He felt the longer he stayed, the harder it would be to tear himself away. And there were things he had to do. The clock was ticking.

****

At the Wright Watson Enterprise Centre on Thorp Garth, a heated meeting was taking place regarding anti-social behaviour in Idle. For discussion in particular was a recent incident of vicious assault on a local man by a gang of youths.

****

Ellen was in her flat packing away some of her things. She'd attended the meeting with Don McArthur earlier that afternoon. It didn't go well. Basically, she was compelled to take the blame for the fact that John Braden had slipped his leash when he should have been under close surveillance. In addition, she'd been unable to provide any useful information regarding his intentions up to and including the 29th October. She argued her case as well as possible, that Braden was a difficult man, elusive, reserved, secretive etc., and that she was sure she could break down his defences in time. McArthur was having none of it. While he didn't actually say her services were being terminated forthwith, reading between the lines, Ellen was in no doubt her work on this operation was at an end. It also seemed clear to her that she was highly unlikely to be employed by CTU at any time in the future. Now she was just waiting for the axe to fall.

****

John smiled as he thought of the pleasure they'd experienced while rummaging through the photographs that afternoon. He was sure Jane knew that he was aware that she'd sorted through them previously to ensure there were none which might upset him or cause offence. There were no snaps of Jane with her mum, or Jane and him. They were all of Jane alone, or John alone, or her mum alone, or photos of the three of them together. All smiling and looking happy. He wondered if Jane had deliberately set out to airbrush their past together. For the first time, it occurred to him that nobody even mentioned his ex-wife at all during his visit.

He stopped at a service station on the way home, and sent a quick text to Jane to thank her for their hospitality, adding that he would call her when he arrived home, at her insistence when he'd left them. He sat in the almost-empty café for a half hour, before pushing his chair back and making his way laboriously to the Gents. Washing his hands, he caught sight of his gaunt face in the mirror. He looked drained.

Don't peg out now, he said to himself. There's plenty work still to do.

It was close to ten o'clock when he arrived home. He parked the car and switched off the lights and engine before phoning Jane to let her know he'd arrived safely. She thanked him, adding,

"Oh, by the way, after you left, Mark and I were discussing names for our baby. We both agreed without reservation. He's going to be called John Braden. John Braden Wallace. We thought you might like that."

He thanked her, trying hard to disguise the emotion in his voice until he'd ended the call. Then he sat in the car and wept quietly. Once he'd composed himself, he dried his tears and, instead of going into his flat, he unlocked the door, threw his bag inside, locked up again and walked to the Draper. He wasn't ready to be alone again just yet. Even Ellen's company would be welcome.

There were only half a dozen customers in the Draper. Ellen wasn't among them, but Clockwork Jimmy was. He made a beeline for John as he stood at the bar.

"Hey, John. Can I have a quick word?"
"Velocity," he quipped, remembering a quote he'd seen attributed to Gordon Strachan, the football manager, when accosted by a reporter with the same question.
"No, seriously. There's something you need to know."
"Just let me get my pint and I'll be over."

Once served, John joined Jimmy at his table.

"So, Jimmy, what is it you need to tell me?"
"It's about Ellie."
"Ellen?"
"Ellen, Ellie. One and the same."
"Go on."
"Well, I know you're going through a divorce, and I think maybe Ellie has been employed to find, or even *plant* some dirt on you. Maybe your wife hired a private investigator or something, you know, to get some sort of divorce settlement."
"The divorce was finalised quite a while ago, Jimmy."
"Well, someone's hired her. And I don't believe it's you."
"What do you mean, 'hired her'?"
"She's an escort, John. That's what she does for a living."
"An escort?"
"Yep. I was at a company weekend 'do' in Birmingham a few weeks ago. At the end of the first night when we'd had a few drinks, two of the lads asked the night porter where they could get some extra 'entertainment'. He passed them a business card, so they went on the web site and booked

her. They said she was excellent value for money. Then they talked me into asking her about pro-rata prices for a quickie. So, I sent a message to her site asking for a quote for a five-minute wank. When I didn't get a response, I realised they were having me on. Just for a laugh, like. Anyway, they gave me her card. Here. See for yourself. Don't know what she's doing up here though. She normally just works the West Midlands area, according to her site. That's why I thought someone must have hired her."
"Thanks, Jimmy. I'm sure it's all very innocent. There'll be a perfectly logical explanation."
"Yeah, you're probably right."

Jimmy moved to sit at another table, clearly embarrassed at what he'd told John. John bought another pint and had just sat down again when Ellen walked in. He nodded to her, but didn't get up to offer her a drink. Noticing he'd left her business card on the table, he quickly slipped it into his pocket before she came over with her drink.

"Hello, John."
"Hi. Sorry I didn't get up. I'm feeling knackered tonight. I think I might be coming down with something."
"Oh, that's a shame. I was looking forward to us having a few drinks and a long chat tonight. I've got a nice bottle of Shiraz at home, and since I haven't had a house-warming party yet, I was hoping me and you could have a small intimate 'do' together."
"Tempting though it sounds, I'll have to pass, I'm afraid. I've had a long day."
"Oh, you've been out?"
"Yes. I had to see an old friend. So, what have you been up to?"
"Job hunting again. Nothing positive yet, but I'm getting some leads."
"I'm sure you'll get what you're looking for."
"I hope so."

I bet you do, he thought, but not from me.

He drained his pint and stood up to go.

"If you can wait five minutes while I finish my wine, John, we can walk down together."
"OK."
"I'll be as quick as I can. You *do* look tired."

They left the Draper together, John giving a sly wink to Clockwork Jimmy on his way out. Jimmy had a look of resignation on his face, knowing full well that Ellie, whatever her motives, was well out of his league and well beyond his price range, and settled for another pint.

****

"You sure you don't fancy a nightcap, John?"
"Positive, thanks. Maybe some other time when I don't feel so tired."

John watched as Ellen closed the door behind her, then walked quickly across the road to his flat as the wind picked up in strength. Once inside, he closed the curtains, poured himself a large whisky and switched on his laptop. Turning the card over and over in his hand while he thought through the implications of what Clockwork Jimmy had told him, he finally typed in the address of the web site. It was unmistakably Ellen, or Ellie as her online persona showed. There were several pages of photos of Ellie in different poses, in various stages of undress, and long descriptions of the services she was prepared to offer at the right price. One line caught his attention. In bold type, it read,

"HONEYTRAPS AND DISCREET SURVEILLANCE ARE SPECIALTY SERVICES. PRICE NEGOTIABLE ON REQUEST."

He thought for a moment. He hadn't hired her, so who had? A honeytrap would not be relevant to his situation. He had no skeletons in his closet that could make him a target for blackmail. But *surveillance*, yes, he could believe that. He considered confronting her face to face with the evidence, or even contacting her through her web site, just to let her know he knew what she was up to. But that could prove counter-productive, he reasoned. Better to play out the charade in the hope that *he* could gain some information on *them*, whoever her paymasters were. And he had a good idea who was behind it. He'd sever ties with her when the time came. In the meantime, he'd remain on his guard, and play their game. And if the time was right, he might even accept her offer of a quick shag. With that thought in mind, he allowed himself a smile, poured another whisky and sat for a while, before getting up to turn out the light and sit in the dark, glass in hand.

Across the road, Ellen saw the light go out, picked up her phone and called McArthur. She informed him she had made one last attempt to lure John into her flat, but without success. She was saddened by her employer's response, but it came as no real shock.

****

Brian Peters pulled his car into the drive at the side of his house. It had been a long day. Very little had gone to plan and there was a danger the operation would fall apart were it not for the fact that McArthur could be relied upon to keep a firm hand on the tiller. He tried to blank all thoughts of work from his mind so he could relax with his wife, Sarah. He knew she hated it when he couldn't relax at home, but it was an unavoidable downside to the job. You could never completely switch off. This night, though, Sarah was able to retain his complete attention from the moment he walked through the door. She announced excitedly she was pregnant.

CHAPTER 8

18th October

“UK unemployment fell by 52,000 in the three months to August to 1.4 million, leaving the jobless rate unchanged at 4.3% from the previous quarter - still at the lowest level since 1975.
The claimant count increased by 1,700 to 804,100 last month, said the Office for National Statistics. Total earnings, including bonuses, rose by an annual 2.2% in the three-month period.
The performance of hospitals across the UK has slumped with targets for cancer, A & E and planned operations now being missed en masse, BBC research shows. Nationally England, Wales and Northern Ireland have not hit one of their three key targets for 18 months. Only Scotland has had any success in the past 12 months - hitting its A & E target three times. Ministers accepted growing demand had left the NHS struggling to keep up as doctors warned patients were suffering.
Players and staff at Leeds United Football Club are to donate a day's salary to help fund a four-year-old fan's cancer treatment. Toby Nye has high-risk neuroblastoma, a rare form of cancer, which spreads rapidly across the body.”

“Broken cloud cover is forecast through the day. Some cloud breaks may form with occasional sunshine, more likely in rural valleys. Intermittent rain may reach the south later. Winds will be light, locally moderate near coasts.”

Either John forgot to set his alarm clock or it went off and he silenced it and went back to sleep. Or it silenced itself. It was immaterial. The fact was it was ten-thirty. He threw off the duvet and rubbed his eyes. His head was throbbing, either from his hangover, or his illness. It made no difference. He didn’t have time to mope; there were things he had to do. He just had to resist the pain. Unsteady on his feet, he nevertheless negotiated a course through to the bathroom and counted out his tablets, swallowing them with a little difficulty and a lot of water.

After he'd showered and eaten a bowl of cereal, he phoned his solicitor and was fortunate to be able to make an appointment for that same day, at 2.15 pm. Having organised that, he could turn his attention to the route the race would take. He took his printouts from his bag and copied the route into his A to Z. then, street by street, he followed it on his laptop using Google's street view, regularly changing the angles to get a panoramic view. He tried to imagine how each scene would look on the day, how dense the crowd would be at each location, but it was impossible to guess. Even the weather on the day could make a massive difference. All he could do was use his imagination. He had to try to put himself in a bomber's shoes, see things through a bomber's eyes, and see if he could identify the most likely sites for an attack. He really didn't have the skills for this sort of work. He knew that he faced an impossible task. But he had to try something.

Hearing some commotion outside in the street, he looked out of the window. A removal van had pulled up and was loading furniture and boxes, the whole operation being supervised by a familiar figure, tall and blonde. She looked up at his window and saw him. She smiled and waved. He waved back and returned to the task at hand.

After lunch, he took his scheduled dose of medication and set off to visit his solicitor. It was a short drive to Shipley and he was able to park up close to the office and present himself in reception with a few minutes to spare. He was aware that for solicitors, time meant money, and he wasn't about to waste his hard-earned cash paying unnecessary bills. At the appointed time, the receptionist asked him to go through. He had dealt with Mr Attenborough in the past, notably during his divorce, and shook his hand warmly.

"So, John, what can I do for you today?"
"My Will, Edward. I think it's time we rewrote it."
"Of course. In the light of your change in circumstance."
"Precisely."
"And I presume you want to write your ex-wife out of the Will?"
"Yes. I want you to be the sole executor, and the sole beneficiary is to be my daughter, Jane."
"I thought you were estranged."
"We were. We are now OK."
"Do you have an address, or any other contact details for your daughter."
"All written down here. Bear in mind that her name will soon change to Jane Wallace. She's getting married early next year."
"That's fine, John. I'll get this sorted as soon as I can."
"Please do it as a matter of extreme urgency, please, Edward. I don't expect to live long."
"That's bad news, John. What sort of timescale are we looking at?"
"Days. Weeks if I'm lucky."
"I'm sorry to hear that, John. Would you mind if we prepare a bill for you before you leave?"
"Leave the office? Or this world?"
"At least you've retained your sense of humour."
"And you've retained your business sense. Of course, I'll pay today."
"Thank you. I'll be sorry to see you go, John."
"Because I'm a good customer?"
"Because you're a friend."

An invoice was hastily prepared and John paid in cash. They shook hands at the door, the solicitor promising that a copy of the new Will would be sent out to him the next day at the latest. All he had to do was sign it, have it witnessed and return it to Mr Attenborough's office.

He drove into Bradford and parked in the Retail Park. He had given more thought to his planned tour of the route, and realised he wouldn't have time to make a meticulous inspection and appraisal of all the various possible threats each particular area may pose. He made a rational decision to concentrate on the start and finish – the areas where crowds would most likely congregate at the highest density. Armed with a camera, an A5 notebook and pen, he headed towards City Hall. As if to remind him of the urgency of his task, the City Hall clock chimed three. He tried to look like a typical tourist, taking random pictures of various buildings and streets, but he knew he stuck out like a sore thumb, walking in a seemingly aimless fashion through the cold and breezy city centre. He began to feel tired and dizzy so went into the nearest coffee house to take a break and consume another large quantity of tablets. He realised he was close to the spot where he had coffee with Amy that morning which seemed so long ago. Perhaps if he'd never involved her, he could have quietly forgotten about the whole mess and just got on with the pain of living his last few weeks. But then he considered that it was the very fact that he felt driven to *do* something which was keeping him alive at all.

Sipping his coffee, he took from his pocket the printout of the race route. It was impossible to check every nook, every cranny. And the route covered four laps of a course. So, one area could be pronounced 'clear' after one lap, but could prove dangerous next time round. He put down the printout and held his head in his hands.

I can't do any more, he murmured. There are people, professional people, who carry out this sort of risk assessment for a living. All I can do is pass on my fears. Let someone else act on them. I've got other things to think about.

"Are you OK, sir?"

He looked up. A young girl on table cleaning duty was standing in front of him, a look of concern on her face.

"I'm fine, thanks. Just lost in thought, that's all."
"Only I was worried. You look so pale. Do you want me to get our first-aider to have a look at you?"
"Only if she's a clinical psychiatrist."
"Sorry. No, she just does first aid. She's probably got some paracetamol, or something."
"I'm OK. Thank you."

He gathered up his printouts, notes and camera, and walked out into the busy street. As he walked along, not a single pedestrian made eye contact with him. Many were texting, or checking their phones as they walked along. Many were just window-shopping. Most were simply minding their own business.

You could walk along here carrying a great big box with the word 'BOMB' written on it and nobody would notice, he said to himself.

Walking back to his car, he stopped on Market Street and consulted his printout. The runners came past the Midland Hotel and went left at the mini-roundabout, before diverting up Hustlergate, then left down Bank Street before re-joining Market Street. Narrow streets. Crowded with onlookers. Tall buildings either side. From that point on, the rest of the route would be packed with onlookers right up to the finish line in City Park. A nightmare to police. He marked a large red X on the printout and drew a circle round it.

By the time he got home it was after four. He parked and locked the car, nipped into the flat to take his medication, came back out and walked up to the Draper, weary and despondent. He was desperately in need of a pint and some company, or at least one of the two.

"Hello, John. Usual?"
"Please, Nick."
"How's things?"
"Fine. I just have a moral problem to solve."

"Good luck with that. I can't even solve crosswords."

He sat at the table with his pint and took out his notepad, turning to a clean page. At the top, he wrote
PROBLEMS

And listed underneath,
Police are watching me. Why? They suspect I'm dangerous. Why? Amy reported me.
Amy reported me as stalker. Why? Over-reacted? Thinks I'm mad? Both feasible.
Ellen watching me. Why? Paid? By police?
Potential disaster. Says who? Me. Can I convince anyone to take the threat seriously enough to take ownership of the problem and take the weight off my shoulders? Who? Police. How? Will they accept my findings? V. Doubtful!

Perhaps better if I die before 29th.

He stared at what he'd written. He couldn't believe he'd written the final line. He'd never been a quitter. He tore the page off the pad, screwed it up and put it in his pocket. He took a long mouthful of his pint, and made his decision. He'd gather all the information he had and dump it on the police. And if they needed his assistance or opinions on any point he would gladly help. But it was their problem. Not his. He finished his pint and ordered a fill-up, just as a familiar figure walked through the door.

"Hello, John. How are you?"
"Hello, Ellie. I thought you'd moved on."
"Going home tomorrow. Some business to settle tonight."
"Would you like a farewell drink?"
"Yes. Shiraz, please."
"Sit down and I'll bring it across."

He paid for the drinks and carried them to the table.

"Thanks, John."

"My pleasure."
"I owe you an apology."
"You don't. You were just doing your job."
"You knew?"
"Yes."
"How did you find out?"
"That's my little secret. Tell me, though, for my own peace of mind. Who were you working for? The police?"
"Yes."
"Why?"
"Because they think you might be dangerous."
"That's what I thought. Anything else I should know?"
"They're not happy their colleagues in the East Midlands spent most of yesterday chasing a taxi going back and forth to the airport."

He couldn't help smiling at that comment as he tried to picture it and inevitably visualized an image of a speeded-up, Keystone Cops-like chase, with truncheons drawn and whistles being blown.

"Good."
"No hard feelings?"
"Absolutely none."
"Me neither. I got well paid for this."
"Well, at least that's something."
"You'll have to excuse me. I have a lot to do tonight. Good luck, John."
"Goodbye, Ellie."

After Ellen had left, he silently cursed himself for not propositioning her for a farewell shag. After all, that *was* what she got paid for. A few years ago, he would never have turned down such a blatant come-on.

You must be getting old, John, he told himself. You're losing your touch.

His phone rang and he dug it out of his pocket hurriedly, guessing who the caller would be. Looking at the screen, he smiled, realising he'd guessed correctly.

"Hello, Jane."
"Hi, dad. Just calling to see if you're OK."
"Yes, love. I'm fine."
"Liar."
"OK, so I'm exaggerating. I'm a bit tired. Had a hard day."
"I had a visit from a policeman today."
"Oh, yeah? Been a bad girl?"
"He was asking questions about you."
"What questions?"
"The nature of our relationship. How you spent your time. General, pointless stuff, really. I'm not sure what exactly he expected me to tell him."
"That I'm a dangerous psychopath plotting to bring about the end of civilisation as we know it?"
"Well, he was certainly probing into your mental state. Your beliefs. Your political persuasion."
"What did you tell him?"
"The truth. That we haven't been in touch for a long time until yesterday. That you wanted to ensure we were reconciled because of your illness."
"Well, that's not quite true, is it? I've wanted to make it all up to you and get you to forgive me for a long time. You just wouldn't allow it. My illness just made it a more immediate problem."
"That's what I meant. Anyway, I told him I couldn't answer his questions as we'd only just met up again after a long time without contact."
"And was he happy with that?"
"Not exactly happy. Satisfied, I suppose. There was nothing more I could tell him."
"OK, thanks. So, how are you? How's Mark? And how's my grandson-to-be?"
"We're all fine, dad."
"OK, love. Keep me informed, won't you?"

"Of course. I'll have to go now, dad. I've still got some ironing to finish before I go to bed."
"Ironing? You *are* domesticated these days. I'm impressed."
"I'll call you again soon. 'Bye, dad."
"'Bye, Jane."

He took a long drink from his glass, happy that he had re-established his relationship with his daughter. They had had some good times together as a family when Jane was just a child. Summer holidays spent not on some warm Spanish beach, but in Cleethorpes, or Morecambe. Life was simpler then. Before the nightmares. Before the mood swings, the anger and the depression. Before the arguments. Before the divorce. Before the illness.

He bought another pint, and then another, sitting alone with only his thoughts for company. He was still there at ten-thirty when he turned at the sound of the door opening. It was E, with a City scarf draped round his neck. He nodded to John and stood at the bar as his pint was pulled. John wasn't really passionate about football these days but still took an interest in the fortunes of his local team so was compelled to ask.

"How did they get on tonight, E?"
"Drew, one apiece."
"Good game?"
"Bloody farce."
"Not a good game, then."
"Bloody ref bloody ruined it."
"Usual story. What did he do?"
"Lost bloody control. There was a bit of a skirmish, and he just went wandering round the field booking everyone who caught his eye. I swear he would have even booked me if I hadn't left with two minutes to go. Bloody disgrace, if you ask me."

John was sorry he'd asked, so didn't pursue it any further and soon E found another unfortunate soul he could vent his spleen on. He finished his pint, took the empty glass back to the bar and left the Draper with a wave to Nick and a smile on his face. He felt sure he could handle just a few more weeks. He felt up to the challenge. The courage and the strength which he'd had in his early years in the fire service, if he could harness it, would pull him through whatever tribulations he had yet to face.

****

In the office at CTU, Don McArthur had listened patiently to the reports from his two colleagues. He tried not to let his anger show, but the dressing-down he'd received for wasting the time of his counterparts in the East Midlands had clearly rattled him. He spoke slowly and clearly.

"One thing we must all understand is that Braden is clearly a very accomplished adversary. He's outwitted us at every move so far. I think it's time we brought him in for some questioning. And I mean *serious* questioning. Not a friendly chat. No tea and biscuits. It's time we took the initiative. We need to break him down and get the truth. Do I make myself clear?"

They both nodded.

"Pick him up first thing in the morning. Oh, and another thing. Ellen Stevenson is no longer working this case. David, make sure we get back all the info she holds on this operation. All of it. No loose ends."
"OK, boss."

With that, McArthur dismissed his officers. He sat upright, his hands palm down on his desk as if he was about to lift himself to his feet. Instead he just sat there, pressing down on the surface of the desk, thinking. It wasn't the first time in the last few days that he'd come to the conclusion that this could be his final operation in charge of the region's CTU. He'd discussed his future with his wife indicating it may be time for him to retire. He wondered if he was losing control, if he was still capable of making the right decisions at the right time. The entire landscape of his work was changing, evolving week by week, and he questioned whether he could still evolve with it. Or whether he was just another dinosaur whose time had come for extinction. He wondered what would happen when he retired. Would he be content to potter around in the garden? Would that be challenging enough for him? Man versus plant didn't get the adrenalin pumping as much as the challenge of preventing terrorists from striking in his domain. At the moment, he really didn't know what the future held for him. Everything depended on what would happen in the next eleven days. All he could hope to do was make the right decisions at the right time and hope, and pray, for a positive outcome. If everything went pear-shaped he, as boss, would have to fall on his sword and retire, otherwise he'd be forcibly retired. His pride would not let that happen.

He gathered up the files from his desk, placed them in a drawer, locked it and slipped the key, the only key, into his jacket pocket. He casually checked the time on the wall clock. It was later than he thought, and the clock was ticking.

****

At his kitchen table, John Braden was composing a letter to Edward Attenborough. It was his insurance policy. Once completed, he read it through a couple of times, addressed an envelope and stuck a first-class stamp on it, put the letter inside, and sealed it. He put on his coat and took the letter down to the post box at the end of the road, ensuring it dropped right inside and was not caught on anything close to the opening. He turned and walked home, smiling, and once safely inside his flat, he took his medication and celebrated with a large glass of malt. Finally, feeling his tiredness beginning to overcome him, he went to bed.

His nightmare was even more vivid than usual. They were making their way up the stairs, the two of them. The smoke was thick and acrid and the landing was engulfed by flames. He could hear the screams coming from a bedroom. Desperate appeals for help, loud at first, and clear, then reducing in volume and being interspersed with coughs and gasps as they inched their way closer to the door. Then came the explosion. And as they broke down the door, the cries had become faint rasping pleas for God as the last breaths left the charred throats of the family of three trapped inside and their burning agonised bodies, huddled close together, fell still. The child must have been about three years old. John woke up, weeping and sweating, the scene fixed firmly in his diseased, pounding brain.

He lay awake for almost two hours before eventually drifting back off to sleep. But even then, the dream returned. As if it was set on repeat, it played over and over in his mind.

CHAPTER 9

19th October

“Spain is to start suspending Catalonia's autonomy from Saturday, as the region's leader threatens to declare independence. The government said ministers would meet to activate Article 155 of the constitution, allowing it to take over the running of the region. Catalonia's leader said the region's parliament would vote on independence if Spain continued "repression". Catalans voted to secede in a referendum deemed illegal by Spain.
The number of crimes recorded annually in England and Wales has passed the five million mark for the first time in 10 years, rising by 13%, figures show. The Office for National Statistics said crimes in the 12 months to June were up from 4.6 million the previous year. It said crime categorised as "violent" rose by 19%, with rises in offences including stalking and harassment.
A man accused of murdering a teenager recorded himself on Snapchat apparently celebrating the killing, a court has heard. Raheem Wilks, 19, was shot dead close to Too Sharps barbers in Harehills, Leeds, on 26 January. Keal Richards, 21, of Francis Street, Leeds, and four other men from the city all deny murder. The city's crown court heard the killing "had all the hallmarks of a gangland shooting".
A man accused of killing a father and daughter in a house fire has been found guilty of their manslaughter. Daniel Jones, 29, set light to a house in Stanley, near Wakefield, in 2016 in a bid to destroy evidence of a burglary nearby. Andrew Broadhead, 42, and his daughter Kiera, 8, died in the fire. A jury cleared Jones, of Knottingley, of two counts of murder but convicted him of manslaughter after more than three hours of deliberation.”

“A dry start with perhaps some brightness in the north. However, cloud will soon thicken from the south to bring rain across all parts by this afternoon, and some of this will be heavy.”

Brian Peters was watching from his front-room window as the car pulled up outside. Quietly, so as not to wake his wife and child, he opened the door, locked it behind him, and dashed down the drive as the car's passenger door swung open for him.

"Morning, Dave."
"Morning, Brian, All set?"
"Yep."
"OK, let's do it."

They drove across town without speaking, only the regular squawk from the radio transmitter breaking the silence. As they neared their destination, Brian finally spoke.

"OK, Dave. This is how it's going to play. We park up close by. We get out and take up positions from where we can see whether or not he's up and about. Once we establish that he is up, we go knock on his door. When he answers, we tell him we'd like him to accompany us to the station – we don't tell him Wakefield – and if he comes willingly, then that's it until we have him in an interrogation room. If he refuses to come, or resists, we put him down, cuff him and throw him in the car. And we do it all as quietly as possible. Hopefully, nobody will see. That OK?"
"Fine by me."
"I'll do the talking."
"Fine by me."
"OK. We're just about there. Let's find a quiet place to park up."

The car pulled to a halt about a hundred yards from John's flat and hidden from view from any of the flat's windows. Brian and David approached the property quietly and on opposite sides of the street, each finding a spot from where, between them, all the windows in the flat were visible. All were dark. They stood in the shadows, collars pulled up, and waited.

****

John woke suddenly. It was already light. He stumbled into the bathroom and retched violently as if to try to clear the smoke and fumes from his lungs. The details of his nightmare were still fresh and clear in his mind. They would never leave him until he too met his end. He knew now that wouldn't be too far in the future. He swallowed his tablets and made a mug of coffee, taking it with him into the toilet before getting showered and dressed.

It was the sound of water running down the drainpipe from John's bathroom which alerted Brian Peters to the fact that someone was up and moving round the flat. He waited fifteen minutes before motioning his colleague to join him at the door. He took a deep breath and rang the bell. They could hear sounds of movement inside, the sound of someone coming down the stairs, before eventually the door opened a few inches and John Braden's face appeared in the gap. It dropped when he recognised the callers. Brian did the talking.

"Good morning, Mr Braden. I hope we're not disturbing you too early, sir. You may remember us, sir. We came when you reported damage to your car."
"Yes. I remember. What do you want?"
"Well, sir. There have been some developments, and we'd like you to come with us so we can discuss them with you."
"Can't you discuss them here?"
"No, sorry, sir. You'll need to come with us to the station."
"Am I being arrested?"
"No, sir."
"In that case, I refuse."
"I'm afraid we insist, sir."
"Who the hell are you?"
"CTU. Counter Terrorism Unit, sir."
"I thought you might be, somehow. I see you're both wearing nice smart shiny expensive-looking suits, so let me just inform you that if you make any attempt to arrest me or

show any violence whatsoever towards me, then your suits will soon be covered in vomit."
"You wouldn't dare...."
"It's an entirely involuntary reaction to the medication I have to take. I can't be blamed for its side-effects."
"Well, if you'll kindly come with us, sir, to assist in our inquiries, we'd be very grateful. And very gentle."
"Let me get my notes and stuff."
"Certainly, sir. Let us in and we'll help you."

Brian Peters pushed hard against the door, catching John off guard. They pushed their way inside.

"You'll need your laptop as well, sir."
"Why? You've already checked it's clean."
"Well, we'll just check again, sir."

Lee followed him into the living room, where John's notes and printouts were piled on top of a folder. He pushed them into the folder and picked up his laptop, handing it to Lee while he put on his coat and took his medication from the drawer, waving the packets at Lee.

"If we're likely to be more than an hour, I guess I'd better take these with me. Don't want to die in your custody. People might wonder what's been going on. Questions will be asked in Parliament. The tabloids will have a field day. Think of the headlines 'Innocent man tortured to death in police custody'."

"You'll be fine with us, sir. We'll take good care of you."

Expecting a short trip into the city centre, or perhaps even just up the road to Javelin House, John was surprised instead to see the car take the ring road towards the M62.

"Where are we going?"
"Wakefield. Our boss wants to talk to you."

John settled back for the trip, knowing there was absolutely nothing he could do anyway. He tried to imagine how the day would go, but admitted to himself he hadn't a clue. He'd play it by ear. That was all he could do.

The trip passed quickly and ended in a car park behind a nondescript building. They entered through a back door and once inside, John noted there were no signs to direct visitors to specific areas. Clearly, unaccompanied visitors were non-existent. They marched down a long corridor at the end of which was a door with a rectangular sign plate attached to it, indicating it was 'Room 3'. They entered. The room was approximately twelve feet square, with a table in the centre, and three chairs. One wall had a large panel of glass.

Typical, John thought. Standard TV drama layout for an interrogation room. Even down to the one-way mirror.

He looked up and saw that in the corner at ceiling height was a camera. He smiled and shrugged his shoulders, and sat down as instructed. He was asked to empty his pockets and put the contents in the centre of the table. He complied without protest; wallet, handkerchief, phone, some loose change, a pen, and various scraps of paper. Lee put them all in a bag and carried it out of the room. As he left, Don McArthur walked in with Peters, who stood by the door. McArthur introduced himself and Peters. Braden responded with a sarcastic 'Pleased to meet you'.

"So, Mr Braden. I imagine you know why you're here."
"I haven't a clue. Perhaps you could enlighten me."
"Well. You already know we're the CTU. We understand you have information concerning an imminent threat."
"Yes. I believe so."
"Mr Braden, I must inform you that this interview is being taped. You are not being charged. You are not under arrest."
"Does that mean I'm free to leave at any time?"

"Theoretically, yes. But if you did that, we'd think you have something to hide. So, why don't you tell us everything you know?"

John Braden left nothing out. He talked them through everything that had happened in a chronological order. He told them which parts of the story were fact, and which parts he *believed* were fact. Finally, he presented his conclusion, that the city should expect a terrorist attack on 29th October, the most likely site being along the Half Marathon course. He answered all the questions which were fired at him in a calm manner. Twice the interview was stopped so that the tape could be changed. John stopped the interview himself at one point to request a glass of water and his tablets.

"Just let me check first that our chemist has cleared them. For all we know, they could be cyanide capsules."
"I hope none of you have had to take any of them to make sure they're not poisonous. If you have, be aware that one of the side effects of taking the blue ones is chronic diarrhoea."

For the first time. Don McArthur gave a quick smile.

"We'll get them to you in just a couple of minutes, Mr Braden. Tell me, what would happen if you were unable to take them within the next few hours, say?"
"Most likely, I'd have a violent seizure. I'd require immediate urgent medical attention, and quite possibly, I'd never regain consciousness."
"It's that serious?"
"It's that serious."
"So, if you're so seriously ill, why are you getting involved in all this shit?"
"I've often asked myself. I should be spending my final days in a pub. Not giving people the impression that I'm an enemy of the state. I'm just trying to help save lives. It's what I was trained to do."

"I know. I'm fully aware of your service history. And your psychological problems."
"So, you think I'm plotting revenge on a society that's turned its back on me because I couldn't do my job anymore? Don't be ridiculous! I'm no more a terrorist than you are Inspector Clouseau."
"So, convince me."
"No. It's up to you to prove what you think I'm up to."
"The world doesn't work like that anymore, John. Things have changed. These days we have to play by the same rules as the terrorists."
"OK. So, what happens now? I get the waterboard treatment?"
"We wait here until you tell us what you're really up to. Or we wait until we've done enough background checks to convince ourselves we've got the wrong man."
"And how long does that take?"
"Depends."
"But why me? I've no affiliation to any terrorist groups. I'm just an average man struggling to cope with the fact that he's dying. I've devoted practically all of my working life to saving others."
"OK. I'll be frank with you. GCHQ has intercepted some chatter which indicates an incident on the 29th, in Bradford, is being planned. At the moment, unless we find evidence to the contrary, you are the prime suspect."
"So, what happens now? Do you keep me in captivity until after the 29th? If you do, you'll have to order more tablets for me. Because as soon as I run out of them, I'll die. But I'm sure you don't give a toss about that."
"Actually, I do. At the moment, we're conducting a thorough search of all recorded information about you. Your phone is being examined. Your laptop is going through a data recovery program which will show everything you think you've deleted and wiped. If there's anything you're hiding from us, we'll find it. And if we don't, but we still have some lingering doubts, there are some interrogation methods, not approved by our superiors, but nevertheless extremely

effective, that we can try out on you. The CIA people swear by the results they get."
"Keep me here longer than necessary and my solicitor will make public to the press what is happening. There'll be a shit storm."
"We can handle that. We have ways of silencing the press, if we convince them it's a matter of national security."
"This is ridiculous! If you believe, from the information you've got from other sources that some sort of attack is imminent, why are you holding me? You could torture me for a week, and then I'll die without disclosing anything useful. You're wasting your time. Go pick on some other mug."
"OK, we'll take a break now. I'll be back soon."
"What time is it now?"
"One-thirty pm."
"How about telling me the truth? I know I've been here longer. You've changed the tape three times. Just don't forget, if you want anything from me, you have to let me take my medication every four hours. You'll get no answers from a corpse."
"I'll be back soon."

McArthur and Peters left the room. John settled back in his chair, making himself as comfortable as the spartan furniture would allow, knowing they were watching him from the other side of the glass. He closed his eyes and feigned sleep as McArthur re-entered the room.

"OK, Mr Braden. Here's your medication. You may take it; it's been authenticated."
"Thank you."
"And here's your mobile too. We're satisfied that's clean. You may call your lawyer if you wish."
"Do I need to?"
"I shouldn't think so. You'll be on your way home as soon as the search of your flat and car has been completed. Oh, and we're already talking to your daughter."
"Leave her out of this."

"It's just routine, Mr Braden."
"Well, one last request, then."
"What?"
"Get me some water."

McArthur nodded in the direction of the mirror, and seconds later, Peters brought in a cup of water, placing it in front of the detainee. John nodded his approval.

"I could do with a magic mirror like that. Does it do everything you tell it?"
"Pretty much."

John grinned and looked at the mirror, then shouted,

"Go fuck yourself!"

And turning to McArthur,

"Let's see how that works."
"OK, Mr Braden. Just take your tablets. We don't want you to get overexcited. You never know what might happen."

Another hour had elapsed before John was allowed to leave and was driven home as the rain started to fall. Conversation in the car was practically non-existent as Lee concentrated on his driving through heavy traffic and heavier rain. John broke the silence.

"What made you decide to work for the CTU?"
"Don't know, really. It seemed like an exciting job. I thought maybe I could make a difference, you know. Save lives. In reality, the job consists of long periods of boredom and pen-pushing, with a bit of action now and again."
"Sounds like my old job."
"Mmm."
"We're both the same, me and you, you know. We both want to save lives."
"The jury's still out on that one as far as you're concerned."

"In that case, when it's all over, I'll be able to say 'told you so'."
"We'll see."

He gave Lee a friendly two-fingered wave goodbye as he drove off. Although it was after four o'clock, and he felt he really needed a pint, common sense told him he should check out the flat first.

He spent over an hour checking everything had been returned to its rightful place, then mindful of the last time the CTU was in his house, he checked everywhere he could think of for bugs. Every electrical appliance was checked and the cover plates removed if he suspected they might have been tampered with. Finally satisfied everything was in order, he stopped to take his medication. He put on a warm coat and walked towards the door, then turned and shouted, "Go fuck yourselves" just in case anyone was listening. He slammed the door, locked it, and went to the Draper in the pouring rain.

****

At the same time, the team in CTU were sharing their thoughts about John Braden. Lee was the first to speak.

"Personally, I don't think he's involved in anything at all. We've seen the medical reports. He's dying with a brain tumour. He's prone to hallucinations which he regards as real, as premonitions, and he interprets the fantasies as facts. There's nothing to suggest he's a threat. And even if he was plotting something for the 29th, he might not even be around to carry it out. What do you think, Brian?"

"I think he might just be planning to go out with a bang, considering his imminent demise. He's got some mental health issues which we shouldn't ignore. It may be that he wants to make a grand statement before he dies, and he's chosen the 29th simply because it's within his time-frame.

The fact that there's a large event on that day is probably coincidental. He's just making the facts fit his fantasies. Maybe he just wants his fifteen minutes of fame. But then again, we've got no evidence whatsoever that he's been in contact with any other co-conspirator or terrorist organisation, nor have we found anything to make us think he's preparing a lone-wolf attack."

Don McArthur listened carefully before giving his opinion.

"We've nothing to go on. Nothing concrete. Ellie couldn't get anywhere. We can't spare the resources to watch him full time."
"There may be another way of keeping eyes on him."

McArthur and Peters turned towards Lee.

"Let's hear it, Dave."
"Well, it's just an idea, but Amy Winston was the only person John contacted about this so-called plot. He trusted her. Maybe we can use her to gain his confidence and disclose more info. Surely it's worth a try."
"There might be some value in that. What do we know about Winston?"
"Freelance journalist. Does work for local and national papers. Clean police record. Unattached."
"If we intend to use her, I want full clearance. Get a check started, Dave."
"OK."

Two hours later, her background check having apparently been completed, Amy Winston was being escorted to the CTU base in Wakefield. She had no idea why she was being invited to attend, but had no intention of declining the offer. The experience might be of use to her in achieving her ultimate ambition.

****

It was nine-thirty when Amy left the CTU building with Brian Peters, who had the task of driving her home. She had answered all their questions and was tired. But at least she knew now that the CTU were taking seriously a terrorist threat on the 29th, and that they believed the Half Marathon was the target. What they didn't yet know was *exactly where* along the route the attack would take place. And they had asked her to befriend John Braden to discover that missing piece of information so they could prevent an attack from being successful. She had agreed.

****

Unusually for John, he'd spent several hours in the Draper. But it had been an unusual day. Tired and drunk, he'd stumbled home and collapsed on his bed, still dressed. He'd fallen asleep almost immediately and woken an hour later desperately needing a pee. Then he sat with his aching head in his hands before undressing, taking his medication, and going back to sleep.

****

Amelia was lying in bed, feeling fulfilled. That evening she had completed a twelve-mile run, in an acceptable time and without apparent difficulty. She'd come home, showered and eaten a light meal, put the kids to bed and spent some quiet time with her husband before they'd gone to bed and made love. Life was good, and she was looking forward to her big day which was rapidly approaching. The posts on her Facebook page were accruing an increasing number of 'likes', and her Just Giving pledges were mounting fast. The tingling sensation she felt throughout her body was not simply the afterglow of love-making; it was also due to the nervous excitement building within her as the day of the race came ever closer.

CHAPTER 10

20th October

“CIA director Mike Pompeo has warned that North Korea is on the cusp of being able to hit the US with a nuclear missile. He stressed Washington still preferred diplomacy and sanctions but said military force remained an option. North Korea claims it already has the capability to strike the US.
EU leaders have agreed to start preparing for trade talks with the UK - as Theresa May admits there is "some way to go" in negotiations. As expected, her 27 EU counterparts agreed at a Brussels summit that not enough progress had been made on other issues to begin formal trade talks now. But by starting internal talks, they are paving the way for them to begin, possibly in December. Mrs May said she was "ambitious and positive" about the negotiations.
A church minister who helped a colleague to abuse women under the pretence of exorcising their demons has been jailed. Laurence Peterson, 59, helped pastor John Wilson, 70, sexually assault six women between 1984 to 2010. On one occasion Peterson barricaded a door to stop the victim's husband entering during one of Wilson's so-called "deliverance sessions". Peterson, of Eric Street, Keighley, was jailed for eight years and six months.
The fate of the former Futurist Theatre in Scarborough is expected to be decided this afternoon. In January, councillors voted 22 to 21 in favour of spending £4m to knock down the former venue which was opened in 1921. In its heyday, the Futurist's stage played hosts to artists including The Beatles and Shirley Bassey, but has been closed since 2014. Officers are recommending that the borough council's planning committee approves an application to demolish it, at a cost of £4m.”

“A good deal of cloud at first, perhaps with the odd spot of light rain in places. Becoming brighter with some sunny intervals developing and it will feel pleasant. Patchy light rain may return from the west later."

He woke suddenly, an image embedded in his brain. Unable to retrieve it he sat up in bed as he felt the hammer-blows of pain in his head. He made his way into the bathroom and took his packs of tablets from the cabinet, counting out the required quantity of each with shaking hands and swallowing the lot along with a glass of water. He went straight back to bed, just to lie still until the tablets took effect. It was becoming difficult to differentiate between dreams and hallucinations because he was never quite sure whether or not he was awake during the night. His illness was getting worse; draining his energy and his will. He briefly considered taking all his tablets at once, wondering if they would put an end to his suffering, or just add another dimension to it. He had to see it through. He owed it to himself, and to the innocent victims-to-be. He hauled himself out of bed, went through to the kitchen and put the kettle on. He opened the window and let in some cold, but fresh, air. He became aware of a ringing in his ears and it took more than a few seconds for his brain to register the fact that it was a real sound, an external sound, and that it came from his phone. He picked it up.

"Hello?"
"Is that John Braden?"
"Yes."
"John, it's Amy. Amy Winston. We spoke a few days ago."
"Yes. What do you want?"
"You wanted me to tell you where I was going to be on the 29th October. Well, I can tell you now. I've been assigned to cover the Bradford races, including the Half Marathon."
"Why are you telling me this now?"
"Because I'm beginning to believe you."
"You don't think I'm a stalker now? A sicko?"
"No. I'm sorry about that."
"So, call me again when you fully believe me."

He ended the call, unsure of her motives for contacting him when she was previously so adamant he was a threat to her. He didn't need her help now. The phone call just confirmed his theory that the Half Marathon was the target. Hearing the rattle of the letter box, he went to the door to pick up his post. Among the junk and flyers for fast-food outlets was the letter he was waiting for. His updated Will and a covering letter from his solicitor. He read it as he ate breakfast, then put it into his jacket pocket to be signed and witnessed later. Having cleared the table, he took out his laptop, notes and street maps to examine them in more detail. He concentrated on the areas he'd previously thought of as high risk, making copious notes under columns heading 'Pro' and 'Con'. He worked throughout the day, breaking off only to make a sandwich and swallow tablets. He finally snapped his laptop shut, gathered up all his notes and printouts and placed them in a suitcase in the wardrobe. He rummaged through the kitchen drawers till he found the suitcase lock he used when he went on holiday, and then spent a further ten minutes searching for the key. Once he'd found a key which fitted, he locked the suitcase and put the key in his jacket pocket. He punched the numbers into his phone and waited for an answer.

"Good afternoon. You're through to reception at Edward Attenborough Solicitors. Barbara speaking. How may I help you?"
"Hello, Barbara, My name's John Braden. I had a meeting with Edward a few days ago. I was wondering if I could have a quick word with him."
"He's with a client at the moment, Mr Braden. Can I ask him to call you back?"
"Please."
"I'll do that as soon as he's free, Mr Braden. Goodbye."

Edward re-read the letter he'd received from John that lunchtime.

Dear Edward,

I have an unusual request to make. I need either you, or your assistant, to call me every day at the same time, say 4.15 pm. If I don't answer, send me a text fifteen minutes later. If I do answer, and include the words 'We had a great evening last week', all is well. If I fail to answer either the call or text, or fail to include the sentence indicated above, then all is most certainly not well.
I have a terrible feeling that the police have an unhealthy interest in me, for reasons known only to themselves. If you don't hear from me, then it's possible I am in their custody. Please do all you can to help if this is the case.
Thanks,
John.

He picked up the phone and dialled John's number.

"Hello?"
"John. It's Edward. I've just read the letter you sent me. It's all a bit cryptic and mysterious. What exactly is going on?"
"Thanks for ringing me, Edward. In all honesty, I really don't know what's going on. I'll tell you what I know if that would help."
"Can you come over to the office?"
"When?"
"Today. After five. I'll wait for you."
"Thanks, Edward. I'll be there."

****

On his way, John stopped off at the Draper and signed his Will in the presence of Nick and Clockwork Jimmy. They countersigned as witnesses.

John was able to park close to the office, and walked in just as the receptionist, Barbara, was leaving. Edward was in reception waiting for him. They went straight into the office but not before Edward had made sure the outer door was locked.

"OK, John. Tell me what's going on."
"I told you I'm dying?"
"Yes."
"I have a tumour, which is causing the odd seizure and hallucination. One of these hallucinations led me to believe that a terrorist attack was imminent in Bradford. I tried to warn a freelance reporter – I believed she was to be one of the victims – but she thought I was a fruitcake and reported me as a stalker. The next thing I know is I've got officers from the Counter Terrorism Unit at my door. They bugged my laptop, my flat and my car, and even tried to set up a sting using a prostitute, because it seems they think I'm the bomber. Yesterday, I spent most of the day in an interrogation room in Wakefield. This morning, the reporter who'd previously branded me a nutter phoned me and told me she now believes me."
"This is all very odd, John."
"Odd is an understatement, Edward. I'm paranoid that the CTU might kill me, or this reporter might kill me. And on top of that, the act of terrorism I saw in my hallucination will cause my death. And finally, if none of the above kills me, my tumour most certainly will. All I'm asking is that if I should die in mysterious circumstances, then you make my fears public and call someone to account."
"OK, John. I'll do what I can."
"Thanks. That's all I can ask. I'm sorry I can't be more specific."
"Can I ask that you make the daily contact? My receptionist is very busy."
"Yes, I understand. I'll do that. Oh, before I forget. The signed Will."
"Ah, yes. Thank you."

As he left the office, John couldn't help but wonder if Edward could now be included along the growing number of those who considered him a nutter. Really, it didn't make much difference. Before he started up the car, he sent a text to his daughter, Jane, informing her she was now the sole beneficiary of his Will, and giving the address of his solicitor. Feeling a headache coming on, he took two more tablets and drove home. Parking his car, he locked up and walked to the Draper.

There were a few customers in, most of whom he knew and nodded to as he walked in. He gave a quiet groan when he saw who was stood at the bar talking to Nick. He walked straight to the bar and ordered a pint, ignoring her.

"I thought I might find you here."
"Why?"
"I asked around. You weren't known as a regular in any of the other bars in this area."
"How did you know I lived in this area?"
"I'm a journalist. We have our sources."
"The police?"
"We don't ask for that sort of information from the police, John. That would be unethical."
"Since when have ethics been important to the press?"
"You'd be surprised."
"So, I guess this isn't a social meeting."
"No. I was hoping we might be able to work together to thwart this attack, or whatever it is that's going to happen."
"Let's get a seat."

They moved to a nearby table, John immediately getting up to visit the toilet. On his return, he picked up the conversation.

"What do you know so far?"
"Only what you told me. That lots of people are going to die on the 29th, including the two of us. And now I've been assigned to cover the Bradford Race Day, which coincidentally takes place on the 29th. So, I'm guessing that may well be the target."
"That's my guess too."
"So, wouldn't it be best for you simply to stay well away from Bradford on that particular day, go on holiday or

something, and then you couldn't possibly die along with all the others?"
"I have to be there. It's immaterial. I'm dying anyway. Where I die makes no difference to me. But what about you? Why don't *you* stay away on the day? Why don't you go on holiday? But don't get on a plane."
"Why not?"
"Nothing. Just a flippant comment. Don't fancy the thought of you and a hundred other passengers falling out of the sky and landing on top of me."
"I've no intention of going away. I can't anyway. I've been assigned to cover the race day, and I've agreed."
"So, ring in sick."
"It's a question of doing the right thing. Regardless of what you think of me, I do have high moral standards."
"Then you're in the wrong occupation."
"Maybe. So, can we work together on this or not?"
"I'll think about it."

His phone rang. Regardless of the fact that he was in the middle of a conversation with Amy, he answered it without a moment's thought.

"Hello?"
"Hi Dad. I got your text. How are you?"
"Just the same, love. How are you and Mark? And little John?"
"We're all fine, dad. I just wanted to thank you."
"You don't have to thank me. You're going to need the extra money. Your mother certainly doesn't need it. And unfortunately, I can't take it with me."
"Mark and I have been thinking. I'd like to come up and stay with you for a while. Just to make sure you're OK."
"Your place is with your future husband. I'm coping fine, Jane. You don't have to worry about me...."

John felt an intense pain in his head, as if he'd been struck by a bolt of lightning. The phone fell from his hand and hit the floor a second before his body did. The convulsions started. Nick phoned 999 as Amy tried to control John's fit. With Nick's help, she rolled him onto his side to ensure he didn't choke. She could hear Jane's anxious voice pleading to know what was happening but simply switched off the phone so that she could concentrate on holding John's thrashing limbs. The seven minutes it took for a paramedic to arrive seemed like seven hours, but he immediately took charge and John slowly regained control of his body. The ambulance arrived soon afterwards and John was rushed to hospital whilst two paramedics worked frantically to keep him alive throughout the journey as the sirens helped clear the traffic obstructing their path. Amy followed in her car.

****

Back in the Draper, John's phone rang. In the commotion, it had been kicked under one of the tables. Nick traced the sound to its origin, retrieved the phone and answered it.

"Hello?"
"Where's dad? What's happening?"
"Dad? Do you mean John Braden?"
"Yes. I'm his daughter. We were just talking when everything went crazy. Is dad there? Is he OK?"

She was almost hysterical. Nick considered how best to phrase his reply. He took a deep breath.

"I'm afraid your dad's been taken to hospital. He's had some sort of fit. You know he's not been very well?"
"Yes. He's still alive, though, isn't he?"
"Yes. He was alive when the ambulance left."
"Do you know where they've taken him?"
"It will be BRI, I guess. That's the nearest A & E."
"Thanks. I'm coming up. 'Bye."

The phone went dead. Across the city, John was battling for his life in Intensive Care. It had taken the ambulance a mere ten minutes to reach the hospital A & E department, and a further ten minutes to clear the bureaucracy and get John handed over and receiving specialist medical attention, during which time his heart had stopped.

CHAPTER 11

21st October

"The Spanish government is holding a special cabinet meeting to approve measures to take direct control of the semi-autonomous region of Catalonia. The meeting comes almost three weeks after the region held a controversial independence referendum, which was ruled illegal by the supreme court. Catalan leader Carles Puigdemont argues that the referendum result gave him a mandate to pursue independence. But Spain's government disagrees and is preparing to take back power.
The World Health Organization (WHO) has appointed President Robert Mugabe of Zimbabwe as a "goodwill ambassador" to help tackle non-communicable diseases. New WHO head Dr Tedros Adhanom Ghebreyesus praised Zimbabwe for its commitment to public health. But critics say that during Mr Mugabe's 37-year rule Zimbabwe's health services have deteriorated, with staff regularly unpaid and medicines in short supply.
A man is to go on trial accused of murdering a mother-of-two. Jessica King, 23, was found dead by police at a house in Oxford Lane, in the Siddal area of Halifax on 27 August. Jordan Thackray, 27, of East Grange View, Leeds, has appeared before Bradford Crown Court where he denied her murder. He was remanded in custody until his trial, which is due to take place on 12 February."

"Initially dry and bright, but blustery showers will soon spread from the west, frequent across the Pennines, more scattered further east. A more organised spell of rain is likely later, heavy in places. Very windy, with gales becoming widespread across the hills."

Jane was exhausted after driving up the motorway in the heavy rain. It was after midnight when she pulled into the car park at the hospital. She found a parking space and pushed coin after coin into the machine until she was sure she wouldn't have to move her car during the night. She ran into A & E and asked if John Braden had been admitted. She was given directions to the ICU and ran along the corridors until she stopped abruptly at the entrance to catch her breath, wondering what lay in wait for her on the other side of the door. She wiped tears from her face and pushed the door open. She could hear voices and the hum of machinery. Nurses were scurrying back and forth, taking rushed instructions from doctors. Finally managing to stop one of them, she asked,

"Is John Braden in here?"
"Are you a relative?"
"I'm his daughter, Jane."
"Will you please take a seat outside for a minute, Jane? I'll get a doctor to come and talk to you."
"Thank you. Can you please tell me if he's still alive?"
"The doctor will see you shortly. Just take a seat."
"But I need to know! He's my dad."

The anguish and desperation in Jane's voice could not have failed to register. The nurse turned and spoke, calmly and compassionately.

"Yes, he's still alive. I'll get someone to talk to you as soon as I can. I promise. Just, please, be patient for a few minutes more."
"Thank you."

Jane did as the nurse requested and waited, watching the second hand of the clock sweep slowly round the face from one to twelve and then round again and again. Watching the chaotic order through the door as it swung open and closed again as staff went in and out, she felt helpless and fearful, alone and tearful.

It was close to two o'clock in the morning when a doctor finally emerged from behind the doors of ICU. His face bore an expression of concern in addition to the overall look of exhaustion.

"You must be Jane."
"Yes. How's my dad?"
"He's stable, Jane. At the moment."
"Can I see him?"
"Not yet. I wouldn't advise it. There are machines, and monitors. It can appear quite frightening. Besides, he's heavily sedated..."
"Sedated? But not in a coma."
"No. When he was admitted he suffered a cardiac arrest. We were able to resuscitate him and he's now breathing without artificial aid. We're hoping he'll recover, although at this stage we're unable to assess how much damage his brain has suffered. You are aware he has a tumour?"
"Yes."
"It may be that his brain has suffered irrevocable damage. We won't know until he regains consciousness. That could take a while. It might be best if you went home. We'll call you if there's any change."
"I'd rather wait."
"Of course."

Jane settled down on the bench in the corridor. Trying in vain to get comfortable enough to sleep, but finding it impossible, she asked a passing orderly if there was anywhere she could get a coffee. He directed her to a vending machine one floor below.

If I can't sleep, I might as well do my best to stay awake and alert, she told herself, but when she reached the machine, it had a hand-printed 'Out of Order' sign taped across the front.

"Just my fucking luck!"

She returned to her bench, pleased to find it still vacant, and laid down, her bag under her head and her coat spread over her for what little warmth it brought. But it was impossible to get comfortable, and instead she took out her phone and checked for any messages. Finding none, she resigned herself to scrolling through Facebook posts. Though it was still dark and early, on a whim she decided to phone Mark on the off-chance he was awake and up. He answered almost immediately.

"Hi, Jane. How's John?"
"He's still unconscious, Mark. I'm sorry for calling so early. You sound really tired."
"I am. I've been worried. You staying till he comes around?"
"Yes. I have to."
"I know. Keep me informed, won't you?"
"Yes. Of course. I'll ring you this evening."
"OK. Take care, love."
"You too. 'Bye."

She closed the call and immediately wished they'd spoken for longer. She missed him and was sure he missed her. But her dad was more important at the moment. When this crisis was over, things would soon be back to normal. She quickly corrected herself. Things would *never* be back to normal. Her dad was dying. She burst into tears.

****

Amy was at home eating breakfast. She'd left the hospital not long after John had been admitted, staying only long enough to be told he was still alive. She'd passed the information to CTU in a brief phone call and was now free to continue with her own agenda. She needed to make the most of the time she had. The clock was ticking.

****

Jane managed to get some sleep and woke stiff-limbed and uncomfortable. She checked the time: 7.45. After she'd composed herself, she went looking for a working vending machine. Fortunately, the hospital café had already opened and she was able to get a cup of coffee and a couple of slices of toast. She freshened up in the adjacent toilets before returning to her post outside the ICU. A further hour had passed before she received the news that her father was conscious and that she could see him briefly. She was warned that he wasn't totally lucid, due to the medication, and that he was constantly moaning something that sounded like 'blew woody' all the time.

"He's been repeating it ever since he woke. Have you any idea what it might mean?"
"No, doctor. I've no idea. Maybe he'll be able to throw some light on it when he's feeling a little better."
"It's probably nothing. Just something he's been dreaming about. I have to be honest with you, Miss Braden. His chances are not good. Most people in his situation would have given up. But he's a fighter. We'll do all we can, but ultimately it's up to him."

His eyes were open and he managed a smile when he saw Jane. She sat at his bedside and held his hand, taking care not to dislodge the line taped to the back of it. He was remarkably lucid.

"How are you, dad?"
"OK. I should be out soon. Just need some tests, then they'll let me go."
"Don't bank on it being soon, dad. You're very ill."
"I know. I know I'm dying. But there are things I have to do."
"Let someone else do them, dad. Tell me what you need to do."
"I need to stop a bomber, Jane."
"Can't you just pass whatever information you've got to the police? Let them deal with it? It's their job, dad, not yours."
"Well, do me a favour, then."
"What?"
"Get my keys out of my jacket. It's in the cabinet. There are keys to the flat and a small one which fits a suitcase in the

wardrobe in the bedroom. Will you go and get my laptop and my notes out of the suitcase and bring them here? Please. It's important. And why don't you have a nap while you're there? You look awful."
"I guess I do. Thanks. I'll do that. I'll get a shower too if that's OK."
"Of course, it's OK. Take your time, Jane. They'll probably put me back to sleep for a few hours. Keep me from being a nuisance."
"What's 'blew woody' mean to you, dad?"
"Blew woody? Blue woody? I've no idea."
"It's just that you were saying it over and over when you were waking up."
"Blue woody? I don't know. Sorry. Oh, and can you also call in the Draper and get my phone? I must have left it there. They'll be open at lunchtime for the City supporters. And call my solicitor – his number's in my phone – and tell him I'm OK."
"Yeah. I'll do all that. I'll come back to see you this evening. You get some rest."
"Thanks, love. I'll see you tonight."

Jane kissed her dad on the forehead and left the room, waving from the door. John realised it was the first time his daughter had kissed his forehead for years. It felt good. He fell asleep in seconds, and remained oblivious to the fact that a small army of doctors and nurses came and went with regularity, checking his monitors, updating his charts and injecting drugs into his intravenous drip.

****

The mood in CTU, Wakefield, was light. Both Lee and Peters expressed the opinion that the possibility of any incident at the Half Marathon would be lessened by John Braden's incapacity. Don McArthur was less certain that was the case.

"You two seem to be forgetting the fact that no-one has yet established with any certainty that Braden is definitely at the centre of any proposed activity. We're all going on gut-feeling here. But that in itself leaves us with too many 'what ifs'. Braden may yet recover sufficiently to be out on the streets on the 29th. And if not, who's to say he hasn't got an accomplice as yet unidentified who may carry out the activity on his behalf. We believe he is working alone simply *because* we have no intelligence of any co-conspirators. Then again, we could be totally wrong, and someone else may be behind it, off our radar. And, of course, we still don't know for certain that there *is* going to be an incident at all. We have to remain alert to all possibilities until that day has passed. Then, and only then, can we stand down. Both of you can consider yourselves on full alert until that day has passed. And let's not forget there are other races in Bradford on the same morning. So far, we've just *assumed* the Half Marathon is the target. It could be one of the others. The Kids race, for example. Just imagine the outrage if that was the target."
"There's also the possibility that Braden has got the date wrong."
"Don't make things worse, Lee. But you're right. That's another possibility to add to the list."

****

Jane parked her car next to her dad's and walked round to his flat. She unlocked the door and locked it again behind her. The heating had been left on all night and the flat was stifling. She turned the thermostat down and opened the kitchen window. Leaving her coat and bag in the kitchen, she went through to the bedroom, opened the wardrobe and pulled down the suitcase. Inserting the key, she opened it. Her dad's laptop, and a file of printouts and other papers were there as he'd indicated. She took them through to the kitchen, spreading them out on the table as the kettle came to the boil. She found coffee and sugar in the cupboard, milk in the fridge, but had the sense to smell the milk before pouring it. It was off. Only slightly, but enough to dissuade her from using it. She poured it down the sink. Sipping her black, strong coffee, she pored over the printouts and read the associated notes. Her dad had made meticulous notes, cross-referenced to timings from the previous year's race. He was able to pinpoint to within a couple of minutes where he expected groups of runners to be. It was an uncertain science, but with the data he had available, he'd made some workable forecasts. His conclusions, at the end, were well-argued and largely backed up by the statistical evidence he'd provided. It was compelling reading. Without knowing why, she took photos with her phone of every single page and sent them to her fiancé, Mark.

"Just in case", she told herself, mirroring her father's evident paranoia. "Like father, like daughter."

She gathered the printouts together and replaced them in the folder, shoving them along with the laptop into a drawer. She closed the open kitchen window and locked it. Yawning, she went through to the bedroom, took a blanket out of the wardrobe and spread it over the bed. She stripped off and slid under the blanket, feeling suddenly drained. Sleep came in minutes.

She woke suddenly. Her phone was ringing. Where had she left it? It wasn't on the bedside table. It must still be in the kitchen, probably on the table. She slipped naked out of bed and walked through. It was almost dark but the street lights were bright enough for her to see her way. It was on the table, as she thought. She picked it up, hearing Mark's calm voice.

"Hi, Jane. How's John?"
"Hi, Mark. God, I'm missing you."
"I'm missing you too. So, how's John?"

"He woke this morning and I spoke to him. He's very ill, and sedated. But he's a battler. The doctor is less optimistic than dad, though."
"Well, you stay with him as long as you need to, Jane."
"Are you sure that's OK?"
"Of course. He's family. He needs you there."
"OK. I'm going back to the hospital tonight. Do you want me to call you when I get back?"
"Please."
"OK. I'll talk to you later. Oh, and the stuff I sent to your phone. Please, Mark, don't delete any of it."
"I won't."
"Thanks. 'Bye, Mark."
"'Bye, Jane."

Jane showered and dressed, cursing the fact that she didn't pack enough clothes for an extended stay. No matter, she could wash her things daily. She would do some tonight, when she returned from the hospital. Realising she hadn't eaten, she made a mental note to call at the convenience store on the way home. Failing that, she could use some of her dad's stock of frozen ready meals. But she had to remember to get fresh milk, at least. She put on her coat, picked up her bag, phone and car keys, stuffed her dad's laptop and notes into a carrier bag, and went out into the cold cloudy evening. Rain was falling and becoming heavy, and the wind was picking up in intensity. As she'd promised her dad, she called at the Draper for his phone, and accepted all the good wishes for John's quick recovery before making a short phone call to his solicitor. Due to it being out of business hours, she left a brief message on his answering machine.

When she eventually arrived at the hospital, she was pleased to find that her father had been moved into a side ward, still in Intensive Care, but nonetheless it was a step forward, a relaxing of the constant need for manual monitoring. The machines were now left to get on with their job while the staff could spend time on other critically ill and injured patients. John smiled when he saw his daughter.

"Hello, Jane. How are you?"
"Never mind me. How are you?"
"Same as ever. Making a nuisance of myself. Asking when are they going to let me out. Why can't we get decent coffee in here? Usual moans and gripes."
"You should be grateful to the staff here. They're the reason you're still alive."
"I know, I know. Oh, and I forgot to mention. Don't drink the milk in the flat. It's probably gone off by now."
"I know. I tried it."
"Sorry."
"No problem. I'll get some on my way home… I mean on my way back to the flat."
"Have you spoken to Mark?"
"Yes. He's agreed I should stay up here for a few days."
"I'm glad. Did you bring my notes? And my laptop and phone?"
"Yes. All here."

She patted the carrier bag and placed it in the bottom of his bedside table.

"Thanks, Jane. I'll have a look at it later when there's nobody around."
"Don't overdo things."
"Wouldn't dream of it."
"Just take things steady, that's all I'm asking."
"OK, boss."

They spent nearly an hour just chatting. John made sure that Jane was aware that his downstairs neighbour Doris, or Bella, had dementia, and when she asked, to tell her that her husband was working late and she should go to bed. Finally, Jane took her leave as she still had to get to the shop before it closed. In truth, she was relieved to get outside. Hospitals were not comfortable places for Jane.

She associated them with pain and death, and was secretly dreading the birth of her baby. She pulled out of the car park on to the quiet road home, keeping just within the speed limit, a habit she'd picked up from her father when she was young and the family, mother, father and daughter were happy together. She stopped off at the convenience store and bought bread, eggs, milk and some biscuits, reckoning there were enough ready meals in the freezer for a few days and that she would replace what she used. Then, as an afterthought, she bought a bottle of New Zealand Sauvignon Blanc. The assistant asked her how her father was.

"News travels fast round here, doesn't it? He's awake and seems OK at the moment. Certainly, a lot healthier than I'd expected."
"Any idea when he'll be coming home?"
"No, not yet."
"It's just that he owes me for a packet of fags. But it will wait. Don't worry about it."

She offered to pay, but he insisted it was John's debt and he must repay it. She promised John would repay it at the first possible opportunity, made a mental note to remind her dad, and thanked him.

On a whim, she stopped by the Draper and walked in. It was busy. Nick was not on duty, but a man behind the bar came around to meet her.

"You must be Jane. How's John?"
"He's better than I expected. Conscious, lucid, smiling. Just looking at him you would never know he hasn't long to live. But how did you know I was his daughter?"
"He once showed me a photo of you. He was very proud of you. He said you were single-minded and wilful. I'm Jim, by the way. This is my pub."
"Oh, I'm pleased to meet you, Jim. I've heard dad speak about you."

"I bet. He's quite a character. Now, can I get you a drink?"
"White wine, please."
"Sit down. I'll bring it over."
"Thank you. How much is it?"
"On the house."
"Well, thank you."
"My pleasure."

Customers made room so Jane could sit at a table. She got the impression that most of them knew who she was, and that they were aware of what had happened to her dad. Jim brought her drink and sat with her at the table for a while, occasionally getting up to serve a customer, but his priority was making sure that John's daughter was OK. She refused the offer of a second glass, saying she was driving and needed to get back to the flat so she could phone her fiancé and bring him up to date with events. She said goodnight and left, driving to John's flat and parking next to his car. She was met inside the bottom door by Doris, who was wondering why her husband wasn't yet home from work. As advised by her dad, she told Doris her husband was working late and she should go to bed. She felt as if she needed to do the same, despite the sleep she'd had during the day. Instead, she opened the bottle of wine, sat at the kitchen table and phoned Mark. He picked up on the second ring.

"Hi, Jane. How are you?"
"Hi, Mark. I'm fine. Just a bit worn out. It's been a stressful day. Are you OK?"
"Fine. A hard day studying, but otherwise fine. How's John?"
"He's looking a lot better. Quite alert, considering…"
"Any idea how long he'll be in?"
"Not yet. I may know more tomorrow."
"So, what are you doing for the rest of the evening?"
"Having a glass of wine, then bed."
"Have you eaten?"
"Yes, I had some pasta earlier."

"That's OK then. You have to keep the baby's strength up."
"I know."
"Well as long as you're looking after yourself...."
"Don't worry about me. I'll ring you tomorrow, OK?"
"OK. Goodnight, Jane."
"Goodnight."

She felt guilty that she'd lied to him about having eaten. In truth, she hadn't really thought about food. She'd get things back to normal in the morning. There was no way she'd go through the horrors of anorexia again. Today was simply an oversight, because she was focused solely on her father's health. It was a one-off. She wouldn't put her baby's health at risk. She opened the packet of biscuits and took a sip of wine, realising at that moment that she hadn't closed the blinds. Standing by the sink, reaching for the cord, she noticed for the first time the photograph hanging in a small pine frame by the window. It was creased and faded, as if putting it in a frame had been an afterthought after it had lain in a wallet for years. She recognised it immediately. It had been taken on a holiday in Scarborough when she was about nine. She was sitting on the beach, between her smiling parents, ice-cream in hand and a great big grin on her face. It brought back memories of happier times with her family. She wiped away a tear from the corner of her eye. She took out her purse and opened a zipped section out of which she took a folded piece of paper. She unfolded it to find herself staring at the same photo she'd just seen hanging in her dad's flat.

CHAPTER 12

22nd October

“The five living former US presidents have gathered for a concert in aid of victims of the hurricanes which ravaged the US this year. Barack Obama, George W Bush, Bill Clinton, George HW Bush and Jimmy Carter appeared in Texas on Saturday. The three Democrats and two Republicans came together behind The One America Appeal, set up to help those caught up in the devastating trails of Hurricanes Harvey, Irma and Maria. It has raised $31m (£23.5m) so far.
Labour will back Conservative rebels over Brexit unless the prime minister accepts changes to its repeal bill, the party's shadow Brexit secretary says. Sir Keir Starmer wants six changes to the bill, which aims to transfer EU legislation into British law. If these are not accepted Labour will back Tory rebels in an attempt to force a vote on the final EU deal, he said.
Proposals by an NHS trust to privatise some services at a hospital in West Yorkshire have been described as "disastrous" by a union. Airedale NHS Foundation Trust said it was looking at setting up a private company to run facilities, estates and purchasing at its hospital in Keighley. A union has started a petition, saying the move would "lead to lower wages and poor conditions for new staff".
A woman has been arrested on suspicion of murder after an 18-month-old boy fell from a sixth-floor window and died. Police were called to Barkerend Road, Bradford, at about 17:10 BST on Saturday. Officers said it "quickly became apparent" the boy had died. A 23-year-old woman arrested on suspicion of murder is receiving medical assessment in custody.”

“A windy start to the day with some blustery showers, but these becoming mostly confined to the hills later in the day as winds ease a little. Some sunny intervals developing, especially in the east, but feeling cool.”

John was roused from a deep sleep by the commotion in his room. His charts, his belongings were being gathered together. His monitors were being disconnected and his intravenous line removed. He began to panic, tearing at what he believed were bonds tying him down. Still drowsy, he was conscious of being wheeled along a corridor and into a ward where the bed was guided into its place in the line and secured. As the fog cleared from his brain, he began to relax. He'd been dreaming he was being kidnapped. He drifted off back to sleep.

He woke a short while later, and was able to take in his new surroundings. He was in a general ward, in fact judging by the appearance of the rest of the patients, he was in a geriatric ward. He stopped a nurse on her way past with a bedpan in her hand.

"Nurse. Excuse me."
"Oh, good morning, Mr Braden. Are you OK, love?"
"Yes. But where am I?"
"This is Ward 3. We had to move you early this morning. They needed the bed in the ICU, and this is all that was available."
"No monitors?"
"No, apparently, you've been stable for long enough now. Your readings are all good. The doctor will be coming to do his rounds in an hour or so. After we get you some breakfast."

And she was off, bedpan in hand, leaving John without water.

From Intensive Care to Intensive Neglect, he thought.

He checked the clock on the wall above the door to the ward. Seven o'clock. Too early to ring Jane. He decided he'd wait to see what news the doctor would give him, when he eventually got around to seeing him. He checked his phone for messages. None. He pulled out his laptop and powered it up to check for emails. Only junk. He powered it down without checking news sites as he would normally do, as he noted the battery was almost dead. He wondered briefly if he could plug it in at his bedside, but reluctantly decided he daren't unplug any of the existing connections. He couldn't be certain if he would be inadvertently disconnecting another patient's life support system.

In time, his breakfast arrived on a tray. A cup of tea and a couple of slices of cold toast with a spoonful of watery, lukewarm scrambled egg. Just like home. He finished it and settled back to wait for the doctor.

****

David Lee was already at his desk when DI McArthur arrived at work. Lee couldn't wait to give him the news.

"Some interesting news in this morning, boss."
"Well?"
"You know Braden is in hospital. Intensive Care. He's been there since Friday."
"Yes. Is that it?"
"No, boss. The thing is, there's still chatter being detected by GOLIATH at GCHQ."

GOLIATH – General On-Line Intelligence And Translation Hypervisor - was the name given to the supercomputer system that GCHQ used to filter all internet and mobile phone traffic, and alert various agencies and departments of any unusual or suspicious activity.

McArthur thought for a moment, weighing up what he'd just heard.

"All this means is Braden is either innocent, or he's not working alone. Go talk to him. See if he has access to a burner phone or computer in hospital."

"OK, boss."

****

John Braden was still waiting to see the doctor an hour later when David Lee arrived at the hospital, asking at reception where he could find Braden. He was mildly surprised to be told Braden was out of ICU and in a general ward, but even more surprised to be told that he would have to come back at visiting time, either between two and four, or six to seven o'clock. He flashed his warrant card and was immediately given directions to Ward 3.

As he walked through the ward doors he could see John Braden in conversation with a doctor, and had the good sense to wait until the doctor had finished. He busied himself chatting up a young nurse, and got her phone number as a reward for his persistence. Looking back towards Braden's bed he could see the doctor had moved on and the patient was waving to him. He walked over.

"I was wondering how long it would be before you visited me. Haven't you brought any flowers?"
"No."
"Grapes?"
"Sorry. This is strictly a business visit. Though I am genuinely pleased to see you're still with us."
"Well, thanks for that."
"First question. Will you be discharged before next Sunday?"
"Not certain yet. But indications are, yes, I'll be back on the streets."
"Well, that's good news. Now, would you mind if I have a look in your bedside cupboard?"
"What exactly are you looking for? Explosives?"
"Phone. Laptop. Any communication devices."
"I have a laptop. My daughter brought it in last night, along with my phone. The problem was, I couldn't use them in IC because they might interfere with the other electronics."

"When did you get moved into this ward?"
"Sometime early this morning. I was here when I woke up."
"Have you used either your phone or laptop this morning?"
"Checked my phone for messages. None. Checked the laptop for emails. Couldn't do anything else because the battery is just about flat, and I daren't plug it in because the sockets are needed for more important hospital-type equipment. You're welcome to check."
"We will. We'll do it at our end. I just want to talk to some of the staff to verify your whereabouts since you were admitted."
"I'm sure they'll all verify I was up at the crack of dawn jogging round the perimeter of the grounds, followed by a hundred press-ups, before finally shagging the matron in the laundry cupboard."
"Been hallucinating again, then."
"Even if it were true you lot wouldn't believe it. Go ahead, be my guest. Check all you want. Oh, and next time you come, don't forget the flowers. And a get well soon card would be nice."

Lee spoke briefly with the staff in ICU, checked the hospital records, and, satisfied he had all he needed, drove back to Wakefield, and was soon at his desk checking the reports from GCHQ. He compared the time stamps on the messages reported by GCHQ against the medical evidence from the Infirmary. It confirmed what he'd thought. He passed the news to McArthur.

"This is it, boss. At the times the messages were intercepted by GCHQ, Braden was under heavy sedation, practically comatose. There's no way he could have made any calls. There's so much equipment in ICU, I doubt if he'd get a usable signal. He didn't get his laptop and phone until last night anyway. I checked while I was there. No incoming messages. He's not involved."
"It's still possible he has an accomplice."
"True. He mentioned his daughter brought his phone and laptop to the hospital."

"No doubt she'll be visiting him sometime today. Hang around at visiting time. Talk to her when she's leaving."
"OK."

****

John Braden lay back in his hospital bed trying to make some sense of it all.

Why me? he thought. What did I do to deserve this?

He considered the situation for the thousandth time. What if he were wrong? What if he'd got the wrong race? What if one of the other races was the target? What if there wasn't a target? And what if there was, but they simply weren't able to stop it? What if all those people really died? Including Amy and himself? Why couldn't he just stay at home and get drunk while listening to the radio? Waiting to hear news of a disaster. The body count rising. But he had to be there. His name was among the victims. The one hundred and three victims. He could change that by being there. Even if he just managed to save one person, it would be worth it. And if he failed? Well, at least he would have tried. He would have done everything in his power, as he had throughout his working life. It was his duty. He thought again of the race routes he'd looked at. Even if he knew for certain which race was the target, there were simply far too many potential sites to adequately police. And far too long a time frame. Far too many people to watch for suspicious behaviour. There must be some way to narrow it down. To increase the odds of identifying the bomber. He would have to go back and discuss it with the CTU team.

He called over a nurse and asked for permission to plug his laptop into the socket by his bed. Permission granted, he got to work, reviewing all he'd done so far, and questioning the assumptions he'd made. He was still making notes when his lunch was brought, and ate as he worked. Only the arrival of his daughter brought a pause to his absorption and assimilation of information. She kissed him on the cheek.

"Hi, dad. You're looking better today. How do you feel?"
"Much better. I hope they'll tell me later today when I can go home."
"Well, they'll let you leave when they think you're well enough."
"So, I'll have to convince them."
"The staff and customers of your local sent their best wishes."
"That was nice."
"And a local shopkeeper told me you owe him for a packet of fags. I thought you'd stopped."
"I have. I haven't had one for.... days."
"Well, you need to stop."
"Yes, boss."
"I'm serious, dad."
"I know. But I think it's a bit late to stop now, don't you? Can't see how stopping is likely to have any impact on my life span at this stage."
"I suppose not. So, there's no point in my lecturing you about the amount you're drinking either."
"None at all."

Jane stayed with him for the full length of visiting time and left reluctantly with all the other visitors in the ward. She was stopped by a man outside the doors to the ward. He showed her his warrant card and asked if he could have a quiet word. She reluctantly agreed, answering his questions but ending with a warning full of anger.

"Look. I don't know what you think my dad might have done, but I can assure you, you're totally wrong. He's a good man. He's spent his life *saving* people, not killing them. And look just where it's got him. Now leave him alone. He's *dying* for Christ's fucking sake!"

She ran off in tears.

John was allowed to eat his evening meal, such as it was, at a table in the middle of the ward. It felt good to be able to get out of bed, though he needed some assistance initially in walking the few steps required. Afterwards, he sat in his bedside chair tensing and relaxing his muscles and occasionally walking a few steps up and down the ward. He even walked down to the toilet on his own, though a nurse kept a close eye on him from her desk by the door. At the same time, she took a call from an external phone. She replied courteously to the question the caller asked. Yes, John Braden is making excellent progress. No, John Braden would not be allowed home before tomorrow at the earliest.

****

Jane returned for the evening visit, apologising for being five minutes late because she was on the phone to Mark. That was only partly the truth. She couldn't decide whether to tell her dad about her earlier skirmish with DS Lee. After discussing it with Mark, she decided to keep it to herself for now. She reasoned her dad had enough on his plate.

"No need to apologise for being late, love. Mark comes first. You're going to marry him and have his baby, remember?"
"Of course. He wants to know when I'll be going back to Derby."
"What did you tell him?"
"That I don't know yet."
"Jane. I'm OK now. If you need to go home, I'll be fine. I can always talk to you on the phone."
"I know. Tell you what, as soon as they discharge you and you're back in your flat and comfortable, then I'll go back to Derby for a couple of days. How's that?"
"I've got a better idea. You go home tomorrow. I'm sure they'll let me out tomorrow. So as long as you can make sure there's some fresh milk in the flat, then I'll be fine until I can get out and about. I'll phone you every day. That's a promise. Then Mark will be happy. And I'll be happy that

you're not wasting any more of your valuable life worrying about me."
"I'll think about it."

John knew he wasn't going to get his daughter's outright agreement. She was far too headstrong for that. She would make her own mind up in her own good time. She was like her father in that respect.

Before she left, she asked her dad to call her in the morning if he was being discharged. If she didn't hear from him, she'd see him at visiting time. He agreed. She stopped on the way home for a takeaway pizza. She needed something to eat while she finished off the bottle of wine she'd opened the previous night. She was adamant she'd go back to a sensible diet once she got back to Derby. For now, comfort food was important. She parked the car in the usual spot next to her dad's and walked round to the door. As she closed it behind her, Bella intercepted her, a puzzled look on her face.

"How nice to see you again, dear, so soon. Have you just been out again?"
"Yes. I've been visiting."
"Well, it was a short visit. I just saw you come in not ten minutes ago."
"Yes, I just popped out."

Poor Bella, she thought, walking up the stairs. She gets so confused.

She put her key in the door and was surprised to find it unlocked. She was certain she'd locked it when she left earlier to visit her dad. She opened the door quietly, little by little. The hall was dark, but there was a dim light in the bedroom. She moved slowly and silently down the hall towards the bedroom door, holding her breath. As she was on the point of turning the bedroom door handle, the light in the room went out and the door was wrenched inwards, out of her grasp. She was momentarily caught off guard as someone rushed past her, colliding with her and she felt a searing pain in her side from the contact as she turned to catch a glimpse of the hooded figure descending the darkened stairs through the open door. She dropped the pizza as her left hand automatically went to the source of the pain, and when she looked down at it she knew it was blood. With her right hand she scrabbled in her bag for her phone and, finding it, dialled 999.

Stumbling along the hall, she edged her way down the steps, fighting hard to remain conscious, holding on to the banister, descending slowly, step by step. Reaching the bottom, she knocked on Bella's door. By the time Bella opened the door, Jane had slumped to the floor, barely conscious and bleeding heavily. Bella knew exactly what to do, having been a nurse before succumbing to the ravages of dementia. Instinctively, she held a towel against the wound, keeping pressure on the site, staunching the flow. She laid Jane on her back, her head supported by a cushion. She talked to Jane constantly to ensure she remained conscious and as comfortable as possible. Jane was more concerned about the welfare of her unborn child than her own wellbeing and tried to remain calm until the paramedics arrived. She was well aware of the amount of blood she had lost and which still seeped through the towel.

****

John was already asleep, blissfully unaware of his daughter's plight. His diseased brain was overloaded from his attempts to sort some kind of action plan from the mass of information he'd sifted through, and his body was worn out from the mass of drugs coursing through it.

****

At home in Derby, Mark was becoming concerned that he hadn't heard from Jane. There was no answer when he tried her mobile. As a last resort, he'd tried John's. There was no answer from John's either. Reluctantly, he gave up. He would try again in the morning.

****

The paramedics, once they'd determined the extent of Jane's injury, concentrated on trying to stabilise her condition and handed her over to the ambulance team when they arrived on the scene. She was taken to A & E at the same infirmary where John was currently staying. Despite the best efforts of the medical team, she died on the way to the hospital. Her baby, tragically, failed to survive.

CHAPTER 13

23rd October

“Japanese Prime Minister Shinzo Abe has promised strong "counter-measures" against North Korea, after winning a decisive victory in Sunday's election. Mr Abe had called an early election for a greater mandate to deal with "crises", including the growing threat from Pyongyang, which has fired missiles over Japan in recent months. His ruling coalition has retained a two-thirds majority in parliament. This paves the way for Mr Abe to amend Japan's post-war pacifist constitution.
Britain's five biggest business lobby groups are calling for an urgent Brexit transition deal, or they warn the UK risks losing jobs and investment. In a joint letter being sent to Brexit Secretary David Davis, the groups, including the Institute of Directors and CBI, will say time is running out. Sources told the BBC the letter is still in draft form, but will be sent in the next day or two. A government spokesman said the talks were "making real, tangible progress".
Drivers of older, more polluting vehicles will have to pay almost twice as much to drive in central London. Mayor Sadiq Khan's £10 T-Charge, which mainly applies to diesel and petrol vehicles registered before 2006, has come into force. It covers the same area as the existing congestion charge zone, bumping up the cost to £21.50 for those affected. Opponents said the scheme would "disproportionately penalise London's poorest drivers"
Towns and villages in West Yorkshire have been hit by flooding in the wake of Storm Brian.
More than a dozen flood warnings were put in place after gale-force winds and heavy rain hit the UK on Saturday night, but these have now been removed. Three homes and business were flooded in the Calder Valley, the Environment Agency said.”

“A dry start in eastern parts, but outbreaks of rain in the west will soon reach all areas. However, drier and brighter conditions with some sunny spells will follow from the west in the afternoon."

John was awake and enjoying a cup of weak hospital tea when a nurse approached his bed, a concerned look on her face.

"Morning, nurse."
"Good morning, Mr Braden. I've just been asked to pass a message on to you. It's about your daughter."
"What's happened?"
"I don't know the details, Mr Braden. I was just told to inform you that she was brought here last night with a serious injury."
"An injury? What sort of injury? How bad?"
"I believe it was a knife wound. That's all I know. I'm sorry."
"Well, can I go and see her?"
"Not yet, I'm afraid. Someone will come to escort you soon."

****

The police had been notified of the break-in and assault by the hospital. The police clerical officer who entered the details on the computer system was immediately made aware of a 'flag' on the address in question, the appended note stating that CTU must be notified of any incident. She called the number and spoke to David Lee. He made a note of the crime number and took some details before thanking the officer for her diligence and ending the call. He left a note on Don's desk, ran out to his car and set off at speed towards Bradford. He cursed silently as he got caught in the rush hour traffic when even with his siren blaring and lights flashing he was unable to make much headway through bottle-necked junctions. It was 09.15 by the time he reached the Infirmary. He parked as close to the entrance as possible, leaving his police authorisation card in the windscreen. A WPC was already waiting for him at the entrance. She introduced herself.

"I'm WPC Armitage. You must be DS Lee."
"I am. Has Mr Braden been informed yet?"
"About the attack, yes. But he doesn't know she's dead yet."
"OK. I suppose I'll have to do it."
"We need him to identify the body. I'm only here in case he needs a shoulder to cry on. I'm not part of the investigating team."
"My team will be co-ordinating this investigation."
"I see. Well, let's get this over with."

They walked up to Ward 3 where they found John pacing back and forth by his bed. He saw Lee and the WPC approach and walked to meet them.

"What's happened? No-one's telling me anything. How is my daughter? They said she'd been stabbed."
"That's correct, Mr Braden. Please sit down, sir."

The look on Lee's face indicated bad news was coming. John sat down in his bedside chair.

"Mr Braden, I'm afraid I have some bad news. Last night, someone broke into your flat. We believe Jane disturbed the intruder and in the scuffle which ensued, she was stabbed. I'm afraid she died on the way to hospital, Mr Braden, despite the best efforts of the paramedics."

John's face drained of blood and he was unable to speak. Then came the tears. And then the anger.

"When I find who did this, I swear I'll kill him."
"We'll do all we can to find him, Mr Braden. You can be assured of that. However, first, there's the matter of identification."
"What?"
"Standard procedure, sir. I'm afraid we need you to identify the body."
"Yes. Yes, of course."

WPC Armitage asked a nurse to fetch a wheelchair, but John insisted he would walk. The three of them went together down to the mortuary. It felt cold down there, with harsh fluorescent lighting, as they stood in a small room, one wall of which had a window whose curtains were currently closed.

"Are you ready, Mr Braden?"
"Yes."

John steeled himself as Lee pressed a button by the window. The curtains parted to reveal the shroud-covered shape of a body. At a nod from Lee, the attendant pulled back the shroud so that John could see his daughter's lifeless white face.

"Is that your daughter, sir?"

John could only nod his acknowledgment. No words would come. Only tears which continued to flow long after the attendant had closed the curtains. Eventually, he was able to ask.

"What about her baby?"
"I'm afraid the baby didn't survive, Mr Braden."
"Dear God."

Both Lee and WPC Armitage were quick to realise that he was on the point of collapse, and supported his sagging body until a wheelchair could be brought. They took him back to his ward and sat with him until he regained some measure of control over his grief and his anger.

"Can someone please tell Mark? I've only met him once, and he'll blame me for this."
"If you would give me his address, I'll speak to him personally."
"Don't tell him on the phone."
"I'll speak to him face to face, Mr Braden. I promise."

"Thank you."

In view of what had happened, it was decided that John should stay in hospital for one more day at least. He spent the day brooding, blaming himself. He was already responsible for the death of his daughter and unborn grandson. How many more deaths would there be before his own death put an end to it all?

****

David Lee was in Derby by lunchtime. Fortunately for him, Mark was at home. He hadn't gone out due to the fact that he'd been trying all morning to contact Jane. Neither could he contact John. The news he received from DS Lee explained why. DS Lee had lost count of the number of people he'd seen fall apart when receiving such news. Mark was no different, and Lee dealt with it in the same detached manner he'd learnt over the years, even offering him the contact details for the local Victim Support group. Dealing with villains was easy; it was the task of having to deal with the victims that made the job so demanding. It felt like a long, lonely drive back to Wakefield during which he constantly asked himself why he continued to do this job. He was no nearer to an answer when he arrived at the CTU building. However, he soon had enough to do to take his mind off the doubts he had about his chosen career. After a quick meeting with McArthur, he was informed he would be liaising with CID in the investigation into the murder of Jane Braden.

DS Peters was furious.

"This means there's just the two of us actively investigating a potential terrorist threat."
"On the contrary, Brian. We've now got more than twice the manpower. The break-in at Braden's flat has to be linked to what he knows. Find out who did it, and what they were looking for, and we've a far better chance of cracking our

case. Look at the bigger picture, Brian. Without CID's help, we'd never get the answers in time."
"Yeah. OK, I get it. There's one thing, though."
"What's that?"
"Well, if someone was going to break into Braden's flat, unless it was just a random, unplanned act of petty burglary, whoever it was would first want to make sure nobody would be in. Yeah?"
"Go on."
"Well, the burglar must have known Braden was in hospital."
"Not necessarily, but go on."
"Well, whoever did it must have known Braden would be out of the flat. Presumably he didn't expect anybody to be in. He just had the knife for insurance. But let's assume he knew Braden, or at least knew someone who'd told him Braden was in hospital, then he'd want to break in *before* Braden was discharged. Look, boss, I know it's just a theory, but if he knew the flat was empty, then presumably he knew why. If that's the case, then he must have known, or at least suspected that Braden was *still* in hospital last night."
"So, what are you waiting for? Find out who his visitors were, who they've spoken to, and see if the hospital had any phone calls about him."
"OK, boss."

He might have something there, thought McArthur after Peters had left. It's a long shot, but at least it's something.

The secure email he had been waiting for came through soon afterwards. The scene-of-crime report from SOCO. He read it carefully, then read it again, highlighting certain passages with a marker pen.

No sign of forced entry. Keys were used. No prints found, except those which have already been eliminated as belonging to the occupier, and the victim, his daughter. Evidence that the burglar was looking for something specific. CD player, CDs and other small electrical appliances were overlooked.

And then the pathologist's report. Knife was long-bladed, at least twenty centimetres, with one serrated edge and a blade width of three centimetres. Killer probably right-handed. Death due to massive trauma and associated blood loss.

The rest of the report told him very little of interest, although there was a sentence which puzzled him, concerning the fact that keys were used. 'Residual traces of a plastic substance were found in and around the lock.' He returned to the SOCO report, and picked up the phone.

"Hello?"
"Mr Braden? It's DI McArthur. I'm very sorry to hear of your loss. Please believe me, we'll do all we can to bring the culprit to justice."
"What do you want?"
"Could you tell me, please, do you have more than one set of house keys?"
"No. Jane was using mine."
"Have you ever lost your keys, then found them at a later date?"
"No. What's this about?"
"This wasn't a break-in, Mr Braden. The burglar had a set of keys."
"Oh."
"Do you know how that could have come about?"
"What are you implying?"
"Nothing, Mr Braden. I just want to know how a burglar could get hold of your keys. Give it some thought, please. I won't bother you any further. Thanks for your time."

Out of courtesy, he contacted DS Lee, told him what he'd learnt, and forwarded to him the SOCO and pathologist's reports.

****

It didn't take long for Peters to get to the hospital and after checking at the desk, he was quickly on his way to Ward 3. He stopped at the nurses' station, showed his warrant card and introduced himself. He was able to speak to all the staff currently on duty and each of them confirmed that only John's daughter had visited prior to her death. It then dawned on him that, since nurses work shifts, he would have to speak to a few more people to ensure he checked every single person who had worked on the ward while John had been a patient. After some initial resistance from Human Resources, he came away with contact details for everyone he needed to check. It was a task which took up the entire evening.

****

McArthur was still pondering how someone could have got hold of John Braden's keys without his knowledge. It was possible that a member of the hospital staff 'borrowed' them while John was in Intensive Care, and had a copy made. But why wasn't the flat broken into then, when it would definitely have been empty. What his colleague had suggested made sense. The intruder must have known the flat was empty. But a member of the hospital staff must surely have known his daughter might be staying there. She visited at every opportunity. She had to be staying locally. McArthur was coming around to the view that someone other than hospital staff had taken or somehow copied the keys without John's knowledge, and that it was possibly done before John went into hospital. The intruder then would most likely have checked he was still in hospital before he entered the flat. He was praying his colleague's inquiries would yield a positive result.

He was still at his desk at 9.30 pm when his desk phone rang. He snatched it from its cradle.

"McArthur."
"Boss, it's Brian. I've spoken to everyone who has been on duty in Ward 3, and guess what?"
"Tell me."
"One of the nurses on duty yesterday remembers taking a call during the evening, she thinks around six, seven o'clock. It was from a member of the public, though she didn't get a name, asking if John would be going home that night. And get this, it was a *woman.*"
"Thanks, Brian. Good work. Get off home and I'll see you in the morning."
"Thanks, boss. Good night."

He put the phone down. A *woman*. That was something he hadn't expected. But then nothing about this case had ever seemed straightforward. He gathered together all the files on his desk, stuffed them in a drawer, locked it and picked up his jacket from the back of the chair. He turned off the light by the door, locked the door behind him and went home.

In his hospital bed, John was still awake. He'd taken his medication but refused a further sedative. He was still going over the events of the last few days, wondering how anyone could have got hold of his keys for long enough to get them copied without his being aware. He mentally replayed every meeting, every conversation, where he might have become distracted. He wanted answers. He was determined to leave hospital if not in the morning, then as soon as possible, even if it meant signing himself out.

CHAPTER 14

24th October

“China's ruling Communist Party has voted to enshrine Xi Jinping's name and ideology in its constitution, elevating him to the level of founder Mao Zedong. The unanimous vote to incorporate "Xi Jinping Thought" happened at the end of the Communist Party congress, China's most important political meeting. Mr Xi has steadily increased his grip on power since becoming leader in 2012.
A British former assistant of Harvey Weinstein says she was paid £125,000 ($165,200) to keep quiet after accusing the movie mogul of sexual harassment. Zelda Perkins told the Financial Times she signed a non-disclosure agreement in 1998 after making the accusations. She said he asked her to give him massages and tried to pull her into bed, but she "was made to feel ashamed for disclosing his behaviour".
A 19-year-old woman has admitted posting online links to propaganda produced by the Islamic State group. Ammber Rafiq, of Elmfield Terrace, Halifax, pleaded guilty at Sheffield Crown Court to four offences of disseminating terrorist publications. She was arrested in April following an investigation by counter-terrorism police into messages she had sent to an online chat forum. Rafiq was remanded in custody and will be sentenced on Tuesday.”

“Rather cloudy and breezy, with the best of any brighter spells across eastern parts during the morning. Cloud then thickens from the west, with outbreaks of rain developing. These perhaps persistent and heavy at times across the Dales and Moors.”

By the time John woke up, Mark had already arrived at the hospital. He needed John’s permission for the body to be released for burial. John had no objection. There were no pleasantries between them and the formalities were completed with John’s signature. He knew there would be no invitation to the funeral, but it mattered little. Revenge was all he wanted. They shook hands briefly, and Mark was gone. They would not meet again. Mark considered him toxic. He was solely responsible for Jane's death, even if only in an indirect way. As far as Mark was concerned, John Braden had ruined his hopes and dreams, his whole future, his entire life. There would never be any reconciliation. The fact that John felt exactly the same way about the person who was directly responsible for Jane's death – whoever it was - never occurred to Mark.

****

In the CTU office, McArthur, Lee and Peters were already working. Peters was checking on the recent activities of Ellen Stevenson and had subpoenaed her phone records for the last week. It transpired that she hadn't been the one who'd made the call to the hospital, and she had been working in the Midlands on the night in question, as her embarrassed punter had reluctantly confirmed.

"OK, so where does that leave us?"
"Maybe the phone call to the hospital was totally innocent after all. Maybe it was just a customer at his pub, wondering how he was."

They looked at their inquiry board. There were lines and arrows everywhere. Every name was connected to every incident, crossed out and inked in again at a different point. They studied and argued passionately, pointing out possibilities, however remote, and eliminated each in turn by consensus until only one name remained upon which they all agreed. McArthur issued the command.

"Go pick her up. Both of you."

DI Lee phoned the newspaper office to ascertain whether Amy Winston was at work, only to be informed she had called in sick the previous day and was not expected back that week. Lee was able to get her home address, and thanked her boss for his help.

****

Lee and Peters parked the Audi a short distance from Amy Winston's flat close to the canal in Shipley. Lee pressed the buzzer and waited. Receiving no response, he called her next-door neighbour.

"Who is it?"
"Police, madam. May we come in?"
"Hold your ID up to the camera, please."

Looking up and to the right, Lee spotted the video camera pointed at them. He motioned to Peters and both officers in turn placed their warrant card in front of the camera. There was a short buzzing sound before the door swung open. They entered, and took the lift to the third floor. A middle-aged woman in jeans and a loose top was waiting outside her flat.

"Morning, madam. Sorry to disturb you at this time of the morning, but we're looking for your neighbour, Miss Winston."
"I'm not her neighbour. I just clean for the lady who lives here."
"Do you know if she's in?"
"Well, I saw her yesterday. She told me she was going on holiday. She was taking a case to a car. I watched her get in and drive away."
"Can you tell me anything about the car?"
"Not really. I only saw it from up here. It was white. A white hatchback. That's all I can say. I didn't know she had a car. I've never seen it before. She usually goes to work on the bus or the train."
"And this was yesterday?"
"Yes. Yesterday morning. Just before lunch."
"Did she, by any chance, say where she was going?"

"Scotland. She said near Inverness."
"Thank you. How did she seem? Was she nervous or anything?"
"No. Just her usual, business-like self."

Back in the car, Lee phoned McArthur. He was less than pleased when told Amy had fled.

"Any idea where she's gone?"
"She told the cleaner next door she was going to Inverness, but that's not necessarily true. The other thing is, the cleaner didn't think Amy has a car. Sounds like she may have hired one."
"OK. Sit tight for a few minutes. We'll get a list of local car hire companies to you. With a bit of luck, her car will be fitted with a GPS tracker."

They used that few minutes to speak to local shopkeepers in the area for any clues as to what Amy might be up to, but everyone they spoke to confirmed she seemed to be a very private person. They decided to speak to her boss, and after receiving permission from McArthur, drove into Bradford, having made an urgent appointment to speak to the editor. He was waiting for them, having made time in his schedule.

"Come in, officers. I hope you will keep this as brief as possible. I have deadlines to meet."
"Of course, sir. We'd just like some further information about Amy Winston."
"Fire away."
"How long have you known her, sir?"
"She's been freelancing for me for about five years, though she was already here when I joined. I believe she's worked with us for almost ten years. HR will be able to tell you precise dates."
"And what was she like to work with?"
"When I started, I believed she had a great future as a journalist. She had a nose for a story. Asked the right

questions. And wrote her stories well. Well-researched and meticulous in detail. I thought at the time she was too good for a provincial daily."

"But she stayed here. Why?"

"She works for a number of publications, not just us. But her work suddenly began to lose focus. The quality dropped. Her enthusiasm seemed to flag. I don't know why. She never raised any problems she might have been having. Anyway, she was still a valuable resource, but it seemed as if she'd lost her ambition."

"Can you remember when all this started, sir?"

"Not really. It was more a gradual decline. The first I noticed was when she filed a story which contained a number of glaring errors. If we'd published, we could have been on the end of a suit for libel."

"Can you remember what the story was about?"

"Yes. It was a local businessman who'd been accused of discrimination. Against a Jewish supplier. Amy was Jewish, you know."

"No, sir. We didn't know that. Can you remember when that was exactly?"

"Maybe three years ago. Amy had just returned from holiday, I think."

"Can you remember where she went on holiday?"

"Tel Aviv. I think."

"Just one more question, sir. I believe Amy is on sick leave. Is that correct?"

"Well, yes. It came as a bit of a surprise to me. She seemed fine, until I called her in to discuss her assignments for the next week or so. I had asked her to cover a dignitary's visit to Harrogate on Sunday. But she refused. She demanded to be allowed to cover the Bradford races. When I wouldn't allow it, she stormed out of the office and the next thing I knew, she'd phoned in sick."

"Thanks for your help, sir. We'll let you get back to your business."

****

They passed the information to McArthur and, before lunchtime, armed with a long list of vehicle hire firms, they were on the move again. The list had been restricted to those companies which did not have any logo or company name visible on the body of the vehicle, the reason being that Amy would not wish to draw attention to herself. While they were checking the addresses one at a time, support staff at CTU were calling other companies, checking whether they had rented out any white hatchbacks in the last few days. As they eliminated companies from the list, they passed the information to Lee and Peters. As a precaution, Don McArthur had informed *his* boss of the situation, and Amy's photograph, description and other relevant details had been circulated to police forces nationwide, with the added caution that she was to be considered A and D – armed and dangerous. He called CID, explained the situation to the commanding officer, and courteously, but forcefully, informed him that CTU were taking over the murder inquiry, but that CID would be required to assist where required. Outranked, the officer reluctantly agreed, and, again reluctantly, arranged for around-the-clock surveillance of Amy's flat.

****

John Braden left hospital before lunchtime, having had to wait until the doctor did his rounds and authorised his discharge. He got into the taxi feeling better than he had for a while thanks to having the correct doses of medication administered at the correct times, rather than the haphazard way he'd been taking them. He'd collected his flat keys from the mortuary, noting that Jane's body had already been removed, no doubt to her adopted home in Derby. He was well aware there was little chance he'd be invited to her funeral, even if it took place while he was still alive, and had said his personal final prayer for her in the mortuary. Right now, what he really wanted was revenge. Someone had to pay.

The taxi dropped him outside his flat and Bella was there to let him in. Strangely, he thought, she seemed remarkably clear-headed.

"Hello, John. Have you been on holiday?"
"Yes."
"Well, while you were away, you had a visitor. She said she was your daughter. Well, she had an accident and had to go to hospital. I haven't seen her since. I do hope she's all right."
"She died, Bella."
"Oh, I'm so sorry."
"Do you remember anything about that night, Bella?"
"Not really. I just thought it was odd that she came in and didn't speak to me, then a few minutes later she came in again with a pizza and said hello."
"She came in twice?"
"Well, yes. Well, I was sure it was her. But now I'm not so sure. She didn't speak the first time and she was dressed differently. The first time she wore one of those hood things."
"What colour?"
"I don't know. Dark."
"Blue, maybe?"
"Yes. Possibly dark blue."
"But it was definitely a woman?"
"Oh, yes, dear."
"Thank you, Bella."

Blew woody. Blue hoodie! That was what he'd said in hospital. Jane told him. He mounted the stairs still stained with Jane's blood. There was also blood in the hallway of his flat. So, she'd come home to find an intruder, who'd stabbed and killed her. And the intruder was a woman. There were only two suspects in his book. Ellen. And Amy. And what was it that McArthur had said? The intruder had a key. He knew he had a habit of leaving his keys on the table when he was in a pub. But they were always in sight. Think, John! Did you ever go for a pee, and leave them unguarded? He couldn't remember. But yes. While he was talking to Amy in the Draper, he'd left his keys on the table and gone for a quick pee. But he wasn't long and they were still there when he returned. He picked up his phone and called CTU. McArthur answered.

"It's John Braden."
"Hello, John. Are you out of hospital?"
"Yes. I've just got home."
"How are you feeling?"
"As well as can be expected considering my daughter has just been murdered along with her unborn child, and I'm dying."
"Sorry. Stupid question. I'm truly sorry, John. So, is there a specific reason for your call?"
"You asked if there was a chance someone could have taken my keys. If I ever left them unattended?"
"Yes."
"In the pub. I went for a pee. They were still on the table when I returned, though."
"Who were you with, John?"
"Amy Winston."

There was silence for perhaps ten seconds before McArthur spoke again.

"John, she's our prime suspect. I presume when she was with you in the pub, she had a mobile phone with her."
"Yes, of course."
"You may not be aware, John, that she probably had software installed on her phone that allowed her to do a scan of your keys so that they could be printed on a 3D printer."
"Is that possible?"
"Yes. I guess that's what happened. Our SOCO team reported finding some residue round the locks of your flat. Later examination proved it to be the same compound used in 3D printing."
"So, I'm responsible for my own daughter's murder."

"No, John. Don't take it like that. There's no way you can be held remotely responsible."
"So, where's the bastard now?"
"We're looking for her, John. She called in sick at work. And now she's disappeared. There's a nationwide search. We'll let you know the minute we find anything."
"Just to let you know, in case your inquiries have not already established the fact, it *was* definitely a woman who murdered my daughter."
"And you know that how?"
"My neighbour told me, and guess what?"
"What?"
"She was wearing a blue hoodie."
"Is that significant?"
"I saw it when I had my last seizure."
"Thanks, John. And John, I can only apologise to you. It was my decision to get Amy to contact you. We just didn't suspect, at that time..."
"We all make mistakes. It's not the first one you've made."
"We'll get her, John."
"Not if I get her first."

John put the phone down, and for want of anything constructive to do, set about trying to clean up the bloodstains.

****

Amy was at that moment holed up in a remote rented cottage in the Lake District. Her hair was cut short and dyed blond. The car was nowhere to be seen. As soon as she'd set off in it, she'd punched in the post code of an address in the Scottish Highlands, and drove north up the A1. She'd pulled off on to a B-road and stopped in a deserted lay-by, where she'd opened the bonnet and disabled the GPS tracker. Then she'd driven across to Cumbria using as many back roads as possible to evade roadside cameras, before abandoning the car in a disused quarry, covering it with branches and continuing her journey for the last ten miles on foot. She'd used the cottage previously, having taken out a long-term rental using a false identity, the owners being happy to let it out to a writer who needed a retreat to work on her projects. She had no close neighbours, and nobody bothered her there.

****

By four o'clock, Lee and Peters had almost exhausted their list of hire companies. They each had two more calls to make. Lee suggested,

"A fiver to whoever lands the right one?"
"Deal."

As it happened, Peters' first call yielded good news. The previous day, they had hired out a white hatchback to a lady named Amy Swanston, for one week. She'd provided appropriate documents which seemed authentic and paid cash. Peters recorded the registration number and asked if the car was fitted with a GPS tracker. It was. He asked if they could give him the car's location, gave his thanks, then held out his hand to Lee.

"You owe me a fiver."

He passed the news to McArthur and drove off at speed towards the A1 North. Lee sensed a chance to get his money back.

"Bet you a fiver the GPS has been disconnected."
"You're on."

They hit slow-moving traffic on the A1 and it was almost six o'clock when they pulled on to the back road and drove to the lay-by indicated by the GPS tracker. The lay-by was empty apart from a burger van. The occupant had only arrived there within the last hour, and so was unable to give them any information. However, it had been a long day, so they allowed themselves a short break for a burger before calling McArthur with the bad news.

"It's been disconnected, boss. There are no cars here."
"I expected as much. OK, make your way back and I'll circulate the news to the regionals."

So, Amy was a professional, as McArthur had half-expected. False documents, different identity, technical skills. So, what did Braden have in his flat that she wanted so badly she was prepared to kill to get it? He picked up the phone and rang Braden's mobile to ask him that very question.

"John? It's Don McArthur."
"What can I do for you this time?"
"I'm wondering what exactly Amy was looking for in your flat. Can you help me with that?"
"No idea. Unless she thought I might have something which could incriminate her."
"And do you?"
"All I have is her work phone number and email address."
"Mmm. That doesn't sound like it's any use. We know you phoned her and we have a copy of the email you sent her. Anything else?"
"The only other thing she might conceivably have been interested in is the work I was doing to try to pinpoint the optimum sites for an attack. She told me her editor had assigned her to cover the race day."
"That's not true, John. The local editor told my men she had been assigned a job in Harrogate which she'd refused and then she'd gone off sick. So, it seems she was definitely planning something for that day and wanted to find out what information you'd assembled. If she thought you'd passed that to us, it might just influence her thinking concerning an attack."
"You mean, she wanted to know if I'd worked out her attack plan?"

"Well, not necessarily. But if she thought you had some very plausible and well-researched theories concerning the best site for an attack, then she would suspect we would ensure we had a very heavy presence there. So, she'd pick an alternate site."
"I get you. What do you need from me?"
"Have you got a scanner?"
"Yes."
"Well, would you mind... No, cancel that. Can I come over to your flat to examine what you've got? Look through your notes and everything."
"OK. When?"
"Within the hour?"
"OK. I'll see you then."
"Thanks, John. 'Bye."

Next, he called Lee and Peters to update them. Peters was to meet him at John's flat while Lee was given time off until Thursday morning. Peters would then get Thursday off to have some time with his pregnant wife before they would all be required round the clock until Sunday.

Lee was dropped off in Bradford and was driven to Wakefield by a uniformed officer while Peters made his way to Idle. Lee drove home, made a quick phone call, packed an overnight bag and drove down to the West Midlands to see his lover, Ellen Stevenson.

****

McArthur was the first to arrive at John's flat. Again, he apologised to John for the grief he'd caused.

"Enough, Detective Inspector."
"Call me Don."
"Well, Don. Look, it's not your fault. It's mine and mine only. I accept full responsibility. I should have kept my mouth shut."

"No, John. What you have done was show an uncommon measure of bravery and public spirit. And I can only apologise for the fact we didn't take you seriously at the time."
"Can I take it I'm no longer a terrorist suspect?"
"You're not a suspect, John. But we do need your help."
McArthur held out his hand, John shook it.

"Thank you. Can I explain why? It's no excuse, but I want you to try to understand what we have to deal with on a daily basis."
"Fire away."
"Do you know how many people are referred to me every year? About one a week. We get End-Of-The-World-ers, conspiracy theorists, alien invasion spotters, clairvoyants and mind readers. All people who see something that isn't there, or foresee some disaster or other. The first question I ask most of them is 'when is your next booking'? Because most of them are simply looking for cheap publicity for their gigs at the local Bingo hall. Then there are the Facebook posters who see evil everywhere and proliferate all sorts of rubbish, most of which did the rounds years ago and have been resurrected because it's the anniversary of the death of someone or other. So why should I believe you? The answer is, I have to examine all the evidence I can muster, and make a judgment call based solely on my experience. You know how much it costs to mount an operation like this? Who pays for it? The public. Do you expect them to thank you if you're wasting their money? These are the things that go through my head every time I'm confronted with something like this. And the fact is, sometimes I get it wrong. Like this time. And I sincerely apologise."
"Accepted. We can't change what's happened. We can't bring my daughter back. Let's make sure we get whoever's responsible."
"With your help, John, we'll do that. You have my word, we'll do all we can."
"Do you drink whisky, Don?"
"Of course, I do. But only malt."

"What about when you're on duty?"
"We're not allowed to drink on duty. But I make the rules, so I can make an exception."

John found two clean tumblers and brought them back with a bottle of 15-year-old Glenlivet. He poured two large glasses.

"A toast, Don. To catching the bastard."
"To catching the bastard. Cheers."

Don noticed something about John in that instant. It was a look of blind, naked hatred on his face, and pure anger in his voice. Before he could comment, the doorbell rang. John rose to answer it, but Don held him back.

"From now, John, you need to exercise caution. I'll get it. I'm expecting DS Peters to join us."
"I'd better get another glass."

A worn-out looking Peters came up the stairs behind Don. He shook John's hand and accepted a glass of malt after receiving a nod from his boss. They spread the notes and route maps on the table and exchanged ideas, sometimes arguing heatedly, sometimes agreeing wholeheartedly, but as usual the final decision had to come from McArthur. He prepared to lay out his theory. John watched him absent-mindedly picking at his fingernails, which were short and ragged. Bitten.

He doesn't give that appearance, but he obviously lives on nervous energy, he thought.

McArthur gathered his wits and spoke.

"I'd like to think we can discount the start and finish as the target. It's too obvious, so Amy will be expecting the site to be flooded with armed officers. So, we need to focus on

less obvious sites which would still draw a dense crowd. Agreed?"
"Agreed."
"Agreed."
"I think we need to be in the city centre where the impact of a blast would be most dramatic. There'll be a large concentration of cameras and camera phones to record the immediate aftermath. Not to mention widespread panic. Which is why my money's on this spot."

His finger pointed at Hustlergate, and he went on to explain what had influenced his thinking.

"We get a sudden narrowing of the course as the runners come up from Market street. It's not too far from the finish line so it's likely there will be a large group of runners there at the same time. And a crowd of onlookers. All packed into a small area."
"The problem with this theory is that Half-Marathon runners cross this stretch four times. How do we know which circuit's going to be the one the bomber will choose?"
"Can I make a suggestion?"

They looked at John, waiting for his input.

"If it was me, I'd go for the first circuit. The runners will still be fairly tightly grouped then, but there'll still be a sizeable crowd. Besides, interrupting proceedings at that point will mean the whole day has to be abandoned. Which means more chaos."
"On the other hand, surely the crowd will be at its maximum for the final circuit, and there'll still be large groups of runners together. It doesn't have to be the leading pack that cops it."
"There's another factor we haven't yet considered. The weather. If it starts pissing down, the crowds will want to watch from under cover. There won't be as many at the roadside."
"So, what do we do? Toss a coin?"

"We keep all our options open and make the call as events unfold. And hope we get it right. And have enough people at strategic points to react quickly to anything suspicious."
"Can we assume we'll be looking for a brunette?"
"No. She's probably changed her hair colour already. If she wanted to avoid detection, changing her hairstyle and colour would be a natural first step."
"So, what exactly do we tell our people to look for?"
"A blue hoodie."

Brian looked at John in surprise.

"A blue hoodie. She was wearing it when she attacked my daughter. My neighbour downstairs told me. And I saw a blue hoodie in my hallucinations."
"Oh, Christ."
"Shut it, Brian. John's been right so far. Blue hoodie, it is."
"Sorry, boss. Sorry, John."
"Don't worry about it. I've got used to being regarded as a loony."
"Well, look. I suggest we wrap it up at that for tonight. If either of you comes up with any ideas, let me have them as soon as possible. I know Dave Lee's on leave but I'll bring him up to date in the morning, to see if he's got anything to add. In the meantime, can I suggest that we all meet formally for a briefing session on Friday at HQ? John, someone will collect you and drive you home again. But let me remind you both, you speak to nobody about this meeting. Is that clear?"
"Absolutely."
"Yes, boss."
"One more thing. We need a name for this operation. There are going to be hundreds of people involved in one way or another, so any communication must address the operation it refers to. Standard procedure. So, any suggestions?"

They looked at each other blankly until Brian's face lit up.

"Coyote."

"Coyote?"
"Coyote. We're dealing with a road race. Roadrunner. Wile E Coyote in the Roadrunner cartoons?"
"Yeah. I see the connection. Operation Coyote it is, then."
"OK."
"Good. John, thank you for joining us on this. Your help is invaluable. If we're not in touch before, I'll see you on Friday."
"Fine by me."
"Goodnight. We'll see ourselves out."
"Goodnight. I'll come down with you. Just to make sure the door's locked. And bolted."

John felt pleased after the meeting. For the first time, he felt justified in airing his fears concerning an impending tragedy and bringing them out into the open. At least now, he thought, someone was taking him seriously. At least now, someone believed him. He checked the time, and took his medication. Then, disregarding the doctor's advice, he poured another small whisky. He went over to the window and looked out. For the first time in quite a while, the skies were momentarily clear. And better still, there was a police car stationed across the street with two uniformed officers inside. He selected a CD at random, loaded it in the player, sat in his chair with his whisky and listened to some old Springsteen tracks.

And then the thought crossed his mind. What if there are multiple co-ordinated attacks? There's no way we can patrol the entire route. That thought kept him awake for most of the night. But when he finally fell asleep, instead of his usual 'burning building' nightmare, he dreamt of a long-gone holiday with Catherine and Jane. Sitting on the beach, eating ice-cream in the sun on a warm afternoon in Morecambe. Building sandcastles. Taking Jane to the sea's edge so that the tide lapped at her calves, but no higher. Keeping a firm hold on her hand to ensure she was safe from the waves when she became anxious that the tide was coming in. A family. A happy family. Times were much simpler then. OK, they didn't have much money as they struggled to pay a mortgage and raise a child, but they were happy. They were a family, a real family, who, whenever possible, went everywhere together and did everything together. But Catherine had divorced him, and now Jane was dead. Despite the problems in the later stages of his marriage to Catherine, there had never been anyone else, even after the divorce, apart from meaningless, loveless short-term relationships and one-night stands. Someone would pay. Someone had to pay.

CHAPTER 15

25th October

"US President Donald Trump is to allow refugees to begin entering the US again, with stricter rules for applicants from 11 "high risk" nations. The decision came as a 120-day ban on refugees expired on Tuesday - a part of Mr Trump's executive orders that came to be known as the "travel ban". Applicants from the 11 nations will be restricted for a 90-day review period. Last month the president announced the lowest cap on refugee resettlements ever set by a US president.
Kenya's Supreme Court is to hold a last-minute hearing to decide whether the re-run of the presidential election can go ahead. The court will hear an urgent petition by human rights activists arguing Kenya is not ready for the vote. The election is due to take place on Thursday. The Supreme Court in September took the unprecedented decision to annul the presidential election and demand a re-run.
A woman who shared Islamic State propaganda over the internet has been jailed for terrorism offences. Ammber Rafiq, 19, of Elmfield Terrace, Halifax, pleaded guilty to four offences of disseminating terrorist publications at a hearing on Monday. She admitted sending a number of links to terrorist publications over the online chat service Paltalk. Rafiq was sentenced at Sheffield Crown Court to 18 months in jail for each offence to run concurrently.
Huddersfield Town fan Adam B sent a £5 note as a reward for Australian midfielder Aaron Mooy after his man-of-the-match performance against Manchester United last week. In an accompanying letter, Adam wrote that "Mooy can keep the money because he played very well and scored". The young fan explained that he had found the five pound note at the stadium and wanted manager David Wagner to pass it on Mooy."

"A mainly dry and bright day, although patchy cloud may cling to the Pennines through the morning. Some sunny spells during the day, the best of these in the east. Feeling cool in the strong breeze, but winds easing later."

John woke up suddenly, the weather forecast on the radio dragging him from his nightmares, still in his chair. The words of a song were floating round in his head. Bruce Springsteen's Point Blank had always been one of his favourites, but he couldn't remember the last time he'd played it.

'You were standing in the doorway out of the rain
You didn't answer when I called out your name
You just turned, and then you looked away
Like just another stranger waiting to get blown away
Point blank'

He looked out of the window and was relieved to see the patrol car still there. He decided to call McArthur to check out his theory. There was no response, unsurprisingly, considering how early it was, so he left a message on voicemail.

"Don, it's John Braden. I've had some thoughts about what we discussed last night. Could you please call me when you're free? Thanks."

He was deliberately vague as he didn't want to say anything which might inadvertently be picked up by someone other than Don McArthur and his team. Don and his two colleagues were the only two people he felt he could trust now. He went for a shower, taking his phone into the bathroom with him and it rang as soon as he'd got his head under the stream of hot water. He turned off the water immediately and reached for the phone hurriedly, knocking it on the floor in the process. He got out of the shower, regardless of the water dripping from his naked body and picked up the phone.

"Don?"

A woman's voice; one he vaguely recognised.

"John? Is that you?"
"Yes."
"John, it's Catherine."
"Catherine?"
"Your ex-wife."
"Yes, of course. I'm sorry. I was expecting an urgent call from someone else."
"Mark gave me your number."
"Oh."
"How are you?"
"OK. You?"
"Devastated. About Jane. Mark rang me yesterday. He blames you."
"I know. I suppose he's right. If I hadn't gone into hospital, she wouldn't have been here when...."

He hesitated, then continued, a lump in his throat.

"...when it happened."

"We can't change anything now, John. I just wanted to call you to let you know about the funeral. It's a week tomorrow, the 2nd of November. I'd like you to come."
"I don't think Mark would want me there."
"It isn't really his decision. You're family. He isn't. And he won't ever be family now, unfortunately..."

There was silence for a few seconds while John could feel her discomfort as she struggled to continue. He couldn't remember the last time he'd known her lost for words.

"Anyway, there's a ceremony earlier in the day for the baby. He has a right to decide who attends that, I suppose, but Jane's funeral is our responsibility. Will you come?"
"Of course. If I'm able."
"Mark told me you were ill. How bad is it?"
"Terminal."

"I'm sorry."
"Thanks. I promise I'll attend, if I'm still alive. Text me the details."
"OK. I hope I'll see you there, John."
"I hope to be there too. 'Bye."
"'Bye, John."

John was sincere in expressing his hope to be able to attend the funeral of his daughter, but was pragmatic enough to realise it was highly unlikely. He was forced to take the maximum permitted doses of his various medications just to get through each day now. His headaches were persistent and often overwhelming and whenever he could focus his attention, it was fully focused not so much on preventing a disaster, but more on bringing Jane's killer to justice. He ate a slice of toast, then lurched across to the sink where he promptly vomited, his stomach heaving, his head swimming.

His phone rang once more. It was on the table, out of his reach, and by the time he was able to summon the energy to clear his head to make his way back across the room, it had fallen silent. He cursed under his breath as he checked for the identity of the caller. As he expected, it was McArthur. Totally drained of energy, he dragged his weary body into the bedroom where he slept until the ringing of his phone brought him back to life.

"Hello?"
"John. It's Don. I've been trying to get back to you all morning. You called me. It sounded urgent."
"Sorry, Don. I'm not able to think clearly just now. Things are getting worse. I'm sorry but I just can't remember why I called you. It can't have been that important."
"Well, if you remember, call me straight away."
"I will."
"Get some rest."
"I was trying to. But the phone keeps ringing."

He put the phone down, made a cup of coffee and rummaged through the cupboards until he found something he thought he might be able to eat without throwing up. A half-empty packet of Rich Tea biscuits. Jane must have bought them. He took two and left the packet out on the worktop. He would eat them later, provided he could keep them down. He checked his watch. Time for more medication. Afterwards, he left a message for his solicitor. It was brief.

"I'm still alive. And the police should no longer be considered the enemy."

****

Shortly after six, David Lee kissed Ellen and got in his car for the drive home via the M42 and M1. He wanted to get back that night so he was fresh to resume work in the morning. As he explained to Ellen,

"If I stay another night, you'll shag me senseless, and I'll never get home."

The previous night and that day they'd talked on and off about how his current case was going, how John was managing, and work in general. She seemed genuinely interested in David's work, and he talked openly, but in general terms, about the ongoing investigation in which she, of course, had played a part quite recently. One hour after Lee had left, she made a hurried phone call, packed a bag and loaded her car, and headed north at speed on the M6.

****

John had spent the day quietly in his flat, conserving his energy. He hadn't been to the Draper since he left hospital and would dearly have loved to just call in for a couple of pints like he used to, even if just to listen to the Foghorn telling his entertaining stories. But times had changed. It was no longer simply a matter of doing whatever he wanted to do. He now had a responsibility to put things right. And if that meant forgoing his afternoon drink, then so be it. He considered taking a glass of whisky. It was tempting, but instead he put the bottle in the back of the cupboard. He would need a clear head and his wits at their sharpest for the days ahead.

****

At seven o'clock that evening, the two plain-clothed officers on surveillance duty close to Amy's flat watched a man enter her block. They sent photos back to HQ, and sat and waited for him to emerge. As they waited, news came back regarding the photos. The man was not known to the police. They decided to talk to him anyway and one of them went up to Amy's flat while the other remained at the entrance.

DC Willis paused outside Amy's door, listening. He could hear music from within and sent a text to his partner outside to join him. As DC Jackson ascended the stairs, Willis knocked on the door. A tall, clean-shaven man probably in his late thirties opened the door. Willis showed his ID.

"Sorry to bother you, sir. I'm DC Willis. This is DC Jackson. Is this your flat?"
"No. It belongs to my girlfriend."
"Your name, sir?"
"Kevin. Kevin Hargreaves."
"And your girlfriend's name, sir?"
"Amy. Amy Winston. Why? What's this about?"
"Where is she at this moment, sir?"
"I don't know exactly. She just said she had to go away for a few days and asked me to call round to the flat when I had time. Just to see if there was any post. Stuff like that."
"Can you get in touch with her at all, sir."

"No. I tried yesterday. Her mobile number is unobtainable. I came over to her flat thinking she might have come home."
"When did you last speak to her, sir?"
"Sunday. Sunday afternoon. I thought we were going to spend the night together, but she said she had to work and more or less ended the call at that. Then she phoned me, about six o'clock. She said she was sorry, but she had to go away. A work assignment, she said. And I haven't seen or heard from her since."
"OK, Mr Hargreaves. Would you mind coming down to the station with us? Just a formality, sir. Make a statement for our records."
"Am I in trouble? Is Amy in trouble?"
"Just routine inquiries, sir. It won't take long."

Before they left, DC Willis called McArthur to update him. McArthur was quick to act.

"Don't leave the property unguarded under any circumstances until we get there with a search warrant. Is that clear?"
"Yes, sir."

DC Jackson drew the short straw, being left on guard outside the flat while Willis took his charge to the station to make a statement. Meanwhile, Peters picked up the search warrant and sped over to meet DC Jackson at Amy Winston's flat. They entered and commenced a thorough search. When he found what he had been looking for, Peters called McArthur.

"I've got it, boss. The 3D printer. In the bottom of the wardrobe. Not exactly well-hidden."
"Get it straight down to the techies, Brian. I want to know what it's been programmed to print, and what was the last thing it printed."
"I'll do it first thing in the morning, boss. The lab's shut now."

"OK, Brian. First thing. And don't let it out of your sight till Riley's had a look at it."
"I take it that my day's leave has been cancelled, then?"
"Yes, Brian. After Sunday, we'll be back to normal."

No, we bloody well won't, he thought.

****

Kevin Hargreaves was not detained for long. It was quickly established that Amy had just used him as a front to maintain the illusion of her having a normal life. In reality, when she whistled, Kevin came running. Having no criminal history whatsoever, he was released without charge with the promise he would inform the police if Amy made contact with him. The CTU thought that was highly unlikely. Amy would no longer have any use for Kevin.

****

Amelia was just finishing her last long training run. She'd completed twelve miles, in good time, without any problems. She was ready now. She felt fit and confident she wouldn't let herself, or any of her family and friends, feel she hadn't given it her best shot. On Saturday morning, she would jog a couple of miles just to loosen up before her big day. Nothing could stop her now. The previous day, she'd received an email from the race organiser providing all the relevant details she needed about the big event, such as where to collect her timing chip and race number. She'd copied a photograph from the race web site and posted it proudly on her Facebook page. She had already accepted pledges for a considerable amount of sponsorship money and was determined not to let anyone down, least of all herself and her two girls who were covering her training as part of a school project on fitness. As soon as she got home and had her shower, the girls would be pleading with her to download the data from her tracker to the laptop so they could print an up-to-date chart of her progress. The kids would take this with them to school immediately after the half-term holiday and watch proudly as the teacher added it to the already extensive display on the classroom wall. And, of course, on that same day, they would have the details of her 'live' run, including her finishing time.

****

John was woken by the sound of his door bell ringing. He rose slowly and painfully from his chair and looked out of the window. The police car was still there and one of the officers gave him the thumbs-up. With some difficulty he made his way downstairs to the door, opening it to find a police officer and Father Brennan. The officer spoke.

"Sorry to bother you, Mr Braden, but this gentleman insisted on speaking to you."
"That's fine. Father Brennan is an old friend of mine. He's welcome any time."

The policeman returned to join his colleague in the car while John led Father Brennan upstairs.

"Would you like a small drink, Father?"
"I'd prefer a large one, John."
"Large malt it is, then."

John fetched the bottle and two glasses to Father Brennan who had already settled on a chair at the kitchen table. He poured a large measure into each glass, and they raised their glasses in a silent toast.

"And to what do I owe the pleasure of this visit, Father?"
"Just checking you're OK, John. It's been a couple of weeks or more."
"I'm fine, Father."

"You're not though, John. I can tell that much by looking at you. You look like shit, if you'll pardon the expression. So how about a little honesty?"
"I'm deteriorating fast, Father. I just need a few more days..."
"Still troubled by your visions?"
"Yes. Things are clearer now, though. And the police believe me. And my daughter has been murdered."
"Oh, dear God, John. I didn't know. I'm so sorry. Does this have any connection with your visions?"
"We believe so."
"Is there anything I can do, John? Other than pray, of course."
"It's out of my hands, Father. I won't even be at the funeral. But I swear, I will get revenge."
"That sounds like you think you know who is responsible."
"I do."
"Then pour another glass and tell me more."

John told him the full story, or at least as much of it as he could be sure of. He was careful not to lay the blame for his daughter's death on anyone but her killer. Everything else was coincidental and circumstantial. The killing, though, was cold-blooded, and though the victim was simply in the wrong place at the wrong time, the intent to kill was no mistake, no accident.

"So, you intend to kill whoever was responsible?"
"I do, Father."
"You know I can't condone it?"
"An eye for an eye, Father."
"True."
"I know it's a bit premature, Father, but will you pray for my soul?"
"I will."
"And one more thing. Stay away from the city centre this Sunday morning."

Father Brennan finished his whisky and prepared to perform the Viaticum – the Last Rites. John was more than ready.

****

Don McArthur looked up at the clock on the wall. It was already nine and he was still at his desk in the office, poring over reports, going through statements. Checking, and re-checking all the data he had. Time was running out and his team desperately needed a break. Whether that break would come as a result of good police work, or just plain good fortune made no difference to McArthur; they just needed a break. The investigation was going nowhere. No new evidence had turned up. No sightings of Amy. No intelligence which might throw some light on the actual *specific* target. Nothing. His worst nightmare was about to come true. He would turn up mob-handed on Sunday with no plan as to where and how the men at his disposal should be deployed. He would simply have to react, and react fast, as incidents took place. He rubbed the nape of his neck with his left hand as he authorised overtime forms with his right.

I'm too old for this. His voice was low and weary. This is it. Win or lose, this is the last one. I'm finished with all this.

He gathered his files and placed them in his drawer, locking it as usual, and slipped the key into his jacket pocket. He rose and walked out of the door, switching off the light as he left.

****

It was late by the time Ellen arrived at the address she'd been given. Her Satnav had misled her more than a couple of times and she'd had to phone for help, but eventually pulled up outside the cottage. Amy was waiting at the door.

They kissed and hugged like the old, intimate friends they were, and went inside with the bags Ellen had brought.

"It's so good to see you again, Amy."
"I've missed you so much. Did you get everything?"
"Everything on the list."
"Let me see."

They emptied the bags and laid out the items on the kitchen table. Batteries, firing cable, switches, boxes of bolts, ball bearings, nails. Ellen stated proudly,

"I did exactly as you asked. I bought everything in small quantities from different stores over a period of time so no-one would suspect anything."
"Good. I knew you'd be careful. And I've got something to show you. Something I prepared earlier."
"You make it sound like Blue Peter."

They walked round to the back of the cottage where a large garage was attached. Amy unlocked the padlock and pulled open the heavy doors. Inside was an old engineering bench upon which were six steel pipes, newly fabricated with one end blocked and welded, the other end threaded along with threaded caps to form a tight seal.

"Let's get to work."

Between them they filled the pipes with a mixture of bolts, nails and ball-bearings. Amy produced her pièce de résistance – a rectangular block of a polymer substance, which she carefully cut into six pieces, rolling each into a ball. She pushed one into the top of each pipe until it was full, screwed the caps on tight and then carefully inserted a fuse wire through a small drilled hole in each cap. She stored the pipes safely under the table.

"We'll do the firing mechanism indoors. We need better light."

They kissed passionately, locked the garage securely and walked arm in arm into the cottage. Ellen opened a bottle of red wine, talking excitedly as she did so. They settled, close together, on the small settee in the living room.

"I can't believe we're actually going to do this. After talking about it all those years ago. It's finally going to happen."
"Let's just concentrate on this last bit before we celebrate."
"I know exactly how I want us to celebrate. Like we did at University."
"We will. After we finish this bottle."

How naïve this girl still is! thought Amy. She still thinks I'm going to blow up a statue in Lister Park.

Way back in their idealistic days as students at Hull University sharing a flat, they'd discussed all manner of things. Their hopes, their dreams for the future. How they would set the world on fire with their revolutionary thinking. And one night, still drinking long after a party was over, Amy had confided to her lover that one day she intended to blow up the statue of Samuel Cunliffe Lister in Bradford's Lister Park in protest at his capitalist principles and employment of child labour. And now Ellen actually believed that was Amy's intention. It never seemed to have crossed her mind that an explosive device packed with bolts and ball-bearings would have a much more sinister purpose than simply demolishing a statue.

Since they graduated, they had kept in touch over the years, meeting occasionally and comparing the different paths their lives had taken. Since the night a couple of years ago when Ellen confided that she did occasional work for Special Branch and had a lover who worked for CTU, Amy had contacted her more often and wanted to know all about her new boyfriend and the exciting work he did. When Amy asked if Ellen had a photo of her lover, Ellen told her that Dave insisted she could not have one under any circumstances as it might compromise his work. Amy told her that it didn't matter; she was only interested. Ellen never realised Amy's motive for being so interested.

"So, when are you thinking of planning your great protest?"
"Sunday. When everybody is in the town centre watching the street races. Manningham will be deserted. It'll be easy. Like a walk in the park."

They both giggled and snuggled closer together as Amy shared out the last of the wine.

"You get comfortable, Ellie. I've got a present for you. Close your eyes. I'll be straight back."

Amy went into the bedroom and opened the drawer in the base of the old pine wardrobe. She took out the long, slim black case. Flicking open the brass clasp, she took out the knife, holding it up to the light which reflected from the narrow gleaming blade. Walking slowly back into the living room she approached the settee from behind and, leaning over Ellen, planted a kiss on her cheek, whispering 'Goodbye' before plunging the knife deep into her unsuspecting lover's neck. She held it firmly while Ellen contorted and gasped for breath, using all her remaining strength to try to free herself from the immense pain, her hand reaching for the wound in an attempt to staunch the flow of spurting warm blood. The desperate writhing soon stopped and in less than a minute she was dead. Amy relaxed her grip and gently extracted the knife, wiping it clean on Ellen's sleeve before replacing it in its case, closing the catch and putting it back in the drawer. She looked at the lifeless body.

"Such a waste of a pretty girl. Pretty, but pretty stupid."

Amy sat with her glass of wine in the chair opposite the settee, staring at Ellen's face, with its wide-open eyes and deathly pallor, the head tilted to one side as if asking why did her old friend and lover do this to her. Her blood had pooled at her feet and soaked into the old, worn carpet. Ellen's bowels had involuntarily relaxed as the life left her and Amy knew that the stench would soon become unbearable but she didn't care. Soon she would walk away. Soon she would be free of any concern for others. Soon it would be over. She got up, went into the kitchen and returned with another bottle and her glass refilled with wine. She sat and held it up to the light. It was dark, like Ellen's blood. She took a mouthful, then spat it at the body of her dead friend.

"Whore!"

She stood over the body and poured the rest of the contents of the glass over her friend's pale face, then turned and walked into the bedroom. She stripped off and got in the shower to wash Ellen's blood off her face and hands. Emerging from the shower minutes later, she pulled on a robe, gathered up her blood-stained clothes and fed them one by one into the living room fire, watching them smoulder and disintegrate in the flames as she sipped a glass of wine contentedly. She picked up a magazine from the rack and thumbed idly through the pages before rising to rummage through the cupboard under the kitchen sink where she found a bottle of bleach. Returning to the living room, she unscrewed the top of the bottle and poured the contents over Ellen's inert body before turning out the lights and going to bed.

Amy rose early in the morning to complete the assembly of the firing mechanism for her device. Her hands were shaking. She knew it wasn't due to the wine. No, it was from the sheer exhilaration which was coursing through her whole body. Her dream, the very reason for her entire existence, was on the point of being realised. Everything she'd ever suffered, everything her family had suffered, everything her *race* had suffered, was about to be avenged. Her destiny was in her hands. But she had to control their shaking to complete the assembly with the meticulous attention it required. She *must* not fail.

CHAPTER 16

26th October

"A United Nations expert has urged Iran's government to stop harassing BBC Persian staff and their families. David Kaye, the special rapporteur on freedom of opinion and expression, confirmed he had received a complaint from the BBC about their treatment. It came after Iran initiated a criminal investigation into 150 BBC staff, former staff and contributors for "conspiracy against national security". A subsequent court order froze the assets of the 150 staff involved.
Australia should consider deploying police to help protect refugees and asylum seekers it has detained in Papua New Guinea, Human Rights Watch says. Australia holds refugees and asylum seekers arriving by boat on PNG's Manus Island and the Pacific nation of Nauru. The Manus centre is due to close next week. Australia has set up alternative accommodation in a nearby town.
Jurors in a manslaughter trial in Leeds were offered £500 bribes to fix their verdicts, a court has heard. Three men, Shahrear Islam-Miah, Abdilahi Ahmed and Haroon Sharif, are accused of approaching jurors after they left Leeds Crown Court as a judge summed up in the trial in February. The trial involved a cash-for-crash insurance fraud which caused the death of one of the vehicles' occupants. The men all deny a charge of conspiracy to pervert the course of justice.
Plans to build a new stadium to be used by rugby league side Wakefield Trinity have stalled over a disagreement with the club's owners, council bosses say. Wakefield Council announced plans for a 10,000-seat venue on the site of the existing Belle Vue ground in September. However, it says the club's owners have rejected "previously agreed plans" relating to rent and management and are pursuing "alternative arrangements"' The club said it planned to take legal advice before making any comment."

"A generally cloudy and cool day for much of the region with outbreaks of rain and light winds. Any longer drier spells are most likely in the north, where cloud may break to give some warmer sunny spells."

A little before 9 am, Brian Peters had reached Bradford University and had parked in a restricted area made available to him courtesy of his police permit. He took the printer up to the third floor, to the lab. The university often provided technical services to the police force. It was a cost-effective method of accessing the latest technology, and the best technical know-how, without the associated infrastructure and payroll costs. The head of department, Dr Martin Riley, took personal charge, ushering Peters into his private office where he quickly connected the printer to his PC. Dr Riley's discretion was assured; he was the go-to man for technical services, and rarely outsourced them to his staff or students unless he was certain there were no sensitive security issues involved. Peters watched with interest as the screen displayed the last print program it had undertaken.

"Keys. Common house keys, by the look of them. Any idea where they might fit?"
"Yes. Can you print them for me?"
"Yes, of course. Go get a cuppa downstairs in the restaurant. I'll give you a call when I've done."
"Thanks, Martin."
"No problem."

Dr Riley got to work while Brian enjoyed a bacon sandwich washed down with a mug of strong tea. The catering assistant didn't understand him when he asked for 'builder's tea'; an older colleague explained and provided an extra tea bag free of charge to give the drink its required strength. He sat alone at a table until his mobile buzzed.

"They're ready for you, Brian. Come on up."

Having collected the keys and with the printer under his arm, Brian returned to his car and called McArthur.

"I've seen Professor Riley, boss. The last things she printed on this contraption were keys. House keys. He's printed copies for me."
"Good work, Brian. Get them round to Braden's. I want to make sure they fit.... Oh, Christ!"
"What's up, boss?"
"We need to get Braden's locks changed. Get over there, Brian. Now."
"Right, boss. On my way."

****

John woke suddenly, sweating and in urgent need of a pee. He attempted to swing his legs out of bed and stand up but immediately dizziness overcame him. He made a grab for the nearest piece of furniture, a pine chest of drawers, but missed by some distance, falling heavily on his side on the carpet. He lay there for a while, breathing deeply, hoping his head would stop spinning and the growing feeling of nausea would subside so he could get to the bathroom for his medication before his head exploded. He tried to stand but was unable. Instead, he pulled himself up onto his hands and knees and made his way laboriously towards the bathroom. He vomited as soon as he got his head over the toilet bowl and crouched there like a sick drunkard until the nausea passed. He scrambled to his feet so he could have a pee. Then, finally, he counted out his tablets and swallowed them, scooping up a handful of water from the running tap to wash them down. Slowly, he staggered back to the bedroom and pulled on his dressing gown. He sat on the bed for a good fifteen minutes until he felt strong enough to stand in the shower, but once there, his strength deserted him to the extent that he had to take the shower head from its mounting and sit in the bath while holding the shower head to allow the water to spray over his body. When he'd finished, he didn't bother replacing the shower head in its mounting; he thought he might as well leave it in the bottom of the bath for future use.

He dressed and went through to the kitchen. Looking out of the window, he was relieved to find the police car was still parked up the road. He thought of inviting the officers in for a cup of tea but decided against it. He found it difficult enough to make a drink for himself, never mind making cups of tea for guests. He took two biscuits from the pack and chewed them slowly. They were already going soft. Encouraged by the fact that he didn't throw up immediately, he rummaged in the cupboard for something more substantial, eventually deciding on a tin of soup. But he hadn't the strength to operate the tin opener. He simply couldn't exert enough pressure to turn the knob. He made several attempts but only ended up with half a dozen holes pierced in the can. He had an idea but wasn't sure he had the balls to try it. In desperation, he picked up his mobile.

"The hell with it."

He thumbed through his contacts list and pressed the Call button. The answer was instant.

"John? What's up?"
"Don. I'm really sorry to call you about this. I know it's not in your remit, but I'm desperate."
"What's the problem, John?"
"I need something to eat."
"That's it?"
"Yes."
"What do you think I am? Your fucking mother?"
"Don, I'm sorry. I can't even open a tin of soup. It looks like I'm no longer able to look after myself. I don't want to go back into the hospital. They'll never let me out again."
"I'll see what I can do. I'll get back to you. And John, make sure you've got the door chain on."

Ten minutes later his phone rang. It was Don.

"John, someone will be with you within the hour. Her name is Whitehead. Detective Constable Lynn Whitehead. Her brief is to ensure you get fed and watered daily and take your medication as prescribed. She's not a nurse, John. Nor is she a tart, so treat her with respect. She's just there to try to keep you alive."
"Thanks, Don. I appreciate this."
"When she turns up, just throw the keys out of the window to her. Don't want you over-exerting yourself with all those stairs. And DS Peters should be with you any minute. Don't open the door to anyone else."
"OK. Thanks."
"Just keep reminding yourself you're only fifty-two, not a hundred and four."
"Yes, boss."
"OK. I'll see you tomorrow. Lynn will bring you to the meeting. Oh, and once she's in place, I'm calling off the guards in the street. You won't need them. Lynn is perfectly capable of doing her job. Be good."

John ended the call, a smile appearing on his face, then fading as he remembered Don's final words. Be good. That was a clear warning, as was the statement 'nor is she a tart'. The truth was, though, that John wouldn't have had the energy to misbehave if he'd been given free licence to do whatever he pleased. Still, he needed the help and would appreciate having someone to talk to if nothing else.

****

Don felt guilty about not telling John the whole truth. He reasoned with himself that now that he'd provided John with a minder, he didn't need to know. And anyway, he could break it to him face to face the following day. He was still getting over the shock he felt when he took the call from GCHQ which informed him that a breach of protocol had resulted in Amy's file being incorrectly marked as clean, when in fact it was still lying on a researcher's desk while he'd taken sick leave. They'd become so used to getting fast and accurate data from GCHQ that this deviation from standard procedure was difficult to accept. However, it had happened. They would carry on regardless.

The extensive check on Amy had resulted in her file being classed as Code Red. Once again Don looked through the main points of the report GCHQ had sent him first thing this morning.

"Amy Winston is to be regarding seriously as a potential threat. Her great-grandparents were German Jews and victims of the Holocaust. Her grandparents escaped Germany in 1936 and eventually made their way to the UK. They changed their family name from Weinstein to Winston in 1939. Amy's father was born in 1948 when the family moved into Bradford and married a local Jewish girl in 1970. Amy was born in 1973. Her mother was verbally abused and frequently physically assaulted by her husband. She bore it stoically until eventually she knifed him during a struggle. Amy was 11 at the time and was put into care, and had to endure jibes and bullying at school. But she was strong-willed. Despite all the odds, she won a place at Hull University in 1991. We believe during this time she came into contact with a Syrian student, Sayid Abadi, and may have had a relationship with him. His name has appeared on the Watch List in recent months. She has never publicly expressed any extremist views but there is a record of her contributing to a radical Islamic website under a pseudonym which we are positive had been used by her previously when at university. Amy never married. Relationships somehow never quite worked out. She worked long hours and refused to be dominated by any man. It is also suspected that Amy Winston was at the heart of a proposed plot to blow up a statue in Bradford's Lister Park which came to our attention while she was at University, though nothing ever came of it. Among her friends, one name sticks out: Ellen Stevenson. It seems they shared a flat for some months and may even have been lovers."

It was the final sentence which stuck out in Don's mind. Ellen had initially been recommended to CTU by David Lee. He had ordered Lee to return immediately to the office from his current assignment.

At eleven o'clock, DS Lee was seated in his boss's office, while Don paced around in silence Eventually, he sat down behind his desk, ready to tackle the problem having chosen his words as carefully as his experienced had taught him.

"Dave. How long have you known Ellen Stevenson?"
"About five years."
"How did you meet?"
"At a party. In Birmingham."
"And how exactly would you describe your relationship?"
"Friends."
"Lovers?"
"Well, yes. We hook up occasionally. Nothing serious."
"And what do you talk about in bed?"
"With respect, sir, I hardly think that's any of your concern."
"Actually, it fucking is. Give me the truth, Dave. Has she ever asked you about your work?"
"Well, yes."
"And what have you told her?"
"Just general chat, really."
"Ever mentioned the case you're working at the moment?"
"Why are you asking me these questions, boss? Has someone complained?"
"Where is Ellen now?"
"I left her in Birmingham yesterday."
"Have you contacted her since?"
"No."
"Well, let me tell you this, Dave. Officers went to her house this morning. She wasn't home. A neighbour saw her packing her car and driving off yesterday, about an hour

after she saw *you* leave. Any idea where she might have gone?"
"Maybe she had another job organised."
"Did she ever mention the fact that she knew Amy Winston?"

The question hit Lee like a hammer-blow. He swallowed hard.

"No, boss."
"Did you know Ellen went to University?"
"Yes. Hull, I think. It will be on her file."
"Yes, it is. And I've just received the file from GCHQ on Amy. She went to Hull University, too. At the same time as Ellen was there. In fact, they shared a flat. And a bed too, apparently."
"Shit!"
"Were you aware of any of this, Dave?"
"No. Honestly."
"Now think carefully before you answer this. Is it possible that you might have disclosed any details of our current operation with Ellen? Pillow talk?"
"I hope not, boss. You think I've been caught in a honey trap?"
"Too fuckin' right. Somehow, Amy's always been a step ahead of us. She's had insider information, Dave."

He stood up behind his desk, towering over Lee, and delivered his verdict.

"DS Lee, you are suspended from active operation with immediate effect. You will hand over to me your ID and service weapon and access card. You will be escorted from the building and in due course will be invited to attend a full disciplinary hearing in line with standard procedure. While under suspension, you will not contact any other officer active in this operation, and if Ellen Stevenson contacts you, you will attempt to discover her whereabouts and inform me immediately. Any questions?"

"No, sir."
"Now fuck off."

Lee was unceremoniously escorted from the building and locked out. He went home, racking his brains trying to remember exactly what he might have disclosed to Ellen during their time together. If he had passed on any confidential information, his career was over and he could look forward to a life as just another night-shift security guard. He'd made a mistake, and he'd have to live with the consequences.

Don sat in his chair thinking about the preliminary report he was now compelled to write. It would be easy for him to lay the blame for any failure of his department to carry out their duties to the highest standard firmly at the feet of DS Lee. But that would be wrong. Not only would he bring the promising career of a young officer to a premature close, but it would be contrary to their whole ethos which was that the team shared the praise for their triumphs and took equal blame for their failures. He left the report in draft form locked in his desk.

****

DS Peters was at John's flat quickly. He used his new keys to let himself into the building, to John's surprise, but had to ask John to release the security chain to allow him into the flat. Neither man made any comment about it, though.

As promised Lynn arrived within the hour. John heard the doorbell and went to the window from where he could see a young woman smiling and waving her warrant card at him. She was carrying an overnight bag. Still, he was taking no chances. He opened the window and shouted,

"Please identify yourself. By name."
"DC Lynn Whitehead. At your service."

She gave a little theatrical curtsey which caused John to smile for the first time that day. He threw the keys down to her and closed the window as Lynn let herself in. He heard her walking up the stairs. She had the courtesy to knock on the door to his flat.

"Come in, please."

She complied and introduced herself again, less formally this time.

"Call me Lynn."
"OK, Lynn. Thank you for coming over so quickly."
"No problem. All in a day's work for us fortunate enough to be part of Don's team. So, what can I do for you first?"
"Could you please open that tin of soup? I haven't the strength and I'm starving."
"OK. Go sit down and I'll bring it over to you when I've warmed it up."
"You sure?"
"Of course. My instructions are to help you for the next few days."
"I presume Don has told you my days are numbered."
"Yes. So, we'll try to conserve your energy. For Sunday. I gather you'll need your wits about you then."
"That's how it seems."
"So, go sit down then."
"Yes, boss."

DS Peters had a few quiet words with Lynn before taking his leave.

John watched from the kitchen table as Lynn set about her task. She was an attractive young woman, casually dressed in jeans and a loose top. The thought crossed his mind that perhaps she could provide some further, more personal, services for him, but he quickly shelved the idea. That sort of exercise would probably kill him. He just didn't have the energy. Still, he found it gratifying that he could still *think* about sex even if the act itself was beyond him.

Lynn had brought her laptop with her, but again had the courtesy to ask John if he objected to her using it in his flat. He had no objections. She quickly powered it up and established a secure connection from which she could safely communicate with her superiors. Her first message to Don was 'Patient fed and watered, and in good spirits. Permission required to leave him on his own for a short time this afternoon to purchase some food. There's not much edible stuff here.'

Permission granted, she took directions from John regarding the nearby convenience store and together they compiled a shopping list. Realising the police car on watch had already left, Lynn locked him inside the flat, promising to be quick. It wasn't until he'd watched her disappear around the corner that panic suddenly overcame him. What if Amy still had her set of duplicate keys? What if she was out there waiting for a chance to catch him alone? He glanced anxiously out of the corner of the window and was relieved to see the police car had returned to its position. He breathed a sigh of relief. He felt safe. His phone rang, breaking the silence and startling him.

"Hello?"
"It's Don. Just letting you know, John. The police presence outside is being reinstated."
"Yes. I know. I've just spotted them. Thanks."
"And a locksmith is coming around to fit new locks shortly. Just a precaution, John. We don't expect Amy to call to see how you are, but she did have a set of keys after all."
"I know. I'd just remembered. I was panicking when you rang. Thank you."
"Don't thank me, John. In all honesty, I'd forgotten about it myself. It was only when Lynn said she'd have to lock you in because you only had one set of keys that it jogged my memory. We're just human, John. We make mistakes."

Don thought immediately about David Lee as soon as those words left his mouth, but John was unaware of the irony.
"No harm done."
"See you tomorrow."
"'Bye."

John sat quietly in his chair, reflecting on his situation. He'd be powerless if Amy came in and it would be over. All he wanted, all he hoped for, was to be able to be there, to look her in the eye, when they took her down. That thought, that one wish, was probably the only thing keeping him alive just now. Revenge is a powerful motive.

****

Don kept telling himself he'd done what he had to do. He'd followed standard protocol. He hoped that disciplinary measures would be taken at GCHQ against whoever was ultimately held responsible for the failure to provide accurate and complete information about Amy Winston. But he still felt bad for DS Lee. The lad had made a mistake. The worst thing was, he'd been in the same position himself when he first joined the force over forty years ago. He'd worked hard and been conscientious, obeying orders to the letter, until he earned a promotion from beat bobby to CID. He'd celebrated in the pub with his mates and on reflection afterwards realised he'd probably drunk too much. He'd boasted about a case he'd just been assigned to, and let slip details which could have proven detrimental to the whole operation. He'd been hauled before his boss and fully expected the sack. He remembered the conversation.

"You've been stupid, Don."
"I know, boss. What more can I say? I've learnt my lesson. It won't happen again."
"Too right it won't happen again."
"Look, boss. I know what you think, but you're wrong. I *can* do this job. And I can do it very well. I've fucked up, but I

promise, it won't happen again. I'm pleading with you here, boss. Just give me another chance."
"I'm putting you on 'sick leave'. Two weeks. Go home. Think very carefully about what you've done, and its consequences. Think about what you want your future to look like. Two weeks today. 10am. Be in my office and I'll tell you whether you'll ever work for CID again, or whether you'll be joining the ranks of ex-cops at ASDA."

And he'd been given that second chance, and never looked back. He picked up the phone and dialled.

"Hello?"
"David, it's Don."
"Hello, boss."
"I've decided you're worth a second chance. But it's between you and me. Just a little favour, let's call it. Interested?"
"Of course, boss."
"Are you at home?"
"Yes."
"I'll be round in about an hour. I'll bring your warrant card and explain fully what I want you to do."
"Thanks, boss. You won't regret it."
"I sincerely hope not. I'm putting my job on the line for you."
"I understand, and I appreciate it. I won't let you down."
"See you shortly."

Don thought carefully about the role he had in mind for DS Lee. Amy had never set eyes on Lee; he was sure of that. He wanted Lee to move freely among the crowds, to look like a spectator. And keep Braden in sight at all times. Whether it made sense or not, he still believed Braden would be a central figure in whatever took place on Sunday.

As Don expected, DS Lee accepted the role assigned to him without question, and expressed his gratitude.

"Don't thank me, Dave. Just do your job to the best of your ability."
"I will, boss. You can count on that."
"That's what I wanted to hear. The stuff we discussed earlier stays between the two of us. I've not written it up, nor will I as long as you do your job."
"Thanks, boss."
"Just one thing, Dave."
"Your firearm stays here."
"I understand, boss. Whatever you say."

He understood all right. McArthur was worried that Lee would shoot Amy on sight, regardless of the consequences.

****

Lynn Whitehead returned with a couple of bags of shopping, placing them on the kitchen table before picking out the items one by one so that John could tell her where they should go.

"Biscuits?"
"Cupboard."
"Tinned stuff?"
"Cupboard."
"Bread?"
"Bin on the worktop."
"Cuddly toy?"
"Conveyor belt."

They both simultaneously burst into laughter. It felt good. John couldn't remember the last time he'd laughed so spontaneously but he knew it must have been weeks ago, before his life changed that day at the cemetery.

"My grandparents used to have a record called The Laughing Policeman. They used to play it for me on their gramophone every time I went to their house. But this is the

first time I've actually heard a policeman, sorry, policewoman, laughing."
"What's a gramophone?"
"Google it. Or better still, ask your grandparents."
"Anyway, we do laugh, just like everyone else. We're just human. Even Don McArthur. You should hear him on the Karaoke at our Christmas do."
"That's something I'd like to hear."
"I'll get you an invite."
"Don't bother. I won't be there."
"Oops! Sorry, John. Me and my big mouth."
"Don't worry about it. It's a fact. Nothing anyone can do about it. Just accept it. I have."
"It must be hard, though."
"No. As long as I, sorry, *we* get the bastard who killed my daughter, my time on earth will have been worthwhile."
"Do you believe in God, John?"
"Yes. I'm a lapsed Catholic. Which reminds me, I need to go to Confession before Sunday."
"Are you up to it today?"
"I think so."
"I'll just check it's OK with the boss."

She'd said it too. 'We're just human'. Just humans, trying to catch monsters.

Having been given permission, they waited until the locksmith had arrived, fitted the new locks and left again. Lynn put the old locks in a drawer, out of sight, and called McArthur to confirm they had been fitted.

"Keep the old locks safe, Lynn. They're evidence. Bring them with you to tomorrow's meeting. I'll take them off your hands then."

As they left the flat, Lynn locking up behind them, John thought for a second before deciding there would be no harm in pushing his luck a little further.

"While we're out, is there any chance of making a quick detour?"
"What have you got in mind?"
"I'd really like to say goodbye to some friends."
"Where do they live?"
"In a pub just up the road."
"No. Not unless Don allows it. But not today. One trip out is enough."
"Just thought I'd ask."
"I'll try to organise it for tomorrow."
"Thanks. I appreciate it."
"It'll cost you a gin and tonic."
"No problem. They stock every brand of gin you've ever heard of, and some that you haven't."
"Then I'll look forward to it – subject to permission being granted."

Lynn's Vauxhall was comfortable and warm for the short trip to John's church. Father Brennan was waiting for them.

"Hello, John. It's good to see you again."
"Hello, Father. I'm afraid this will be my last visit."
"I'm sorry to hear that, John. I assume your health has deteriorated."
"Yes. To the point where I think I probably only have a couple of days left."
"Then, I'll take your confession and afterwards we'll have a last glass of malt together."

Lynn sat quietly in a pew waiting for John to return. He did so with a smile on his face and the smell of whisky on his breath.

"Take me home, please, Lynn. I'm now fully prepared for whatever I have to do."
"What? Even the washing-up?"
"Even the washing-up."
"In that case, I'll call Don now to see if we can fix a quick visit to the pub."

"The Gods are smiling on me today. Hope they're still around on Sunday."
"The Gods might not be there, but at least the CTU are on your side."
"Well, let's go to the pub to celebrate that, then."
"Wait until I've got approval from Don."
"Ask him if he wants to join us. They don't do Karaoke, though."
"Good. I hate Karaoke."
"Me too. Though I can do a passable rendition of some of Frank Zappa's stuff."
"Never heard of him."
"Shame."
"I prefer to listen to The Sound of Silence."
"Me too. Preferably with a barely audible background sound of beer being slurped."

Lynn made the call, but, as John expected, permission was refused. As DI McArthur justified his decision, there was no valid argument against it.

"She's still out there, John. And while she's out there, we need you safe at all times. Once we have her in custody, or can be certain she's no longer a threat, then I'll take you to the pub myself and treat you to as many pints as you can handle."

John knew exactly what Don meant by saying 'certain she's no longer a threat'. He meant dead.

"So, John. The pub's out."
"Never mind. They don't open until 4pm anyway."
"So, what would you like to do instead?"

Lynn stood smiling at him. He was sure she could read his mind, but equally sure she would reject outright his suggestion of sex.

"I suppose we could listen to some music."

"Have you got anything that was recorded within the last ten years?"
"It's highly unlikely?"
"Then how about a game of cards?"
"Strip poker?"
"OK, but you'd better turn the heating up. You'll feel very cold, very quickly, in just your underpants. I'm the Poker champion at CTU."

They played cribbage for a couple of hours. Lynn won every game. In his defence, John could always claim he was unable to concentrate fully. That much was true. He'd been trying desperately to remember the last time he'd experienced fulfilling sex. He was sure it hadn't happened since his divorce, nor in the final months of his marriage, and though he'd had sex with several women since, it was simply a mechanical act from which he gained little real pleasure apart from the primal gratification of pure animal need. The more he thought about it, the more he realised there wasn't much real pleasure in his life at all. He was just waiting for the inevitable release.

"Your play, John."
"Sorry?"
"It's your go. You're miles away. You OK?"
"Yes. Sorry. I think it's about time for my meds."
"So it is. I'll go get them."
"Thanks."
"Then I'd better get some food sorted. You hungry?"
"Yes."
"Me too. Steak and salad OK?"
"Perfect. There's a bottle of Malbec in the rack if you'd care to open it."
"I'm not sure that's a good idea at the moment."
"It's on prescription."
"Liar."
"It is. They've just spelled it differently, so it sounds like some expensive and powerful anti-convulsant drug."
"One small glass, then."

"It's a deal."

Lynn opened the bottle and let it breathe while she set about making the meal. John watched, helplessly.

They sat at the table, eating in silence. It felt uncomfortable, and John was unable to cope with the obvious tension. His head dropped and he sobbed quietly. Lynn's left hand touched his right hand gently.

"It's OK, John. Do you want to talk about it?"
"I wouldn't know where to start," he blubbed. "What a mess. Why me? What did I do to deserve this?"
"John, it's OK. I'm not here to judge you. Just talk. I'll listen. And don't be embarrassed. I've seen plenty grown men crying. I was in the Army before I joined the CTU. I've seen men have their limbs blown off and suffer unimaginable physical pain. And I've seen the other side of it as well. The mental pain. The feeling of helplessness. The feeling that the whole world is caving in and you're carrying that weight of responsibility on your shoulders."
"But I don't even know if it's real. Or just all in my head. All I know is I'm going to die. And I'm resigned to that. That doesn't matter. It's the fact that somehow I've been selected to play the role of Cassandra."
"I don't agree, John. *We* believe you. Nobody believed Cassandra's prophesy, but *we* believe yours. We have very reliable data which tells us that what you've predicted could well happen. But we can prevent it, John. But only if you stay with it. Help me with this. Please."
"I don't want to be the one who decides who lives and who dies."
"You're not the one who decides."
"I *am*. I had another vision last night. I saw more names."
"What were the names, John?"
"I'm sorry. I can't tell you. It wouldn't be fair. Look what happened when I told Amy she was going to die. That's what started all this crap."

"No. It was going to happen anyway. Amy has been planning this for a long time."
"And you know this how?"
"Intelligence reports from GCHQ. Trust me, John. If you hadn't uncovered the plot, we wouldn't be in such a good position to counter it. So, you've done us a favour. And if we get a result on Sunday, you'll be responsible. You'll be a hero."
"And if we don't?"
"We will. We're all confident we will."

John wasn't convinced, but left his fears unspoken. They could only do their best. That was all anyone could ever ask. He drank his wine in silence, leaving his meal unfinished.

****

Don McArthur was eating his evening meal with his wife when he first broached the subject.

"Do you still want to move to Spain, Janet?"
"Well, I suppose it would be nice while we're still young enough to enjoy it. Why are you asking now?"
"I think it's time I retired."
"I agree. I've been telling you for long enough."
"I know. I just feel that now is the right time."
"Your current case, whatever it is, is getting you down. I can see that."
"It is, and once it's over, I think enough is enough. The job's getting too much for me. It's draining me. Sucking the life out of me. And I'm making mistakes."
"So, hand in your notice in the morning."
"I can't. I have to see this operation through. Too many lives depend on it."
"How long is it going to drag on for?"
"It should all be over on Sunday, God willing."
"Well, let's hope so. As soon as it's over, we'll book a holiday and go house-hunting in the sun."

"I'll look forward to that."
"Me too."

Don was relieved he'd made the decision, the correct decision. He secretly wished the decisions he had to make every day at work were as straightforward.

****

Earlier that day, Amy had walked to the nearest village from where she'd caught a bus to Kendal. Her research had shown there was a shop close to the main street which could supply what she needed – a bicycle. She also purchased suitable clothing and a helmet, surprising the shopkeeper by paying cash. She rode the bicycle back to the cottage, marvelling how confident and competent she was though she'd not ridden a bicycle for many years, since she was a teenager, in fact. She knew she was fit enough to ride it to Bradford, in two stages. Her itinerary was already planned, and so far, everything had gone to plan. Nothing could stop her now.

CHAPTER 17

27th October

"The US government has released 2,800 previously classified files on the assassination of President John F Kennedy in 1963. President Donald Trump said the public deserved to be "fully informed" about the event, which has been the subject of numerous conspiracy theories.
But some documents have been withheld at the request of government agencies.
Spanish Prime Minister Mariano Rajoy has called on senators to approve direct rule over Catalonia, amid an escalating crisis over the region's push for independence. He said he wanted to dismiss Catalan leader Carles Puigdemont, his vice-president and all regional ministers. Mr Rajoy's speech was met with applause in the Spanish senate, where his Partido Popular has a majority.
Leeds will hand in its bid to become European Capital of Culture in 2023 today. Every year, two cities are designated Capital of Culture by the European Union and organise a series of cultural events. Leeds is up against Nottingham, Dundee, Milton Keynes and Belfast.
Tree protesters are gathering outside Sheffield court where three campaigners are due to appear this morning. Calvin Payne, Siobhan O'Malley and Green Party councillor Alison Teal are all accused of breaking a high court injunction and taking "unlawful direct action" to prevent the felling of trees."

"After a chilly start, it will be mostly dry with some good spells of sunshine, and with light winds it will feel pleasant. However, the odd light shower is still possible over coastal areas during the morning."

They were gathered in the Major Operations Room in Wakefield, McArthur, Lee, Peters and a couple of analysts from his team, along with six Special Operations personnel. They were waiting for Lynn Whitehead to arrive with John

Braden, having been told there would be a slight delay as he'd had a bad night and was currently experiencing a severe bout of vomiting, but they were now on their way – in a private ambulance. McArthur paced the room nervously, sweating, doing his utmost to appear calm and in control. Inwardly, he feared the worst. And he didn't want John's death on his conscience, even if it was considered collateral damage.

"They've arrived. They're bringing him in now."

All eyes turned to the clerical officer who'd made the announcement, holding the door open to allow John to be brought in – in a wheelchair, pushed by Lynn Whitehead. The concern was evident on Don's face as he went to greet him.

"Thanks for coming, John. How are you?"
"I feel like shit."
"You look like shit."
"I know."

It was true. John's unwashed hair was greasy and uncombed. He hadn't shaved for days. Traces of vomit were visible on his shirt and jacket and his face had a deathly pallor. His hands were gripping tightly the arms of the wheelchair and the veins were prominent.

"Will you all stop gawping and get started before I shit myself again?"
"OK. Can we get you anything before we start, John?"
"A glass of water?"

At a nod from Don, an analyst was dispatched to the water cooler before everyone assembled in front of the enlarged street maps taped to the wall. They showed different parts of the route to be followed by the runners. Several areas had been circled in red marker pen. McArthur cleared his throat and started his briefing.

"Please don't think that we in this room are the only ones who will be present on duty on Sunday. At this very moment, several other groups are receiving a similar briefing, and each group will have responsibility for policing a particular area. The aim for every group is the same: to prevent a terrorist attack from taking place and take the perpetrator into custody. Alive, if possible. That, of course, is the ideal outcome. Failing that, our role is damage limitation."

"Excuse me, sir."

One of the Special Ops officers had a question.

"Yes, Johnson."
"You said perpetrator. Singular. Are you saying we're looking for a lone wolf?"
"We believe so. The perpetrator is known to have an accomplice but we don't expect her to be directly involved."
"Her?"
"Yes. She is known to us. We believe she's in hiding. It's all on the fact sheets which will be distributed shortly and I'll answer any questions at that point. In the meantime, please allow me to ensure you all know your roles and positions for Sunday."

The Special Ops officer blushed, acknowledging McArthur's mild rebuke.

"OK, this area here is the one which this particular team has been allocated. I personally believe it is the most likely location for an attack to take place. And so does my colleague over there."

He indicated John, who gave a nod of the head in acknowledgment before McArthur continued.

"Each fact sheet has a name on it. Please ensure you take the one with *your* name on it. It will tell you your *specific* role, your position and the name of your partner. Before you leave this room, speak to your partner and ensure you both know exactly what he or she is responsible for, his or her location, etc. Your life, and the lives of several others, could depend on how well you work with your partner. Make sure you get it right. If either you or your partner gets it wrong, you will both be held equally accountable. Is that clear?"

The murmured response indicated it was clear.

"OK. Any questions?
"Where are the sharpshooters?"
"In the positions indicated on your fact sheets. Let me make it perfectly clear that they will not have permission to fire unless they have a clear head shot and there is no danger to the public. By that I mean, they will only fire if it appears the perpetrator is either unarmed or has already discharged an explosive device."
"I notice we appear to have a civilian among us. Would you kindly explain why he's here?"

All eyes were on John. He started to speak but McArthur hushed him and responded.

"John is here at my request. He brings a different perspective to the investigation and has up to now proved invaluable in getting us to this stage. Look upon him as an informed and incisive behavioural analyst. On top of that, he knows the perpetrator better than anyone here in this room, and has a direct interest in capturing her. Come Sunday, he'll be as focused as any of the rest of you. None of you here bear any responsibility for him or have any authority over him. He reports directly to me. Is that clear?"

Nods and grunts from those assembled indicated that it was, indeed, clear. McArthur continued.

"Now you've all either trained for this sort of situation, or in some cases, have actual experience of similar scenarios.

Let me remind you that the lives of many people are at stake. So, do your job, and do it well. Any more questions?"
"You said 'her' again. The perpetrator is a woman?"
"Yes. Her photograph is included with your fact sheets, though obviously she will be in disguise. Her name is Amy Winston. Meeting over."

Before she left, Lynn handed John's old door locks to McArthur. He took them to his desk, took the printed keys from an evidence bag in his desk, and tried them in the locks. They were a little stiff, like all new keys invariably are, but, as Brian Peters had already told him, they released the locks.

****

On the drive back to Bradford, John was silent. His head was pounding and every bump in the road made him feel nauseous. He asked Lynn so stop the ambulance. When she did, he threw open the door, leaned out and was violently sick. Lynn called McArthur immediately.

****

Amy had left the cottage early that morning and was now cycling in a leisurely fashion along the lanes of the Yorkshire dales. Before she left and under cover of darkness, she drove Ellen's car into the garage, and dragged Ellen's body round the back of the house where she heaved it into the driver's seat. Taking a five litre can of petrol, she liberally doused the body and the seats before setting the timer under the driver's seat. She packed the panniers of the bicycle and rode off, safe in the knowledge that the cottage would receive no visitors before the explosion took place, since she'd left strict instructions that no-one should disturb her while she was working at the cottage, and her rental period did not expire until Sunday.

Forty miles away, the timer had reached its pre-set time and ignited a small incendiary device in the car. Burning fiercely, this immediately ignited the petrol fumes, engulfing the cabin of the car, and its dead occupant, in flames. Within minutes, smoke and flames had spread to the structure of the garage, and from there to the cottage itself. Before long, the petrol in the car's tank exploded. Smoke and flames from the building could be seen miles away and the fire brigade was quickly alerted, but by the time they'd reached the scene and extinguished the fire, only the walls of the cottage and garage remained standing. When they found the charred remains of a human body in the car, the police were notified, and SOC officers were dispatched to the scene. Their preliminary report that the body of a woman had been found in a burning building was intercepted by an alert Inspector at Penrith headquarters. The vehicle registration details showed the car was owned by a Miss Ellen Stevenson, a name he recognised as having been circulated by CTU. He immediately relayed the information to Don McArthur in Wakefield in accordance with instructions. Within an hour, Ellen's dental records had been sent to Penrith, and the body was confirmed as being that of Miss Stevenson. A post-mortem examination was quickly arranged and the preliminary cause of death was confirmed as being due to a deep knife wound to the neck and subsequent trauma. A murder hunt was established and all data was shared immediately with CTU in Wakefield.

****

DS Lee sat in the chair opposite McArthur's desk. He had no idea why his boss had called him in, but McArthur's face told him he should expect bad news. He hadn't been expecting this, though.

"David, I'm sorry to have to break this to you, but a few hours ago, a woman's body was found in a burnt-out car in the Lake District. I'm afraid she's been positively identified as Ellen Stevenson."

Lee's face drained. He was unable to speak, and just nodded his understanding.

"The information we have so far, David, is that she was murdered. They think she had been dead for a number of hours before the car was deliberately torched."
"You're sure they haven't made a mistake. Could it be someone else?"
"It's Ellen, David. It was her car, and she's been identified from her dental records. There's no mistake."
"Fuck!"
"As yet we have no evidence to prove it, but my thinking at the moment is that Amy may have been responsible."
"You think she was using Ellen for information about the current operation? That she was no use to her once she'd got all the information?"
"That's what I'm thinking. We've established that the building where the fire occurred was rented out to a woman in her forties. A writer, who did not wish to be disturbed, apparently. SOCO reported that they found a quantity of ball-bearings and evidence that the garage was being used as a bomb factory. There were pieces of steel pipe, and so on. I'm still waiting for the full report to come through."
"Well, at least we know she wasn't in Scotland, and now she's on the move again. To Bradford, I expect."
"And to cap it all, John Braden is back in hospital."
"How bad?"
"Very bad."
"Will he make it for Sunday?"
"Touch and go."
"Well, if he does, I've a favour to ask."
"Go on."
"I want you to change my operational role for Sunday. I want you to put me with John and PC Whitehead."
"For what reason?"

“Assuming he’s well enough, and, knowing him, he will be, we both have the highest motivation to get Amy.”
“Don’t make this personal, David.”
“It *is* personal. All I’m saying is that, together, Braden and I will both be extremely focused on a positive result. It means more to us than to anyone else on the team.”
“Leave it with me, David.”
“Thanks, boss.”
“Another thing, David. Don’t shave. I want you looking unkempt on Sunday. You’ll receive further instructions nearer the time.”

CHAPTER 18

28th October

"The first charges have been filed in the investigation led by special counsel Robert Mueller into alleged Russian interference in the 2016 US election, media reports say. It was not clear what the charges were and who they targeted, CNN and Reuters reported quoting unnamed sources. Anyone charged could be taken into custody as soon as Monday, CNN said.
Computer scientists have developed artificial intelligence that can outsmart the Captcha website security check system. Captcha challenges people to prove they are human by recognising combinations of letters and numbers that machines would struggle to complete correctly. Researchers developed an algorithm that imitates how the human brain responds to these visual clues. The neural network could identify letters and numbers from their shapes.
A collapsed academy chain that ran 21 Yorkshire schools was "dysfunctional" and led by "inadequate" managers, a confidential report has revealed. Wakefield City Academies Trust (WCAT) said at the start of September it was giving up its schools because it was unable to rapidly improve them. A leaked report, written by the trust's interim CEO Chris Pickering, also said it operated "on a basis of fear" and had fostered a "blame culture". WCAT refused to comment on the report.
A burglar from Halifax has been jailed for more than five years after he admitted his crimes in court yesterday. In February this year David Lamb, 40 of Jubilee Road in Halifax, used a Peugeot 108 stolen in a burglary in Elland to drive to Hebden Bridge where a house was burgled while the victims slept in their bed. Their BMW was stolen by others he was working with and he took other items from their house away in the Peugeot - which he then crashed."

“Much of the region will be dry with some bright or sunny intervals, especially in the east, although thicker cloud may bring a little drizzle to the Pennines. Strong and gusty winds developing with gales across the hills.”

The news and local weather forecast played on John’s radio alarm clock before eventually silencing itself. He didn’t hear it. He wasn’t there. He’d spent the night in a private hospital near Bingley and was still sleeping, sedated. Following the previous day’s meeting he’d felt progressively worse, complaining of headaches and nausea. DC Lynn Whitehead had stopped the ambulance on the way home, called McArthur, and, on his instructions, changed course towards Bingley, where medical staff were waiting to treat him. McArthur called Lynn frequently for updates, and finally drove to the hospital himself, staying overnight so Lynn could get some sleep. He was still there at the bedside when John awoke.

“Good morning, John. Good to have you back with us.”
“Where am I?”
“Hospital, John. You felt unwell yesterday.”
“I don’t remember.”
“You were at a meeting. In Wakefield. Regarding Operation Coyote. You remember Operation Coyote?”
“Yes. Yes, of course.”
“Thank God for that. Do you remember anything else?”
“Yes. It just seems to be yesterday that’s a bit of a blur.”
“That’s probably due to the hole in your skull.”
“What?”
“They had to drill a hole in your skull, John. To relieve the pressure. Your head was about to explode.”
“You’re kidding.”
“Only a little. But it seems the procedure was successful. Your headache isn’t as severe?”
“No. it’s… tolerable, much better than yesterday.”
“Unfortunately, the pressure will start to build up again, John. This is only a reprieve.”
“It will do, if it gets me through tomorrow.”

"What's tomorrow?"
"You don't have to test me, Don. I'm perfectly aware of my role tomorrow."
"There's been a slight change, John. You'll be teamed with Lynn and David Lee. There's been a further development."
"Which is?"
"Ellen, the woman we had keeping an eye on you, was found dead yesterday. We believe Winston killed her."
"Ellen? Why would she kill Ellen?"
"They were friends, John. They knew each other at university. Unknown to us, of course."
"So, they were working together while Ellen was working for you?"
"We believe Ellen passed information to her, yes."
"What has this to do with changing the teams tomorrow?"
"David Lee had a soft spot for Ellen."
"A soft spot? You mean they were lovers?"
"So it seems."
"Christ! What a mess!"
"I admit it. We've made mistakes. But we still have a chance to put it right. And you and Lee are our best chance, to be honest."
"O, what a tangled web we weave when first we practise to deceive!"
"Walter Scott?"
"Walter Scott."

****

McArthur stayed at his bedside until John fell asleep. He spent some time speaking to the senior doctor in charge, although it was not so much a conversation as a list of demands. The doctor reluctantly agreed, no doubt persuaded by McArthur's repeated use of the phrase 'a matter of national security'. Satisfied there was no more he could do, he drove home to spend a few hours catching up on his sleep and relaxing with his wife before receiving an urgent call from Wakefield.

"Boss, we've got two teenage boys in custody. They've been arrested on suspicion of preparing an act of terrorism."
"Where did you get them, Brian?"
"They were picked up in Northallerton this afternoon. We've got them until Wednesday."
"Brian, do you think they have anything you do with Operation Coyote?"
"Too early to tell, boss."
"I'm on my way."

He arrived within the hour and went straight to the interview room. Peters was waiting outside.

"What have we got, Brian?"
"Two young lads. Their names were raised after GCHQ intercepted some online conversation. We passed it to the local police to keep an eye on, as it seemed to be low level stuff. But it seems that something recently came to their attention and they raided the lads' homes in Northallerton and seized a number of items which are currently being examined in the labs. At the moment, though, we have found nothing to link them to our current investigation."
"Good work, Brian. Pass on our thanks to the North Yorkshire lads, will you?"
"Of course, boss. At the moment, they're carrying out raids at a number of other properties in the area."
"OK. Keep me informed."

That's all we need, he thought. We're slap-bang in the middle of a serious investigation and a couple of fourteen-year-old kids give us more work to do.

****

Lynn was at his bedside by the time John woke up. Every time she saw him he looked to have aged by several years. The decline in his health was accelerating, but his brain, surprisingly, was still alert.

"HI, John. How's it going?"
"Hello, Lynn. I'm fine, thanks. Got a bit of a headache, but only because some clown has been using a power drill on my skull."
"At least you're looking better than yesterday."
"I don't know what it is they've got feeding through these tubes into my veins, but it feels like liquid electricity. My whole body's tingling."
"Well, my mobile needs charging. I wonder if I could just plug it in. In your arse, maybe?"
"Even if you did, I probably wouldn't feel a thing. But I don't think you'd want your phone anywhere near your ear afterwards."
"Probably not."
"What are the arrangements for tomorrow?"
"If you're able, we'll be picking you up at 7.30, and you'll be spending a few hours in the company of me and David Lee."
"I'm sure that will be fun."
"Fun is the last thing we expect it to be. Peaceful and without incident is what we're hoping for."
"I've a feeling we're not going to get that."
"Well, at least we can hope. As long as we do our jobs, that's all anyone can expect of us."
"Is it too late to get my suit cleaned?"
"You won't need your suit, John. We'll all be dressed down for the occasion. We've got clothes ready for you."
"Made to measure?"
"Made to blend in with the crowd."
"I'm not wearing a shell suit for anybody."
"Relax. We've got a nice off-the-shoulder dress for you."
"Perfect. No-one will give me a second glance in that. Unless my tits are hanging out."
"We'll make sure that none of us draw attention to ourselves."

Lynn left him briefly for a cigarette while he was examined once again by the doctor. He seemed satisfied that John was in as good a condition as his illness would allow, and told him so, while re-calibrating the amount of drug flowing through the catheter into his vein. John answered stoically all the doctor's questions about how he was feeling, but was finally obliged to ask.

"Will I see tomorrow, doctor?"
"I'm optimistic, John, yes. But it's not something I can guarantee."
"Just try to keep me alive till then. After that, I don't care."
"I understand. Would you like to see a priest?"
"Not necessary. I've said my goodbyes, and I'm fully prepared to meet my maker. Just get me to lunchtime tomorrow."
"I'll do my best."
"Thank you."

****

Amy had spent the night in a B & B on the outskirts of Skipton. She'd told the proprietor she was a writer on a short fact-finding cycling holiday following the course of the Leeds Liverpool canal towards Liverpool, for an assignment for a women's health and fitness magazine. She left the B & B after breakfast and cycled towards Shipley, keeping to the towpath as long as possible, out of sight of any traffic cameras. Her route had been well-planned; no-one gave her a second glance as she cycled along at a steady, but leisurely, pace, looking for all the world like any other fitness-conscious weekend exerciser. She stopped for a light lunch at a canal-side pub close to Riddlesden and stayed for a couple of drinks, waiting until the light began to fail before continuing her journey in the dark to Shipley. Now back on familiar territory, she had a choice of no-questions-asked lodging houses, and had selected one just off the Coach Road, quiet and discreet, and un-registered. In truth, it was a room in an ex-council house which had advertised on Airbnb and she'd paid through a difficult-to-trace PayPal account. It suited her purpose.

****

Amelia had returned home from an appointment with a sports physiotherapist. She'd had a massage and felt well and relaxed about having to face the challenge of her imminent Half Marathon. Her evening meal of pasta and chicken was shared by the family in a show of solidarity. She decided to forgo her customary Saturday evening glass of wine. Her husband, though, less strong-willed, poured himself a small glass of Merlot to a chorus of disapproval from the twins. Later, she put the kids to bed, had a bath and an early night, while her husband had a second glass of wine and watched TV for a couple of hours.

****

Don called Lynn for an update on John's condition and received a very pleasing report. John was alert and chatty. He'd undergone some intensive psychometric testing which indicated he had sound decision-making, cognitive and reasoning skills. Lynn passed her phone to him so that he could talk to Don in person.

"Don't worry, boss. I'll make it."

"Glad to hear it, John. We only get one shot at it. If we pull it off, we're all heroes. If we fail, lots of people die. On top of that, I get forcibly 'retired', and CTU's regional budget will be severely cut. This time, though, we've got the full backing of the Home Office and support from the Met. They're bussing in marksmen and loads of officers who'll act as stewards and the like. We're mob-handed on this, John. You need to be with us to see it through."
"I'll be there. Count on it."
"I'll let you get some rest, John. I'll see you tomorrow. Lynn and David Lee will escort you to your position."
"Lynn tells me I'll be in fancy dress."
"Not quite. Let's call it disguise."
"See you tomorrow."

Don ended the call and immediately rang the doctor. He was able to confirm Lynn's statement that John had responded well to treatment and was in better shape than expected.

"You'll call me if there's any change?"
"Yes. Of course."
"Thanks. Just one more thing...."

McArthur's voice adopted an ominous tone.

"It's imperative we get him on duty with us in the morning in a fit state. Sharp. Coherent. Do you understand? Many lives may depend on how he performs in the morning. I can't stress too much how important this is."
"I understand. We'll do all we can."
"One more thing. Don't allow him to shave or wash his hair. I want him unkempt and scruffy."

****

John had been thinking. He asked Lynn if she could do him a favour.

"Could you possibly get one of the clerical staff to type something up for me?"
"Probably. What do you want?"
"If I tell you, can you write it down and get it typed?"
"Yes, OK."
"OK. This is it. Address it to my solicitor, Mr Edward Attenborough, in Shipley. You'll need to look up the address.

'Dear Edward,
In the light of the sudden death of my daughter, Jane, I wish to make an amendment to my Will. My entire estate, less your fees, of course, is to be left to the Bradford Burns Unit to use as they think fit.

Signed Date:

John Braden
Witnessed Date:

Lynn Whitehead

Dr James Morrison'

That should do it. If you could get it typed up and I'll sign it, then pass it to you to sign and date, and ask the doctor to do the same, I'd be most grateful. I'll send a text to Edward to tell him to expect it. Would you do that, please, Lynn?"
"Of course. I'll even get the hospital to post it for you."
"Thanks, Lynn. That's another loose end tied up. I'll tell you what, this dying business doesn't half help you focus."

The Burns Unit was the natural choice, really. John had been in the crowd on 11th May 1985 and had watched the horror unfold from the stand on the opposite side of the ground. It was one reason why, shortly after, he applied to join the Fire Service. He wanted to make a difference. He'd never regretted it, regardless of the way his life had panned out.

At his insistence, John was put into a wheelchair and wheeled into the Day Room to watch the football highlights on television. Although not a huge football fan, he was visibly pleased that Bradford City had won and allowed the nurse to put him to bed where he fell asleep within minutes. Lynn slept in the guest quarters with instructions she should be woken immediately should there be any change in John's condition. There wasn't and he slept through the night. He was the only one. McArthur, Lee, Peters and Lynn Whitehead all had a restless night.

Amy had a pleasant meal in a pub in Eldwick. Rather than risk being seen and recognised so close to home, she'd chosen to get a taxi and go a little further afield. She was too close to achieving the notoriety she craved to jeopardise her mission by bumping into someone she knew.

CHAPTER 19

29th October

“Security forces in the Somali capital, Mogadishu, have ended a 15-hour siege of a hotel stormed by armed militants. The gunmen entered the building after two bombs were detonated in the area. At least 20 people were killed, and it is feared more bodies will be found as security forces search the hotel. The Islamist militant group al-Shabab said it had carried out the bombings. Two weeks ago, 358 people died in the worst attack in Somalia since the group launched its offensive in 2007.
The head of the UN food agency has appealed for aid to avert a humanitarian crisis in the conflict-wracked DR Congo province of Kasai. David Beasley told the BBC that more than three million people were now at risk of starvation. He warned that hundreds of thousands of children could die in the coming months if aid was not delivered. Violence flared in August 2016 after the death of a local leader during clashes with security forces. It has forced 1.5 million people from their homes, most of them children.
A Labour MP has claimed it was "the better educated people" who voted remain in the EU referendum. Barry Sheerman, who has held the Huddersfield seat since 1979, made his comments during the BBC's Politics Show programme. Mr Sheerman said: "You can actually see the pattern, all the university towns voted remain." Pudsey Conservative MP Stuart Andrew, who was also taking part in the debate, described the remarks as ‘snobbery’.”

“A dry day inland with some good spells of sunshine, but cloudier towards the coast with the odd shower. Feeling much colder than of late in the northerly breeze.”

John was grateful for the extra hour of sleep he’d managed courtesy of the clocks being put back due to the end of British Summer Time. With the assistance of a nurse, he walked the short distance to the dining room, where Lynn was already waiting, seated at a table, thumbing through messages on her phone. She switched it off as John reached the table. He was a little surprised by the clothing she was wearing. He would have considered it to be on the scruffy side of casual, but was too polite to comment. At that point it dawned on him why he had not been allowed to shave or even comb his hair. He sat down unaided and thanked the nurse for her help.

They both opted for the full English and engaged in light inconsequential conversation until it arrived. Neither of them made any allusion to the day ahead, until John, eating heartily, made the comment.

"The condemned man ate a hearty breakfast."
"So did the probably-condemned woman."

They both smiled.

"Don't worry, Lynn. You'll be OK. DS Lee and I will look after you. I owe you that much. And before you say anything, let me say I really am grateful to you for looking after me these last few days. You're the reason I'm still here, still chasing the bitch who killed my daughter."
"Thanks, John. I was only doing my duty, but I have to admit it was one of the more pleasurable assignments I've had to undertake. When you've finished your breakfast, you can try on your outfit for today. It arrived last night."
"Can't wait."
"I can't wait to see you in it either."

He was unimpressed. Old, worn corduroy trousers, thick cotton shirt, heavy pullover and old, scuffed trainers over thick woollen socks. And a heavy, baggy, quilted anorak-style outer coat. And finally, a beanie hat to cover his bandaged head.

"I look like a tramp."

"Precisely. No-one's going to give you a second glance. Wait until you see Dave."

DS Lee arrived shortly. He was dressed in a similar fashion to John, with down-at-heel shoes and scruffy clothes. He unzipped his outer coat to show John that he was wearing body armour underneath.

"That's the reason for the bulky coats, John. Not just to keep us warm. Here, try yours on for size."

They both put on the armour, Lynn helping John with his before expertly fastening hers. David then laid out the scenario.

"When we get to our chosen site, we're going to sit in one of the empty shop doorways, as if sheltering. To all intents and purposes, we're a family of down and outs. Winos, just keeping warm until the off-licence opens. The only difference is, we'll be wearing earpieces through which we'll receive orders and info from the boss. Yours, John, just looks like an old NHS hearing aid. Ours are practically invisible. We sit in the doorway and observe. If we spot our target, we report it and wait for instructions. However, the safety of the public is paramount, so if we have to act, we act fast, and face the consequences."

They nodded their agreement.

"OK, if we're ready. Let's move."
"Just give me a couple of minutes to say goodbye to the staff."
"OK, John. Please be quick."

John said a quick thank-you and goodbye to the staff before the doctor pulled him aside for a quiet word.

"Mr Braden, just let me make it perfectly clear. You are NOT cured. I'm releasing you from the hospital against my

wishes, and my better judgment. On the orders of your friend McArthur, you've been pumped full of drugs I would not normally prescribe for a man in your condition. They are the sort of stuff soldiers were given in Iraq to keep them pumped up. That's their sole purpose, John. They'll keep you stimulated for a few hours only. Then, I'm afraid the pain will set in again, and it will probably be pretty unbearable. Take as many painkillers as you need to control it, but realistically, John, you only have a few hours. I'm sorry."
"Don't be. A few hours will be enough. Thanks for all you've done to get me to this stage. I appreciate it. Do I have to sign any release papers?"
"No need, John. DI McArthur has signed them on your behalf. Good luck, John. And goodbye."
"Goodbye."

He rejoined the others in the black Audi and sat in silence throughout the ride into Bradford. They parked in the car park at the rear of John Street Market, a public car park which had been commandeered for the day by the CTU team. They reported first to the Mobile Incident Centre, a huge truck with blacked-out windows, filled with electronics, which was the nerve centre of Operation Coyote. McArthur was there directing operations. He looked composed, probably due to the fact that SO15 had granted him the necessary manpower and equipment he'd requested for the operation. He wished his team good luck, shook John's hand and sent them to take up their allotted positions. They were pleased to note that all vehicle access to the race courses was blocked by refuse collection wagons. This was not simply a traffic management measure; its purpose was to prevent the kind of carnage caused when a terrorist drives a heavy goods vehicle into an unsuspecting crowd.

In less than ten minutes they were in position on Bank Street, sitting on the steps outside an empty shop unit. Two doors up, there was a similar empty unit. They took in their surroundings. Barriers ran the length of Bank Street, along

Hustlergate in one direction, and on to Market Street in the other. The barriers were there to keep the runners on their intended course, and to keep back spectators. There was a gap in the barriers at the top of Bank Street where a marshal was on duty to supervise pedestrians who wished to cross the road, to ensure they only crossed when there was a suitable gap between the runners to allow them safe passage. David informed John that the marshal was not one of their people, but was one of the paid staff employed by the race organisers. It was implicit in Dave's words that their presence as far as the marshal was concerned was as mere spectators. There was a handful of genuine spectators at the bottom of Bank Street and a few customers at the coffee shop in the chairs outside. It was a bright, but cold morning. John seemed disappointed.

"It's too quiet. There should be more people about."
"There will be, John. It's early. Wait until the races start."
"And it should be raining."
"What?"
"In my dream. I expected it to be raining."
"It is. Look at the pavement. It's raining pigeon shit."

Lynn was right. The pavement was spattered with fresh pigeon droppings. High above them and all around, the ornate Victorian buildings had been constructed to feature a plethora of architectural details, carvings and statuary which provided perfect roosting places for pigeons.

"OK. I'll concede that point. Let's wait till the races start and hope there's more activity. If not, I've possibly gambled on the wrong spot."

He checked his watch. 8.15.

Amy, too, had appreciated the lie-in. She'd eaten a light breakfast at a café in Shipley and was cycling towards Bradford on Canal Road. She had planned her route, and the time it should take, very carefully. Before reaching the

City centre, she'd turned off on to Valley Road with the intention of avoiding detection by traffic cameras as she made her way to the place where her diversionary tactic was scheduled to take place. She checked her watch. She was on time. Prematurely, she allowed herself a brief smile. As she cycled past the Tesco superstore, a Range Rover pulled out without looking, causing Amy to swerve and brake abruptly. The car behind her braked sharply but still had sufficient impetus to hit the back of Amy's bike and send her crashing to the tarmac, where she lay dazed for a moment. The Range Rover sped away. The occupants of the car which had hit her got out to help her to her feet.

"I'm so sorry. You braked so suddenly I couldn't stop. We're getting you an ambulance. My wife's calling one now."
"No need. I'm fine. Just bruised."
"But your leg...."

Amy looked down at her left knee. Her jeans were torn and blood was clearly visible. She shrugged it off.

"I'm fine. I don't need an ambulance. I need to go. I'm in a hurry."

Her bicycle, though, had suffered some damage. The rear wheel was buckled. The bike was unusable. She cursed, limping away, wheeling the bicycle into the car park until she reached a spot by Smyths Toys store which was sheltered by trees. Here, hidden from view of the car park, she carefully emptied the contents of the panniers on the grass, and unzipped her bulky padded outer coat. Underneath, she wore a hoodie on the outside of which she'd sown six deep pockets. She carefully placed a pipe in each, working as quickly as she could. She fixed the fuses and ran the wire down through the lining of her outer coat so that it emerged inside her right-hand pocket. She attached the switch and fastened up her coat. She rolled up the left leg of her jeans, took out a handkerchief and tied it as well as she could over the gash in her knee. That would have to suffice. She'd already lost valuable time. She'd have to re-think her plans. It was already 9.30. She calculated it would take her another twenty minutes at least to reach her intended final destination, and as she'd already lost twenty minutes due to the collision, she no longer had time to get across to the Multi Storey Car Park on Hall Ings, where she'd intended to create a diversion by detonating a small incendiary device under one of the parked cars. Instead, she limped across to the Forster Square Retail Park where a large number of cars were already parked up. She watched as a family drew up in an SUV and walked off towards the city centre. She gambled on them spending at least an hour away from their car. She casually made her way across to the unattended vehicle, checked that no-one seemed to be watching her and dropped to her knees by the driver's door. She took the incendiary device from her backpack, primed it and attached it magnetically under the car. She walked away apparently unnoticed and made her way towards the city centre.

****

John, Dave and Lynn had listened via their earpieces to every communication from control. Race registration had been going on since 7.45. There were long queues in City Park, but nothing suspicious had been reported. There was a massive police presence around the Park, both uniformed and plain-clothed, and marksmen placed on the roofs at strategic points. The atmosphere among the crowd was relaxed and happy, as the number of people in City Park steadily increased.

The warm-up session had passed without incident and so, too, had the Kids Race which started at 9.15. The relief in McArthur's voice was evident as he passed on the news to his team. In each communication, though, he emphasised the need for everyone to remain vigilant. The Bank Street team didn't need reminding, checking the time constantly while watching carefully as pedestrians came and went.

The tension among the trio rose at 9.40 as McArthur's voice announced that the Half Marathon runners had just set off. The tension intensified with the further announcement at 9.55 that the 5K and 10K races had just started.

"Another ten or fifteen minutes and we should get groups of runners through. Dave, Lynn, brace yourselves. If it's all going to kick-off, it's going to happen soon. She's close. I can sense it."
"Take it easy, John. Just stay alert."

They listened to the flood of updates coming through their earpieces, reporting the progress of groups of runners, how they were bunching at certain points and spread out at others. The information was pretty much as John's research had predicted. The real problem, though, lay in the fact that the spectators had congregated mainly at the start and finish and there were no real crowds at other points along the course.

Would that influence Amy's thinking? John was wondering aloud. Does she have a plan after all, or is it going to be totally random?

He dismissed these thoughts. There was absolutely no doubt she had a plan. She would only abandon it if it became unworkable. The fact that the crowds were thinner than expected gave her a little less cover, that's all. She would risk it without doubt. She'd come too far not to go through with it now. But she would almost certainly have a Plan B.

Amy was doing her best to ignore the pain in her knee and tried to walk normally so as not to draw undue attention to herself. So far, it seemed nobody had given her a second glance. She arrived at her chosen site just before 10.05. She'd skirted the course by crossing Cheapside and walking up Kirkgate to its junction with Bank Street then turning left, slipping unnoticed behind the marshal on duty at the end of Hustlergate and settling in position in an empty shop doorway close to the junction. She checked her watch again and looked at it for a full thirty seconds, breathing a sigh of relief as she heard the distant explosion from the direction of Forster Square Retail Park. She smiled. All going to plan. When the runners arrived, all she had to do was unzip her coat, step forward towards the barriers, and pull the trigger.

She watched as a number of people started running along Market Street, running towards the source of the explosion. Security forces, she imagined. She could hear the far-off sounds of sirens as emergency vehicles converged at the car park from which flames and thick smoke were emerging. The smoke was not yet visible from where she stood but the few spectators huddled nearby were talking quietly to each other, some of them visibly nervous.

Dave Lee listened in to the frantic messages from the security forces from his position on Bank Street. He'd seen this scenario before in training. The odds were that this was a diversionary tactic, to reduce the number of security officers at designated sites and cause general panic. It took almost three minutes before the voice in his earpiece informed him.

****

A video image of the site of the explosion appeared on the main screen in the control centre, where McArthur was simultaneously watching the drama unfold while relaying information to his teams. He dispatched one of his units to the scene, along with fire and ambulance services. He hoped he had gambled correctly by removing a unit from City Park rather than one from the closer, but less heavily-manned sites. He was following his instincts, but also ensuring none of the prime sites were left unguarded. He sent a brief message to his units.

"Stay alert, everybody. I think this could just be a diversionary tactic. Do not leave your positions without my authorisation."

****

The seconds ticked by before John noticed the woman at the corner of Hustlergate. She was wearing tinted glasses and had long, curly ginger hair. She looked familiar. He watched as she walked down to the doorway of the vacant shop further up Bank Street from his position. He noted that she walked stiffly, with a slight limp, and that one knee of her jeans was torn and matted with blood or mud. She took up her position in the doorway, looking left towards the junction with Hustlergate. She hadn't noticed him, or his associates, and if she had, then she assumed they were simply casual onlookers with nothing better to do until the pubs opened. He watched her intently, ignoring the strung-out stream of runners going past to the cheers and shouts of encouragement from spectators. His eyes remained fixed on her as she lifted both arms up to the back of her neck and inserted her hands under the collar of her coat. When they emerged, they were pulling on fabric, releasing it from under her coat and pulling it over her head. John whispered to his colleagues.

"The blue hoodie."

He motioned in her direction.

"Standing in the doorway…."

Information came through their earpieces.

"Runners coming down Church Bank. Tightly grouped. Be prepared."

Dave answered in a hushed voice.

"Possible sighting. Not yet confirmed. Doorway on Bank Street, near junction with Hustlergate."
"Confirmation required now."
"Reinforcements needed here. Now!"

John couldn't help himself. Confirmation was required. Someone had to act, and act soon, before the runners arrived en masse. His instincts took over. His dream, his vision, his hallucination, his premonition or whatever it was, was unfolding as if in slow motion before his eyes.

'You were standing in the doorway out of the rain'

He called her name, knowing full well what would happen next.

"Amy."

'You didn't answer when I called out your name,
You just turned and then you looked away'

She looked at him for a second, then turned her attention back to the runners approaching up Hustlergate.

'Like just another stranger waiting to get blown away,
Point blank'

He spoke quietly to Dave.

"Tell McArthur. Identity of target confirmed. Stop the runners before they get here."

As Dave relayed the information, John stepped forward and moved unsteadily towards Amy, hoping to stop her before the bulk of the runners arrived. She turned back to look straight at him. At the same time, Dave and Lynn crossed to the opposite pavement through the gap in the barriers by the coffee shop at the junction of Market Street. With Amy's attention fixed firmly on John, they made their way up to the gap on the corner of Hustlergate, where Dave took the marshal's elbow and engaged her in conversation, pulling her around the corner and out of sight before showing his warrant card. Having gained her full attention, he explained what had to be done.

"On my orders, you and Lynn, here, will step out into the course and stop runners from going down Bank Street. I don't care how you do it, just fucking stop them. Divert them, anything. I don't care. Just don't let them, or any spectators, go down Bank Street. Clear?"

They nodded agreement.

****

John was still three or four yards from Amy when he felt his energy dissipate, like a battery running out of power. He felt sick, and dizzy, his head pounding. His legs gave way and he dropped to the ground, face down. And a seizure started. Amy stood, transfixed, a smile spreading across her face as she watched his body convulse.

Across the street, at the junction, Dave gave the order, and realising Amy's attention was fixed firmly on observing John's death throes, ran at her, his rage apparent in a guttural roar. He tackled her like the rugby player he used to be, his arms round her, trapping hers tightly against her body as his momentum pushed them back towards the shop doorway. The glazed door shattered under the impact of the two bodies and they fell through into the shop, still tightly entwined.

****

Lynn and the marshal did all they could to stop the surge of runners racing towards them, diverting them straight forward, rather than left down Bank Street. Other officers raced to the scene and joined them. Between them, they stopped the flow. Barriers were repositioned and the route amended so that the runners could re-join Market Street at the next junction, and the race continued without further ado. Most of the runners were unaware that anything untoward was taking place. One, though, had memorised the route, and listening to her favourite music through earphones, skipped through a small gap in the barriers down Bank Street as she had expected to do. She was not prepared for what happened next.

****

Amy was kicking, struggling and swearing as Dave had her in a vice-like grip. He knew he had to keep her immobilised until the cavalry arrived. If she could just manage to get her hand on the trigger, he knew he would be blown to pieces. He was prepared for that. At least he would take Amy with him and get his revenge for Ellen's and Jane's murder. And John's agonising final moments.

****

John was already dead as Amy's hand, deep in her pocket, managed to locate the trigger at the very moment when Amelia was running past outside, concentrating on the music and her pace, oblivious to the drama being acted out around her. In the instant that she heard the explosion, she was hit by flying debris and shattered glass. She was dead in seconds after her head was almost separated from her body, a sharp shard of glass cutting deep through skin, muscle and bone as the rest of her body was peppered with wounds inflicted by solid metallic objects. By the time Amelia fell dead to the ground, Amy and Dave had both died, Dave's body armour shredded by the force of the explosion at point blank range and their body parts spread randomly all over the area.

As the dust started to settle and silence descended, the City Hall clock chimed the quarter hour. The scene in the area around Bank Street was one of pandemonium, as reinforcements were quickly on the scene. The street was taped off and guarded by uniformed officers as the Bomb Squad ensured the area was safe, before Scene of Crime Officers took photographs and measurements, and bagged up evidence whilst ambulance staff dealt with minor injuries as they waited for permission to remove the bodies. The empty shop had absorbed most of the impact of the explosion, so that outside in the street only a small area was impacted. Unfortunately, Amelia was simply in the wrong place at the wrong time. Collateral damage. Police took statements from the few spectators who had remained at the scene. None were able to provide much useful information. They were simply too shell-shocked by what they'd witnessed.

Lynn and the marshal were both traumatised. Lynn was accompanied home by a colleague to provide support. The marshal was given a sedative and taken to hospital. McArthur and Peters took charge of wrapping up Operation Coyote with mixed feelings. They had prevented numerous casualties, but had lost one of their team, and also the man largely responsible for uncovering the plot in the first place.

****

Andrew and the twins had waiting excitedly on Market Street for a sight of Amelia when they heard an explosion. Dressed warmly, they carried cards bearing her race number to hold up as they cheered her past. Amelia had promised to look out for them and give them a wave. She never arrived. It was another twenty minutes before they found out why. Inconsolable, they were taken home and offered support and counselling.

AFTERMATH

30th October

John's radio alarm broadcast the news and weather as always. It included a brief mention of a terrorist incident in Bradford City Centre in which it was thought that there were four fatalities as a result of an explosion, and several casualties with minor injuries caused by flying debris from the blast.

On this first morning after half term, the school administrator took a phone call from Andrew, the contents of which she relayed to the class teacher. It stated simply that Amelia Walters had died the previous day and her twin girls would not be returning to school for a while. The school, and all the young pupils from their class sent hand-written messages of support. In fact, it would be another fortnight before the twins returned to class. Amelia's parents were at Andrew's house every day to look after their grandchildren while Andrew made arrangements for the funeral, reorganised his work commitments and attempted to re-build his life. By the end of the day, members of the press, both local and national, were camped outside the Walters' home.

In the City Centre, Bank Street was re-opened and the empty, damaged shop made safe and boarded up. For the surrounding area, it was business as usual, though the general collective mood was a mixture of sadness and anger.

The early edition of the Telegraph and Argus carried a front-page report of the incident under the headline 'TERROR BLAST IN CITY CENTRE', accompanied by a picture of the damaged area. Inside the paper, the editorial was, as expected, written to mourn the dead and condemn the perpetrators, while issuing a call for all communities to stand together as citizens against this outrage. None of the victims were named, as the police had not yet released their carefully-worded statement. The centre pages of the T & A carried photos of the runners and the attendant crowds in City Park.

Brian Peters was given the day off to spend with his family. He would have taken the day off even without authorisation. He was exhausted and mentally shattered. Don McArthur was in the video-conference room at CTU nervously preparing to present his report to his superiors and a representative from central government. The national press would receive their briefing soon afterwards.

At 3.15 the video link was established. McArthur introduced himself, took a deep breath, and commenced.

"I will go right back to the beginning of this Operation, which was given the name 'Coyote'. Please allow me to take you through events to the conclusion, at which point I'll be happy to answer all your questions.
We were first alerted about a man named John Braden, who had been reported to the local police force by a local freelance reporter named Amy Winston for stalking and harassing her. It appears he believed he'd had a premonition, and told her she would be killed on the 29th October in some catastrophe. A local officer gave us the details, fearing Braden might be the architect of this catastrophe. We asked GCHQ for background gen on Braden, but there was nothing to suggest he was a terrorist. Nevertheless, we thought it prudent to check him out. We had him followed everywhere, put a tracking device under his car and hired the services of a female we'd used successfully in the past to perhaps discover more about him and his plans. He thwarted all our attempts."

McArthur paused for a moment to take a drink of water. He would have preferred whisky. He continued.

"Then Braden had a seizure and was hospitalised. He was diagnosed with a brain tumour and given only a short time to live. While he was in hospital, someone broke into his flat and murdered his daughter who was staying there while Braden was in hospital. We believe the intruder was Amy Winston, looking for incriminating evidence about herself or at least what Braden had worked out about the impending attack. GCHQ also intercepted some chatter concerning the forthcoming incident, which could not have come from Braden as it was transmitted while he was heavily sedated in hospital. At that point our attention switched from Braden to Amy Winston and we soon discovered that a request for an extensive background check on her had wrongly been signed off by GCHQ as clear, when, in fact, it was still waiting to be processed. When it finally came back, it confirmed our fears that she was a latent terrorist. A nationwide hunt for her failed to locate her."

So far so good, he thought, but here comes the awkward bit.

"By the time we discovered where she'd been hiding, in a cottage in Cumbria, she'd moved on. The cottage had been torched and a woman's body was found inside. That woman was Ellen Stevenson, who we'd previously employed to keep an eye on Braden. It turned out that she and Winston had known each other since attending the same university, a fact which should also have been conveyed to us by GCHQ. Winston evaded detection until the day of the race when my guys, including Braden, on his last legs, I should add, spotted her where Braden had predicted. My DS, David Lee, sacrificed his life by rushing her and knocking her into a vacant shop premises, and holding her still while other officers diverted the runners. By the time she managed to pull the trigger, the area had been almost cleared of targets.
The full body count was surprisingly low, thanks in no small measure to the bravery of DS Lee and the courage of John

Braden in sacrificing his life to save many, many others. The fatalities were:
John Braden, though post-mortem examination established that it was his tumour that had killed him.
DS David Lee, who died from massive injuries having taken the full force of the explosion at point-blank range.
Amy Winston, the suicide bomber.
Finally, there was one civilian casualty – Amelia Walters, a competitor in the Half Marathon, who apparently ignored calls to stop, or divert her course, and instead ran down Bank Street just as the explosion occurred.

In addition, there was the murder of Jane Braden, John's daughter, who had simply been in the wrong place at the wrong time. We should also include Jane's unborn child, who didn't survive the attack on her pregnant mother. And of course, there was Ellen Stevenson, murdered in a cottage in Cumbria. So, seven deaths in all.
And while I deeply regret those deaths, apart from the bomber's, of course, the body count was far less than we had feared. If we hadn't been able to take her down, the death toll could easily have been more than one hundred. In fact, John Braden had forecast a death toll of one hundred and three. Considering the fact that there were around one thousand competitors and several thousand spectators at the event, I have to conclude that Operation Coyote was successful.
That's it. Any questions?"

"Do we know if Amy Winston had any connections with any known terrorist group?"

"Not at the moment. We know that we can link her to Israel, but we, in conjunction with GCHQ, are still investigating."

There were no further questions. Instead McArthur was ordered to provide a full written report, on completion of which he would be put on 'gardening leave' pending a full enquiry. At least, so far, Lee's indiscretion had remained concealed. He wanted it to remain that way. He closed the conference call, and sat at his desk, patiently typing up his report. He took his time and was very thorough, including as much detail as possible. Until, that is, he got to the point about Ellen Stevenson's role in the operation. He worded it as carefully as he could.

"We decided to bring Ellen in so that we could keep a closer watch on John Braden. Braden was a divorced man, living alone and as far as we knew, he had no regular close female friends. We have used Ellen on several occasions before, with a great deal of success in eliciting personal information from suspects. A 'honey-trap' if you like. However, on this occasion, she reported that she was unable to extract anything of any use from Braden, and her involvement in the operation was curtailed. We were totally unaware of her friendship with Amy Winston and must hold GCHQ to account for that failure. However, at that time, Braden, not Winston, was the suspect. We are unable to determine what information, if any, about the operation Ellen was able to pass to Winston. I do not personally believe she had any access at all to any information about Operation Coyote."

He saved his input and read through it carefully, making minor amendments where he thought appropriate. Once he was totally happy with it, he saved the final document, printed a hard copy and signed it. He placed the document in the secure post bag. As an afterthought, he printed a second copy to pass to DS Peters. Peters would in time be asked for his version of events and it was vital that his version coincided with the 'official' report. Checking his watch, he realised that he still had more than an hour before the post would be collected. He sat at his desk, head in hands. He'd made a serious error of judgment in allowing Amy to get too close to Braden, an error which led directly to Jane Braden's murder. And knowing her killer had keys to John's flat, he'd neglected to get the locks changed immediately, an error which could have had deadly consequences. He now felt unable to continue in the job with the guilt he would have to carry for the rest of his life.

He opened a new document and typed out his letter of resignation. He checked, printed and signed it before folding it in two and placing it in the secure post bag.

He pulled on his jacket, gathered up the folders from his desk and locked them in a drawer. Taking the post bag with him, he locked the door and walked downstairs, leaving the post at the collection point. With a heavy heart, he got into his car and drove out of the car park. He had one more task to perform before his day's work was over. While driving, he rehearsed over and over the words he wanted to say to perform his thankless task. Though he'd done it a number of times in the past, it never got any easier. He dreaded it. He had already arranged for a female uniformed officer to meet him at his destination.

He stopped the car at the roadside by a smart, well-maintained semi-detached house with a manicured lawn at the front alongside a driveway on which stood DS Lee's black Audi. He only had to wait a couple of minutes for a second car, with a uniformed female officer inside. Together, they walked up the drive where DS Lee's parents were apparently expecting them. They were ushered into the kitchen and offered a cup of tea. They declined. McArthur could feel the tension in the air, so came straight to the point.

"Mr and Mrs Lee, my name is McArthur. Detective Inspector Don McArthur. It's about your son, I'm afraid."
"We expected as much. He told us he was working yesterday on something dangerous. He also told us not to go near the City Centre. Now we know why. He's dead, isn't he?"
"I'm afraid so."
"When we heard the news last night that a bomb had gone off during the races, we tried to get hold of him but he didn't

answer his phone. So, we phoned the police number he'd given us if we ever needed him in an emergency, but all we get was a recorded message."
"Yes. I'm sorry about that. We were overwhelmed with calls, mostly from the press. We had to cut them off."
"Yes, we understand that. But when David didn't get in touch and didn't come home last night, we knew. And then someone brought his car back and left without our noticing."
"Mr and Mrs Lee, David died a hero. His prompt action saved countless lives while he selflessly sacrificed his own."
"Can you tell us exactly what happened?"
"I'll tell you what I can, but the Official Secrets Act prevents me from revealing the whole story. During the last few weeks, we got wind of a plot to cause an explosion in Bradford and over the course of time we established when and where it was likely to take place. David specifically asked to be stationed at a specific site yesterday morning, the site we had reckoned was the most likely site for this atrocity to take place. His instincts were correct; he was able to identify the terrorist and force that terrorist into an enclosed area so that the spread of the blast was restricted. Unfortunately, when the bomb was detonated, he was right next to it. He died instantly. I will be recommending that he should be honoured by being awarded the highest possible service award for gallantry. On top of that, and I know it's no consolation, you will receive a significant amount of money as a 'death in service' benefit. I know he would like that to be used to commemorate his life in some way. He was one of the best men I've ever had the honour of serving with."
"Thank you, Detective Inspector McArthur. Do you know when we'll be able to see our son?"
"I'm sorry to say this, but I think it would be best if you were able to remember him just as you last saw him. I'm afraid you wouldn't be able to recognise him now..."

Unsurprisingly, Mrs Lee burst into tears and was instantly comforted by her husband. The outpouring of grief was too much for McArthur to bear.

"Please don't hesitate to get in touch with me should you need anything. If you wish, WPC Gledhill, and a team of other officers in rotation will remain outside your house for the next few days to keep the press at bay."
"We would appreciate that. Thank you."
"One other thing. Over the next few days you'll hear a lot of news about what happened. Some will be downright lies. Most, though, will be pure speculation. I've told you the truth, but please keep it to yourselves until Scotland Yard issue an official statement. All you need to focus on is the fact that your son was a hero, who died doing the job he loved."

They left Mr and Mrs Lee in tears, clinging tightly to each other, consoling each other. McArthur drove away, leaving the constable outside the door to keep watch over the house. Once out of sight, he stopped the car at the kerbside and let the tears flow.

****

Over the next few days, more details of the events of the 29th were drip-fed to the press, before the official press release was made available. It was brief, emphasising the hard work and dedication of the police and CTU, with special mention being made of DS Lee's act of heroism. John Braden's death was also noted, along with the sad death of Amelia Walters, an innocent victim. John's death was said to be unrelated to events on the day, but instead due to a chronic illness. The mood in the Idle Draper when it was announced that John had died was one of general sadness and the atmosphere was sombre. Even Foghorn Barry was subdued. John's role in the operation was never made public. It would be several more weeks before the bomber was officially named, at which point the deaths of Ellen and the pregnant Jane were linked to the incident.

Sadly, there was yet another fatality. Mark Wallace was found dead at his home in Derby two days after the funerals of his fiancée and unborn son. The coroner's verdict was 'Suicide probably as a result of the sudden deaths of those close to him.'

****

Don McArthur's resignation was accepted and he was allowed to retire on full pension. Shortly afterwards, DS Peters' request for a transfer to CID was approved. Lynn Whitehead continued to work in the CTU, but was re-assigned to an administrative position, where no 'field work' would be required. Special Branch, and their corresponding agencies in other countries met at a summit meeting to review counter-terrorism strategies and the need for increased information-sharing across borders.

****

Shortly before Christmas, McArthur's CTU team, or rather those who survived Operation Coyote, met in the Idle Draper for a final drink together. The decision to meet at the Draper was unanimous and, naturally, most of the conversation revolved around John's role in the operation. Many of the customers knew John, but not his involvement with the operation. Still, they responded enthusiastically to Dons' request.

"Ladies and gentlemen, would you please raise a glass to honour our friend and also our colleague. To David Lee and John Braden. Heroes both. To fallen heroes!"
"Fallen heroes."

Glasses were raised and emptied, only to be refilled immediately.

Eventually, Peters felt obliged to ask the inevitable question.

"So, what do you reckon, boss? Did you actually believe Braden knew what was going to happen?"
"Do I believe in premonitions? No. But he got some things right. He knew there was a planned attack. He identified the terrorist from her blue hoodie. He knew when and where it was going to take place. And he knew the names of two of the dead."
"But he was way out on the number of casualties."
"Really?"
"Absolutely. He reckoned there would be 103 casualties."
"What about the runner who was killed by flying glass?"
"What about her?"
"Didn't you notice the runner's number on her shirt?"
"No."
"It was one-one-zero-three. 1, 103. Only one digit out. How's that for coincidence?"

THE END

Printed in Great Britain
by Amazon